HOME IS WHERE YOU PARK IT

Blueball Band of Brothers # 3

MARIKA RAY

Home is Where You Park It

Copyright © 2024 by Marika Ray

First Edition: January 11, 2024
Cover Model: Victor
Photographer: J. Ashley Converse Photography
Cover Artist: Jennifer Olson

Ebook ISBN: 978-1-950141-70-8
Original Paperback: 978-1-950141-71-5
Special Edition Paperback ISBN:

DESCRIPTION

He's a giant of a man who grunts for words and barks out orders, yet circumstances require I be his fake girlfriend and spend the weekend with him in an isolated cabin.

And of course there's only one bed. Just my luck...

But I need this commission check that only Boston can guarantee me. So I hike up the mountain 'til I can't feel my legs, eat questionable canned beans for sustenance, and vow to simply ignore him for two days. What I didn't count on was a freak blizzard to lock us in the cabin for a bit longer. I also didn't expect to discover that beneath all those muscles and long hair and smoldery looks, Boston has a soft heart and a sad past that makes me itch to fix it.

And of course we have to snuggle to preserve body heat. My luck is turning...

We find more—ahem—creative ways to pass the time, and holy snowstorm is Boston creative! We both know this charade ends when we get off the mountain, so we use our time together wisely.

Turns out there's one final twist: he's my best friend's estranged brother. Yep, my luck has officially run out...

CHAPTER ONE

oston

I WAS GOING to kill my best friend. And considering my skill set, that wasn't an empty threat.

> Lincoln: Better clear it with Keva first.

I stared at the text message reply, letting the hurt and anger build until I thought I was losing my mind. I'd hiked all the way over to the main road to get a signal long enough to text Lincoln about wanting to come out to visit.

You see, my best friend had gotten married to my little sister. I'd tried to keep them apart, back when I thought it was just a fleeting attraction, but turned out those two were the real deal. I'd finally given them my blessing, but not until my sister had frozen me out of her life for punching Lincoln in the face and scaring him away for five years. It was a long story, but suffice it to say, I had crow to eat and I was doing my best to get going on that, but my sister was being a mighty pain in my ass.

I shoved the phone back in my pocket and started hiking back to the tent I'd set up yesterday morning when I got into town. I finally had the military in the rearview mirror yet somehow found myself still doing special assignment undercover work. Men normally fucked up a lot of things in their lifetimes, but I'd double-downed on the stupid and found myself without a family or a career. Being here in the small town of Blueball was the start of getting some sort of family back. Namely, my sister. This was my most important mission ever and I wasn't going to go in there guns blazing without at least scoping out the situation first.

The dark green tent was right where I'd left it, a sad, temporary home that was on par with my life recently. I reached inside the tent and grabbed the one clean T-shirt I had left, putting it on and throwing the old T-shirt and the jacket back inside. It was cold out here this time of year, but I'd always run hot. At the last minute, I threw my cell phone back in the tent, zipped it up, and hiked out to where I'd squirreled my truck away behind a thicket of bushes near the highway.

I needed to clear my head and an ice-cold beer sounded like just the thing. Not in Blueball though, as I hadn't told anyone I was in town. Far as my sister and my best friend knew, I was still on the East Coast. It was better that way. I needed to get the lay of the land. Figure out a way to get back into my sister's life and help her the way I should have years ago. I'd find a weakness and then I'd swoop in to save the day, thus getting back into her good graces.

So Auburn Hill it was. And the only bar that little town had to offer was called The Tavern. It was as old and crusty as you'd assume from the name, but the beer was cold and the bartender was as ornery as I was. If memory served, he wouldn't try to engage me in conversation and that was all right with me.

The place was hopping, the sound level so high the second I opened the door, I almost walked right back out. My stomach let out an unholy rumble and I pressed on, finding an empty spot at the scarred bartop and bellying up. It took a few minutes before a tall female bartender spared me a glance. Looked like the owner had had to hire help since I'd been here last.

"What can I getcha?" the bartender asked over her shoulder as she poured a stout.

"Beer. Light. Whatever you got on tap."

The woman smirked, but spun back around to the taps after sliding the stout to a guy two stools down from me. "Watching your girlish figure?"

I huffed through my nose. "Somethin' like that."

At six foot four and two hundred seventy-five pounds, I wasn't even close to a girlish figure. They'd called me Tank in the military and I had no plans to shave muscle off my frame anytime soon. The bartender slid a light-colored pint in my direction and opened a tab for me before effortlessly going down the bar and serving everyone else. The first pull was long and glorious. The beer slid down easy, and by the time I was on my third pint, I'd ordered some greasy bar food too. A man could only have so many cans of tuna in a tent before he needed a hot meal.

When my belly was full and I'd had enough beer to temporarily forget about my sister and the nephew she'd hid from me out of spite, I scanned the dance floor for some prime people-watching. One couple was entangled so lewdly in the far corner I wondered if this bar would be the location their future unborn baby was conceived.

A woman a decade or two older than me was getting rowdy in the middle of the dance floor. She had a smile on her face that endeared everyone around her, like she was the town mother everyone loved. But the woman also had some moves. Her flashy sneakers moved faster than my eyes could track. She whooped, and next thing I knew, the younger companion dancing next to her helped her up onto the empty stage that must have held some live bands over the years.

The crowd cheered and someone turned the music up even

louder. I winced, but not even the eardrum-breaking bass could make me leave. Not when my eyes were firmly trained on the young blonde laughing up at the older woman. The blonde threw her hands in the air and danced like she was alone in her bedroom with zero inhibitions. Her hips swiveled from side to side in a pair of skintight jeans, and her breasts jiggled freely below a skimpy tank top. Fuck me, but that woman was blessed with all the right curves in a tiny little package.

Before I could talk myself out of engaging with the world around me, I found myself on my feet, moving through the throng of bodies to get up behind the blonde. She swiveled in a full circle, those hips leading the way. Her face was just as pretty as her body, full lips curved into a permanent smile, soulful brown eyes sparkling under the overhead lights, and pure joy stamped across her features. I stood there like an idiot, an unmoving mass of muscle while everyone around me danced. She must have seen me, but instead of being repulsed or afraid, she sidled up next to me and bumped me with her hips. It was like being hit by a bolt of lightning.

"You gotta move your feet!" she shouted up at me, a tinkling laughter lining every word. She hip-checked me again and I managed to do exactly as she suggested. "There you go!"

Well, fuck, now I wanted to dance just to get her to smile up at me like that again. It felt awkward as fuck, but I gave it a shot. The blonde smiled up at me, this time laying her hands on my biceps and squeezing. Pretty sure she was trying to shake me, but I was like a redwood firmly planted. She threw her head back and laughed.

"Loosen up a bit and let your whole body feel the beat."

I tried that and only felt like an ape dragging his knuckles. Leaning down, I had to shout to be heard over the music. "I don't think my body does that."

The woman's gaze dropped down my body, so slow and methodical, I felt it like a physical touch. When her gaze shot back to mine, there was a heat there I desperately hoped I wasn't imagining. Something about this woman was making my head woozier than the beer.

"You might be right. Do you trust me?" she shouted up at me.

I shrugged. I didn't really trust anyone these days, so that was a bit of a loaded question. Thankfully, she didn't wait for an answer. She just threw her arms up onto my shoulders as far as she could reach and pressed her tight little body against me. I felt every single one of her curves like she'd branded me.

"Move with me," she murmured from at least a foot below me. Her hips swiveled to the side and I tried to follow, just to keep myself pressed against her body. "That's it!" She kept moving and I kept following, not caring if I looked like an idiot if it kept her tits pushed against my stomach. The view from up here was fucking fantastic.

The song switched and still she stayed. We danced through two more songs and there was absolutely zero chance she didn't feel my reaction to her behind my fly. The little minx finally shot me a wink and then ground her body against my erection. My body jolted and I tried to pull away. I wasn't here to get laid. I was here to settle things with my sister.

"Song's not over yet," the blonde said with a twinkle in her eye I wanted to capture with a photo. She smiled up at me and I forgot why I was trying to leave. Pretty sure I never wanted to leave this woman's presence. She was happy and wild and fucking *joyful*. When was the last time I met someone who felt joy? What must it be like to go about life that happy?

Her tongue darted out to lick her bottom lip and my gaze followed. My body tightened and she pressed in closer. Her head tipped even further back and the ends of her hair tickled my arm where it was banded around her waist. I felt myself tipping forward and not one part of me wanted to stop it. So I didn't. I bent down low and laid my lips on hers and felt the shock ripple through my veins.

She opened immediately and suddenly my tongue was

fighting for dominance with hers. The kiss spun out of control. Her hands gripped my shoulders with a bite from her nails. My hips ground against her soft stomach and my dick begged for more. One hand slid from where it was gripping her hip and found the curve of her ass. My body shivered, picturing that mound of naked flesh in my hands if I got her someplace more private.

The woman pulled back enough to nibble on my bottom lip before smiling up at me. "All this dancing and no breaks. I have to visit the ladies' room."

And then she was gone, ripping herself away from my arms and spinning on her cowboy boots to walk away from me. My jeans were indecently tented, and given my size, I drew attention. As I watched my mystery woman saunter away, I tried to piece together what she'd said. It was the wink she'd given me as she said "the ladies' room" that clued me in. She wasn't walking away.

She was finding somewhere more private.

Exactly what I'd been wishing for.

I edged away from the dance floor in the direction of the restrooms. I paused to pull my wallet out and check to make sure I had protection on me in case things went the direction my brain had gone. Thank fuck I did. I slid the wallet in my back pocket, adjusted things in the front, and marched to the hallway leading to the restrooms.

It was quieter back here and darker. Perfect for finding out this woman's name before we fucked. I had standards, you know. Low ones, but some standards existed. Except once I got back there past the doors to the restrooms, the woman was standing with her hands on her hips and the bottom of one boot pressed up against the wall behind her. Her smile had so much sass and happiness when she caught sight of me, I lost my train of thought.

As I stepped up between her legs and my hands landed on

her hips, I couldn't think of a damn thing except getting my hands on more of her naked flesh before I died from blue balls.

Sadly, I never paused long enough to find out her name.

udrey

"I REALLY SHOULD BE WORKING on my mailers tonight," I said absentmindedly to my reflection in the mirror in my tiny bedroom. But when Nikki Hellman called with an invitation to dance the night away, you didn't say no.

Nikki was a force to be reckoned with. She was also my stepmom. No, that wasn't right. Half mom? Sorta mom? It was a long and twisted story. Suffice it to say she was the mom I wished I had growing up. I winced. That made me sound super ungrateful for the mom I did have, who had grown leaps and bounds in the last few years. I was grateful for her, I really was.

A knock on my door had me spinning around on my boot heels. Madi, my roommate, stuck her head in my room with a look I knew all too well. My stomach sank and my skintight going-out jeans rubbed my skin wrong.

"Hey. Mind if I come in a second?"

I nodded and slid my driver's license into my front pocket, along with a twenty-dollar bill I'd planned to use to splurge on a fancy coffee drink next time I got a new real estate client. Instead, it would be going toward not-quite-cold-enough beer tonight.

Madi leaned against my doorway, looking her usual gorgeous self in a flowy dress and suede boots. The gold necklaces and bangles on her wrists just added to her bohemian flair.

"I, uh, might be a few hundred short this month."

I tried to ignore the new turquoise ring prominently displayed on her middle finger that must have cost a pretty penny. The woman was the life of the party, everyone's friend, and the best damn masseuse west of the Mississippi. But she couldn't manage her money to save her life, a personality trait I should have picked up on before we moved in together.

"Madi," I breathed quietly, not quite sure what to say. Being behind on her half of the rent wasn't okay, but what was I supposed to do? Lecture a grown adult?

"I know, Aud. I'll get it to you just after the first though. I have a packed schedule next week. I'm so sorry." Considering there were tears in her eyes, I didn't have the heart to be a bitch about it.

"I know you'll get it to me." I stepped over to put my hand on her arm. "Besides, I still have a little left over from my first real estate deal."

It wasn't much, considering most of that commission had gone to fixing all the maintenance things on my old clunker of a car that I'd been putting off for years, but it would have to do. I was eternally grateful my best friend Keva had agreed to use me as their agent to help her and her husband buy their first house. Now I just needed to drum up more clients.

Madi put her hand on mine and squeezed, eyes instantly clearing. "Thank you. I have an opening Tuesday. Free massage?"

I grinned. "I'd love that." And I would. Madi had magic hands.

She left and I finished getting ready, just spritzing on my favorite perfume when Nikki honked from the front curb outside our bottom-floor condo. I ran outside, locked the door, and headed for her SUV. She waved wildly out the windshield, dressed in a bright blue shirt with feather earrings that were already tangled in her fresh bob haircut. Nikki was old enough to be my mom, but she was still pageant-girl pretty. In fact, she seemed to have aged in reverse since she and Jason got married. That man was proof that the addition of the right person could do wonders in your life. Jason was also my boss and working wonders in my professional life.

"Ready to light the town of Hell on fire, baby doll?" she hollered the second I opened the car door and slid inside.

Like I said, Nikki was a force of nature.

"Something like that," I said back with a bright smile.

I leaned across the console and gave her a hug, still amazed how well we got along. I loved this woman. She had every reason to hate me, considering her ex-husband had been carrying on with my mom for years while they'd still been married. Nikki could have blamed me for my father's sins, or at least let her pride keep her at a distance, but not this woman. She reached across the awkward gap and pulled me into her vortex of love and acceptance exactly when I needed it the most.

"Getting your first real estate deal is huge, baby. If we didn't celebrate this momentous occasion, I'd never forgive myself." Nikki put the car in drive and headed toward The Tavern, the only bar in her little town.

"Well, thanks, but I plan to get a whole lot more of them."

"Damn straight, and we'll celebrate those too."

A beat or two of silence took over and that had Nikki glancing over at me curiously. "You don't seem that excited. What? You don't like money?"

I blew out a breath between my lips. "Of course I do. Just feel like making enough of it is taking too damn long."

"Oh, honey, don't stress about that just yet. You're only twenty-six. You got decades of money stress ahead of you. Believe me." Nikki snorted. "Enjoy being single and having that sexy bod of yours. Get out there tonight and shake that ass and let loose. The money thing will still be there later."

I huffed out a laugh. "I know. I just feel restless. All my brothers are married, my sister is off at college, my friends are starting to get paired off, and here I am just sitting around the same town I grew up in. Doing nothing."

Nikki let out a gasp more appropriate for me having confessed a murder. "Doing nothing? Girl, you just got your real estate license faster than anyone Jason's every worked with before and your first client before the ink was dry on said license."

I opened my mouth but Nikki cut me off by throwing her palm up between us. Oh dear, I'd thrown Nikki into a rant. She was known for a good rant or twenty and I should have known better than to get her going.

"Furthermore, can we talk for a moment about how being young is wasted on the youth? Girl, I can't get out of bed without stretching my legs first or else they'll cramp up like the dickens. I keep tweezers in my car console to catch the stray chin hairs when I'm stopped at a red light, because damn, natural light is like a spotlight on those suckers. I lost my waistline somewhere around forty-five and have no hopes of finding it again. I spent all my cellulite-less, tiny-waisted, high-energy years on raising five babies, and now that I do have the time and the money to shake my money maker all night long, I have to drink electrolytes every other glass of wine just to survive the night. So, how about you dial back the responsibility just for one goddamn night and enjoy your youth so I don't have to strangle you?"

She turned into the bar parking lot too fast, the SUV jostling us every which way before she squealed to a stop in a parking space and turned to face me. There was a sheen of sweat on her top lip that only added to the energy popping from her pretty face.

I put both hands up before she really got going. "Message

received. Save your energy for the dance floor, Nikki. We got some money makers to shake."

"Now that's what I'm talking about!" Nikki shot me a wink and we both climbed out of the car.

She paid for the first round of drinks, despite my arguing about paying my own way. Something about her being older and wiser and able to throw her weight around at her advanced age. I decided relenting was better than brewing another rant. By the time I got to my fourth drink, I wasn't feeling a damn thing but free and happy. My family and money troubles were long forgotten when the DJ played my favorite song. Nikki hopped up on the stage to dance, to the hoot and hollers of our fellow citizens. I wasn't quite that free. I'd enjoy the song from down here, thank you very much.

A strong presence had me turning around halfway through the song. A man, larger than I'd ever seen, stood directly behind me. I was used to large males. I had five older half brothers who were no strangers of the gym, but this guy eclipsed them all. And he was staring at me like he wanted to lick the sweat off my neck while ignoring the beat of the song entirely.

I couldn't have that. Not to my favorite song.

"You gotta move your feet!" I shouted up at the man.

I swiveled my hips and bumped him, earning me a grunt but no dancing. I tried again a few beats later and he began a pathetic little shuffle that barely passed as dancing. It was like watching a handsome sasquatch try out a hip-hop class. I threw back my head and laughed.

"There you go!"

He seemed to warm up a bit, joints looser. My vision was slightly blurry, but even so, I could tell he had a handsome face. Wild brown hair down to almost his shoulders. Dark brown eyes that caught the bright lights from above. And shoulders. Dear God, the man had an upper body that looked like it was half mountain instead of human. Ignoring all the stranger-danger warnings my brain would have been pumping out under sober conditions, I put my hands on his biceps. Just to see what a man like that felt like.

Heaven.

He leaned way down to get close to my ear, the scent of pine trees and cologne adding to the mix of sweaty bodies. "I don't think my body moves like that." His voice was deep, guttural. A slash of vowels and consonants in my ear that had me shivering.

As he straightened back up, my eyes went on an adventure, cataloguing the trim waist below the T-shirt, the well-worn jeans that couldn't hide tree trunk thighs, all the way to the black boots that weren't merely for fashion based on the scratches. Wanting to feel that body of his against mine was my only thought. I slid my hands up his arms and over his shoulders, surprised when I couldn't reach much past the very tops of his shoulders. I was short, a condition I was used to by now, but damn, this guy was a giant.

His hands landed on my hips, his thumbs touching in the middle of my stomach without even trying. I found myself pressed up against miles of muscle, and despite his size, the man let me lead. No more words were exchanged. We just danced through that song and the next. And the next. His hips kept time with mine, his feet moving just enough to keep up.

It was the hip swivel I began on that third song that changed things. There was a new mountain of something between us and it was located behind the fly of his jeans, growing and pressing against my stomach insistently. My gaze flew up, way up, to his. He blinked and jolted back like a gentleman. My fingers made the decision for me, gripping his shoulders like a lifeline.

"Song's not over yet," I said flirtatiously. Apparently, part of Nikki's rant had buried into my brain. I was simply enjoying my youth with this gorgeous man and I wanted more enjoyment. I smiled up at him and licked my lips. His gaze dropped to my mouth and, like a fly to honey, that man was coming in for a kiss.

He was incredibly gentle, his lips barely grazing mine before I licked his bottom lip and took things up a notch. He deepened the kiss right there on the dance floor, tasting like something I'd never had before. Something rich and deep and addictive. His hands gripped me harder, his cock digging into my stomach with a desperation I felt between my legs. When his big hand cupped my ass and squeezed, I knew I had to get out of there before I dry humped this man in front of everyone Nikki'd grown up with on the dance floor of The Tavern.

I pulled back with a dazed smile. "All this dancing and no breaks. I have to visit the ladies' room."

I shot him a wink which I hoped he'd interpret correctly. I wanted him to follow me. To what end I wasn't sure. I wasn't about to have sex in a public place, but I needed more of him away from prying eyes. I felt his gaze on me as I pushed through the crowd and headed for the darker corridor that led to the restrooms.

I didn't have to wait long. The man found me in the back corner waiting for him just a minute later, stepping right up and picking up where we left off. For his lack of dancing skills, the man could kiss, I'd give him that. My nose felt numb and I'd forgotten to keep my moans quiet. I truly didn't even remember there was a world outside of the little cocoon this man had made with his large body. I couldn't see light beyond the width of his shoulders and that was just fine by me.

When he bent low to trail those lips along my neck, I finally got my hands on his long hair. I made a fist and pulled on those strands, holding him against me. His lips found a spot behind my ear that made my knees go weak. My skull cracked against the wall as I threw my head back in bliss.

"Easy," he murmured against my skin. But then he shoved his hard thigh between my legs and nothing about that would make me take it easy.

The ache between my legs lit into a forest fire of want. I rocked my hips shamelessly against his thigh, the perfect friction to give my clit exactly what she needed.

"That's it, baby. Ride my leg and let me hear you."

Fuck, he could make me orgasm just whispering in my ear like that. The man should be a telephone sex operator. Did they have those still? I wanted to slap myself for even wasting time on that thought. I had him right here in the flesh, whispering in my ear and doing things with his lips that shouldn't be legal. How could a leg be doing what the most expensive vibrator in my drawer couldn't? And if his leg could do all this, what the hell could his cock do?

My eyes rolled back in my head and I was gone, an orgasm ripping through me like a forest fire out of control. The man bent down and captured my cries with his mouth, swallowing them down and taking advantage of my mouth until I pushed him back an inch so I could catch my breath.

"Oh my God."

His cocky grin was the thing of legends. It turned his face into something dangerously handsome. The kind of face that makes you do uncharacteristic things just to get another scrap of his attention.

"Didn't even get you naked yet, baby."

My poor, abused, worn-out, orgasm-blissed body shivered. Little hussy.

"Audrey, honey?"

Nikki's voice down the hallway had my eyes widening. Oh shit. I was in the hallway at the bar. I'd just ridden a strange man's tree trunk leg to orgasm in a public place. I was pretty sure that wasn't the kind of marketing Jason had been alluding to when he said I needed to get my name out there to garner new clients.

I cleared my throat and pushed the hulking man away from me. "Yeah? I'm here!" I called back.

She came rushing down the hallway with only one earring and her hair a tangled mess, barely sparing the man behind me a glance. "Ace is here. He's not happy with us. We better go."

Ace was my oldest half brother, and the most responsible of them all. He didn't like it when his mama went out dancing and drinking. He'd probably lecture us on the car ride home about it being some kind of safety violation. Nikki grabbed my hand and towed me down the hallway.

I spared a glance over my shoulder to my mystery man. He was watching me go, his heated eyes looking like he could have gone all night rocking my world if I'd just stayed. I shivered again, this time because my brain was finally kicking in. He was exactly the kind of man who could distract me from my goals in life. The exact kind of man my father had been. A home-wrecker. A disrupter.

I wanted a man who had a nine-to-five job and a desire for two point five kids, and white picket fences.

That guy looked like he wanted my damn soul.

CHAPTER THREE

oston

BY THE TIME I reached my camp in the woods, I still hadn't gotten the woman out of my head. The replay of her shocked gasp, followed quickly by a moan, echoed in my head far louder than the chirp of the male mockingbird in the tree branches above. I shifted the front of my jeans, but that didn't let up the pressure on my straining erection. I huffed out a breath through my nose. Leave it to me to hunker down in a town called Blueball and end up with an actual case of blue balls.

I'd only gone out to get a cold beer, and yet somehow found myself up close and intimate with a woman far hotter than I had any right to be with. Don't get me wrong, I'd messed around with plenty of women during my time in the military, but I'd gotten to a point where all that shit was a tired game I didn't want to play any longer. My goal was to mend fences with my sister and best friend, not bring gorgeous women to orgasm in the back of a seedy bar. Easiest way to fuck up a mission was to take your eye off the ball.

I blamed her, of course, for my boot being distracted and landing right on a small tree branch just outside my tent. It was that echoing snap that led to the cocking of a shotgun some twenty feet behind me. I froze, one boot on that damn branch with my hands in the air. Leave it to a fucking woman to get me so distracted that I failed my first personal mission out of the Army.

"You can stop right there, fella."

My senses were in overdrive. The voice belonged to that of a male, older, perhaps well into his seventies. The wind came from the east, and based on the scent of whiskey in the air, he was upwind from me slightly. My phone was in the tent, five paces in front of me. Weapons were also in the tent. Which meant I was up shit creek with only my charm to get me out. Which meant I was fucked.

"I mean no harm."

"Mhm. Interesting statement for a guy poaching on my land."

"I'm just passing through, sir. Trying to find my sister actual-ly." I inhaled and went for it. "I'm going to turn around so you can see I mean no harm."

I kept my hands up as I began to turn around, ever so slowly. I didn't know if this guy was feeling jumpy on that trigger. He came into view, a crotchety old guy with skinny arms under a worn-out Henley, holding up the kind of firearm that means business. His white hair was wild around his face and not even the old Army hat jammed on his head could hide it.

"You're a big fella, but not too big for a couple buckshots to teach you a lesson."

I used one of my raised hands to point to his head. "You Army?"

He dipped his chin once and I knew I had him.

"Me too. Just got out. Like I said, I'm on a mission to find my little sister and make amends."

The shotgun wavered and then he dropped the nose to the

ground. "Just got out, huh? That's not the hair of a man just out of the Army."

"Yes, sir. Last few years were spent in Italy with undercover assignments that allowed for hair growth. Twelve years total. Left home at eighteen when my parents died, leaving my sister behind. I'd like to reconnect with her, which is why dying tonight would be unfortunate timing."

The man's mouth hitched into something of a smile. He showed teeth, anyway. "Who's this sister?"

"Annabel. Actually Keva Annabel Mooney." I fumbled, forgetting that most people called her Keva and not Annabel like I did. I'd started calling her by her middle name when we were kids. She said she felt like a princess when I used her middle name. Guess she grew out of that when I'd been away.

The old codger cracked up. "I know Keva. Good girl, that one. Same with her son. You're about a mile too far out. She just moved out of the camping place next door and into a house down the road."

I dared to drop my hands, glancing at the large black watch on my wrist that could do just about anything except make me pancakes in the morning. "Probably too late to head over there now. Any chance I can stay one more night before clearing out?"

He scratched his cheek, the whiskers there making a rasping sound in the quiet night air. "How about you come on up to my cabin first? See if you can sip a whiskey before I let you stay."

I dipped my head, hiding a rare grin. Tonight just kept getting weirder. "Sure." I stepped closer, realizing the old man was barely five feet tall and therefore making me feel like I towered over him. "I'm Boston, by the way. Boston Mooney, but my Army friends call me Tank."

He cackled and kicked the shotgun up to lie against his shoulder. I flinched, but he had it under control. "No shit? That's what they called me."

"Boston?"

He swatted his veiny hand through the air. "Nah. Tank."

Then he turned on his heel and marched through the shrubs, assuming I'd follow. I shook my head and caught up, not wanting to lose him in the dim light of the quarter moon. He didn't say another word until we came around a particularly dense copse of trees and there lay a cabin, more rustic than the damn tent I'd been sleeping in. Smoke lazily flew into the dark sky from the rickety chimney, but the porch looked promising with two wooden rocking chairs and a sturdy overhang. My old friend leaned his shotgun against the front door and sank into a chair, gesturing me to the other one. I sat, and he poured whiskey from a glass container. I wasn't about to ask where he got it and if it was going to punch a hole in my stomach lining. I'd survived worse overseas.

"Pete Williams the Third. Seventy-six years old and planning to live well into my hundreds." He lifted his glass in the air and I did the same before taking a sip. I was prepared to wince but it went down smoother than the beer tonight.

"Not bad, Pete, not bad," I muttered, letting the glass rest on my belt buckle while I stared out at his view of limitless trees.

"I like my privacy, that's for sure. I can go weeks without seeing anyone out here. Just the way I like it."

I could appreciate that sentiment. I didn't much like people either. "How long were you in?"

Every serviceman knew what that question meant. "Six years. Mostly 'Nam."

I winced. "Glad you made it out."

Pete coughed, the sound so phlegmy and deep in his chest it had me worried about him collapsing dead right there in his rocking chair. "I was glad too, until I realized everything after was the hard part."

I frowned, not following. "How so?"

Pete took another sip of his whiskey before answering. His bushy white eyebrows were sticking out like a fuzzy creepy crawler across his forehead. "My body was fine, but my head was fucked up, fella. Took me years to get my shit together, but not before my wife walked out and all I had was this land and this cabin."

"Ah." I took a sip and pushed away the panic that always creeped in when I thought about my own ability to settle into civilian life. "I'm sorry. I've never been in love but I imagine losing your wife would be hard."

Pete scrunched up his lips, looking like he was rearranging his dentures. "Love's the only thing that matters."

I dipped my head to the side. I wouldn't go that far, but an old man had a right to rummage through his own life philosophy.

Pete batted his hand through the air, his voice turning angry. "You young things think everything is so important. The job, the car, the house. You get so busy you don't even bother to make sure you have the one person by your side that will be there when all that other shit is gone." He shifted so quickly in his chair, I tensed. "You best make things right with Keva."

I dipped my head. "Yes, sir." All my plans were to do just that.

"I don't know what you did, or why there's space between you, but you need to clear that up right away."

I nodded again, not really caring for the lecture, but respecting my elders just the same. We sat there for another twenty minutes, both of us staring out into the night and sipping our whiskey. The minute the last sip hit my lips, Pete looked over and nodded.

"You can stay another night."

I opened my mouth to thank him but he beat me to it.

"Only if you come back and tell me how you fixed things with your sister."

I bit back the grin at his bluster. I had a sense that the old man was lonely, a feeling I could understand all too well.

"Deal."

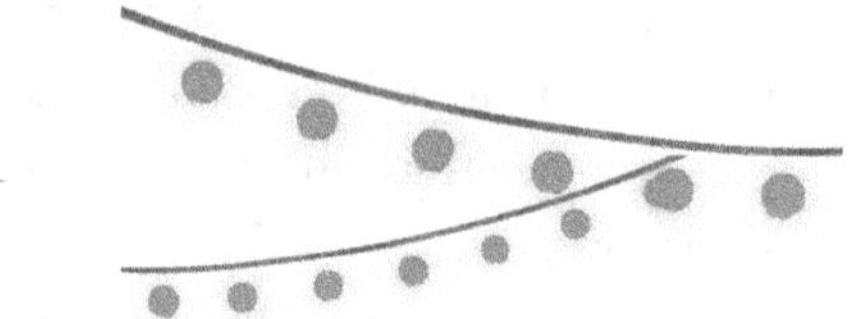

The time for hiding out and learning the lay of the land was up. As dawn broke across the sky, I climbed out of the tent and packed up my things. When the pack was secure across my back, I hiked down to the road and threw it into my truck. I gave one last glance back at the land, trying to catch sight of Pete's cabin and not seeing it. The guy had a huge expanse of land and he'd sure tucked that cabin away, all right.

I put the truck in reverse and got back out on the main road, heading toward Glamper's Paradise. I had to clear the air with Lincoln first and then hopefully get the invitation to talk to Annabel. When I found him, he was in a conversation with another guy wearing a Glamper's Paradise T-shirt. He was probably Gannon Hart, the original owner of the glamp-site. I turned off the engine and watched them both turn my way. The breath whooshed out of my lungs as Lincoln's expression turned to a smile. Relief at a warm reception was palpable.

I climbed out of the truck as the two men came over. Lincoln and I did the back-slapping hug we were known for. Then Lincoln introduced me to Gannon. The two were now partners in this business, a move that had been good for Lincoln based on the way he looked like he was happy and content with life.

"So, you're back?" Lincoln asked, with what sounded like excitement and not anger. I hadn't treated him well when I found out he slept with my little sister. I thought I'd been protecting Annabel when I told him to stay away from her, but that had turned into an epic cluster that I was currently trying to dig my way out of.

"Yeah. I hope so. Not sure what I'll be doing, but I hope to stay here in Blueball. With family." My words hung in the air, hope like a ticking time bomb in my chest.

Lincoln put his hand on my shoulder. "I'd like that. And given enough time, I think Keva will too."

"You need a job, Boston?" Gannon interjected.

I dipped my head, immensely glad Lincoln had welcomed me back. I had high hopes I could win back a spot in Annabel's life too. "Yep. I have some money saved, but not enough for very long."

Gannon looked at Lincoln. "Maybe we have some things around here we could hire Boston for?"

Lincoln cocked his head. "I don't know. Building out is kind of on hold until we can figure out which way to expand. The land to the north is ideal, but we don't even know who owns it."

I frowned, looking out at the glamp-ground and getting my bearings. "Land to the north, you say?"

Both men looked over at me, but it was Gannon who spoke. "Yeah, that's where the lake is that our guests keep sneaking over to. Plus, there's so much land there, we could double our trailer sites without compromising privacy."

Hope built in my chest. Scattered thoughts coalesced into a vague plan. "I think I can help you out there. I could get you that land."

Sure, I had no idea if Pete was in the mood to sell off part of his land, but I desperately wanted to do something to prove I had worth. That I could help Lincoln and, by extension, Annabel. I'd make the promise now and worry about failing later.

Gannon put his hands on his hips and grinned. "You get me that land, and we'd need another partner to help us expand."

The unspoken offer had all of us grinning.

"Count me in."

Gannon pulled on the bill of his hat, seeming pleased. "Let me just call our realtor over and let's put this plan in action, then."

I swallowed hard. I'd have to sweet-talk Pete to even get this idea off the ground, but I had a feeling he could carve off a few acres and still be the recluse he aimed to be well into his hundreds.

Things were finally looking up.

udrey

"I'm not even thirty yet," I grumbled to the universe at large, sliding out of bed and squinting at my reflection in the mirror.

The thick black eyelashes on my left side were smashed against my cheek, making me look like I had a muscle tone problem. I really needed to start taking my makeup off before bed. Even when I'd been at the bar the night before. Especially then. Jesus. Wasn't I a little young to already be a hot mess?

I wandered into the bathroom and washed my face, releasing my lashes and hearing my pores sigh with satisfaction. The shower scrubbed me clean from all the sweaty dancing last night, but it did nothing to scrub clean my brain. I'd spent the entire night twisting in my sheets remembering that lumberjack of a man. He'd had me hot and sweaty and ready for round two.

For a girl who said she wanted to find Mr. Forever, I sure did dry hump a stranger the first chance I got without blinking a goddamn eye. I wrapped a towel around myself and exited the bathroom, shaking my head at myself. Madi skid to a stop in the doorway, looking just as tired as me.

"Morning, Aud." She didn't meet my gaze, which was always a bad sign. "Have a good day at work." And then I was looking at the back side of the bathroom door as she locked herself in and the shower started again.

Back in my bedroom, I stepped into a racy pair of red lace underwear, my only concession to style and the free spirit of a twenty-six-year-old. I topped it with a wrap dress that gave a hint of boob but was overwhelmingly professional. Paired that with sandals and thin gold hoop earrings and I was ready for another day of pounding the pavement to find clients. Whenever my brain would skip right over to my mystery man, I'd corral it back in line. Last night was simply a mistake I could chalk up to being young and stupid. No harm, no foul. Just a quick make-out sesh in the back of a bar. Every girl has done that a time or two, amiright?

My phone dinged with a new text message as I grabbed a yogurt out of the refrigerator. I checked it, hoping a new real estate client would materialize out of nowhere.

Nope. It was the landlord.

Big Bad Landlord: You're short.

My jaw dropped open. "Dude, I know, but that's rude."

Then my brain kicked in and I realized he probably wasn't randomly commenting on my height. I logged in to our account on my phone and saw that Madi had only transferred over half of her half of the rent, not just a few hundred short like she'd warned me yesterday. My stomach tightened into a knot. I hated drama. Hated money issues. Hated confronting my roommate for the bazillionth time about being more fiscally responsible. With a few taps to the screen, I transferred over the money to make us even for the month and made a mental note to get those monies back from Madi before she spent them yet again. The girl went through cash like Keva went through insults with Gannon.

Speaking of Gannon, my phone buzzed again, and even though I was almost afraid to look at it, I did finally check it once I finished my yogurt and dumped the empty container in the trash.

Gannon: Hey. Can you come over this morning? Might have a real estate deal for you.

My fingers were shaking with how fast I typed back.

Me: On my way!

When I arrived at Glamper's Paradise, there was a cluster of people right by the entrance. My best friend Keva; her husband, Lincoln; Gannon; and a tall-looking man I couldn't see because his back was to me and he was currently in an intense huddle with Gannon. I climbed out of the car and came over to give Keva a hug. She returned it, but kept a stiff frown on her face that was unlike her lately. Since Lincoln had come back into her life, she'd been so happy it made my heart melt.

I opened my mouth to ask her what was wrong. That was when Gannon and the stranger lifted their heads and looked in my direction. Oh, sweet baby Jesus, no.

"Hey, Audrey, thanks for getting here so quick." Gannon stepped over and gave me a hug while I stared in disbelief at the hulking man over his shoulder. "Audrey, this is Boston, Keva's big brother. Boston, this is Audrey, Keva's best friend and our resident realtor."

Poor Gannon. He had the best of intentions doing these introductions but the guy was clueless. I gave Boston the best smile I could, but all I could think about was his lips on my neck last night. And wonder if those jeans he was wearing were the same ones he'd worn last night. The jeans I'd rubbed myself all over. My face went hot and I wanted to turn right around and run away.

"Hey, Audrey." The man's voice was nothing but a familiar

rumble of noises as he leaned forward with his hand outstretched. Even in the early light of day, his voice still made me shiver.

I took his hand, the calluses there reminding me of how they'd felt skimming across my skin. I lifted my gaze and allowed myself to look him fully in the eye. He had a smirk to his lips that pissed me right off. And thank goodness for that cocky smirk as it had my spine straightening and the cobwebs lifting. I would not be embarrassed any more than he would. If he could smirk and pretend last night never happened, then I would too. I'd outsmirk the giant like my life depended on it.

"Hi, Boston. Lovely to finally meet you. I've heard so many things over the years." I tilted my head in Keva's direction and watched the smirk slide right off his face. *That's right, asshole. Keva has had plenty to say about you.* Boston abruptly let go of my hand and I tried not to miss the warmth of it.

Gannon rubbed his hands together. "Boston here thinks he can get the owner of the land up north to sell to us. That's where you come in."

I blinked my gaze away from Boston and tried to focus on what Gannon was saying. I knew Glamper's Paradise had done well since they opened, and I knew they wanted to expand, but if what Gannon said was true, this could be a huge deal for them. And me.

"I don't see how Boston can promise that when he just got to town," Keva said, folding her arms across her chest and over her developing baby bump.

Everyone's attention slid to Boston, who looked at Keva like she pushed him and made him drop his ice cream cone on the hot pavement. He was wearing a form-fitting navy-blue Henley with the sleeves shoved up his impressive forearms, looking more manly than a *Thor* movie poster and yet his face looked like that of a contrite ten-year-old boy.

"I promise you I know the owner, and I think he'd be interested in hearing our offer."

Keva lifted a dark eyebrow. "And I think you're getting involved in something that's none of your business."

Everyone watched the two of them like we were front row at a tennis match. Which gave me time to wonder how the hell this mountain of a man could be Keva's brother. I knew her history and I knew her brother was in the military. This guy had long hair he kept tucked back in a manbun that shouldn't have been hot but very much was. Nothing about that screamed military to me.

Not that I'd ever tell the tale, not even to my best friends, but I'd once been a bit tipsy and flirted with my half brother. Before I knew he was my half brother. It was totally innocent and he knew who I was, so he shut that down hella quick, but still. Talk about embarrassing. Now I'd gone and dry humped my best friend's brother—whom she'd had a falling out with—without knowing who he was. I really needed to start asking for a full history before I flirted with a guy.

Boston's thick shoulders dropped. "Now, Annabel."

"Don't you Annabel me, Boston Mooney! You can't just waltz in here like some white knight and think we'll all just welcome you with open arms like Gannon."

I winced. I'd welcomed him with open legs. Normally, my loyalty would be with my best friend. I just hadn't realized who Boston was. And now that I did? I sure as hell was not going to be telling Keva I'd made out with her brother and couldn't stop thinking about him last night. I'd lived enough family drama to last two lifetimes. I didn't need to step in the middle of someone else's.

Lincoln held up his hands before Boston could respond. "How about we just let Audrey and Boston work together and see what can be done?"

Keva narrowed her eyes at her husband and then back at Boston. But she dipped her head in agreement. Boston didn't take his eyes off Keva's face. Gannon clapped his hands like all was decided and moved away with Lincoln. I waited there awkwardly, realizing I'd have to work with Boston, but his attention was still on Keva. He grabbed her elbow as she turned to walk away. If I wasn't so highly attuned to his voice, I would have missed the rumbled whisper.

"Let me help you and Lincoln, Annabel."

Keva looked up into his face for a long moment and then pulled her arm away. She and Lincoln headed for her car, which left just me and Boston at the entrance to the glamp-site.

I watched Boston watching his sister. He didn't turn my way until her car had turned down the street and was out of sight. It was almost adorable, if I didn't know better. Keva had repeatedly told us how her brother had abandoned her years ago and didn't put in much effort to stay in touch. But that wasn't the vibe I was getting from the huge man as he watched her like he wouldn't be able to breathe unless he was somewhere in her vortex. Interesting.

Nope! No, Audrey, I scolded myself. I was a serial peacemaker, picking myself up after turning myself inside out trying to keep my own family together. I'd learned my lesson and had the scars to prove it. Families just had to figure their own shit out without outside help.

"That went well," I drawled.

Boston's gaze snapped to my face, his jaw locked in granite. "She'll come around."

I made a noncommittal noise. Keva was as stubborn as a geriatric mule.

Boston put his hands on his hips, looking around like he was that ten-year-old boy lost at the grocery store and trying not to cry. I wasn't a hard-ass, even on my best day, so I put my hand on his arm, snatching it back when I felt a jolt of electricity singe my fingers.

"Give her some time. Getting this deal will support Lincoln, which will soften Keva."

Boston nodded. "That's what I'm counting on. Let's hike up there."

He spun on his boot and walked in the opposite direction, all man-on-a-mission without a backward glance. I stared down at my cute sandals and dress.

"Yeah, I don't think so."

Boston froze, then spun back around. I started to wonder if I'd imagined him dancing with me last night. Today's version of Boston looked like he wanted to swipe soot under his eyes, wrap a scrap of cloth around his head, and play Rambo in the woods until everyone around him followed his orders.

I lifted my eyebrows and pointed at my attire. "Let me do some research on the property first and then perhaps tomorrow we can talk to the owner. When I'm more appropriately dressed for hiking."

Boston sighed, his thick chest lifting and deflating. "Fine." He walked back over, barking out further orders as he pulled his phone from his back pocket, making it look positively tiny in his huge hand. "Give me your number."

I smiled saucily. "My, my, Boston. You have to at least buy me a drink to get my number."

His head lifted and he didn't look amused. He looked like he wanted to crush the phone in his hands, toss me over his shoulder, and hike to the top of the mountaintop just so he could howl at the sky. I was about to have mercy on him—he didn't seem the type to understand teasing—when he leaned in and whispered at a decibel that ensured all the squirrels in the vicinity knew our secret.

"What do I get for the orgasm, then?"

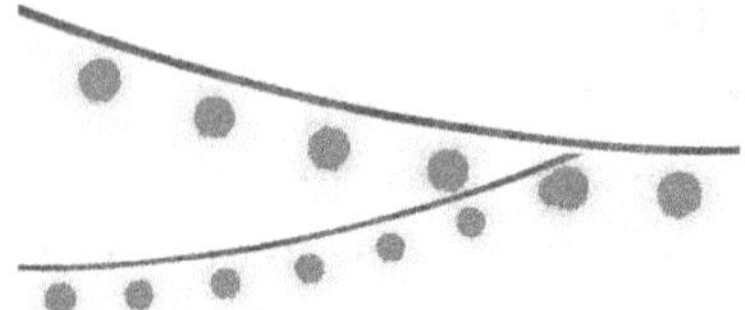

Bossy Boston: I'd prefer we not tell my sister
that we met at The Tavern.

Me: For once, I absolutely agree with you.
Seems like she has plenty of reasons to be
mad at you already without us adding to them.
Not that it's any of my business.

Bossy Boston: For it not being your business,
you sure have lots to say.

Me: Has anyone told you that you might make
more friends if you're not rude when moving to
a new small town?

Bossy Boston: I don't need friends.

Me: Don't be ridiculous. Everyone needs
friends.

Bossy Boston: Not me. I prefer silence, which
usually happens with less people around.

Me: Which is why your behavior at The Tavern
was curious. If you prefer to be alone, why
come dance with me?

Me: Boston?

Me: Your silence is rude.

oston

"You should think about eating more protein. You're about to blow away in the wind," Pete said through his dentures.

I looked down at my bare chest—I'd taken my shirt off immediately upon hiking up the mountain to go see the old man —and wasn't quite sure why he'd say that. I'd been doing all the push-ups, pull-ups, and squats I could, even while living in a tent since I was discharged. I was pretty sure I hadn't lost any size.

"Bah!" Pete swiped a hand through the air and sank into the rocking chair he'd occupied last night. "I'm teasing you, boy. You should remember to try to laugh at least once per day."

I shook my head at the loner. I'd barely known him a full twenty-four hours and yet I felt a kinship. "Is that like an apple a day keeping the doctor away?"

Pete chuckled but it was mostly a thick cough. "Yep, except laughter keeps you from being constipated."

I chuckled, leaning back to send my chair rocking. "I'll keep that in mind."

"My wife tried to teach me that, but I was ornerier than most. Felt like I didn't have anything to laugh about when I came home from Vietnam."

I eyed the whiskey glass he balanced on his thigh while he rocked. My watch said it wasn't quite noon yet. It wasn't a mystery how a lot of guys took up drinking when they left the military. Wasn't easy to blend back in as a civilian. "I can see why."

Pete harrumphed. "My wife was smart. I just didn't want to listen. Didn't want to feel better. I was a wallower and I'm not ashamed to admit it." Pete turned his bushy eyebrows on me. "Hope to God you ain't a wallower too. Too damn young to ruin your life like that."

I shook my head. "Nope. Not a wallower. In fact, I'm trying to get a job here in Blueball. Settle down in a little place off the beaten path." I eyed the old man, wondering how receptive he'd be to my idea. "You ever think about selling some of your property?"

Pete snorted violently, nearly sloshing his whiskey out the sides of the glass. "Got a developer up here every couple of years sniffing around. Got more money burning a hole in their pockets than they do sense. Want to put up high-rises as far as the eye can see. Do I look like I give a rat's ass about high-rises?"

"No, sir, you do not."

"No, I do not," Pete spat. "I want to live the rest of my damn life in peace. Keep this land wild so the next generation has a place to play in nature instead of some glass and metal structure with temperature-controlled, filtered air blowing in and screens in every single child's hands before they learn to talk."

I nodded, letting him catch his breath from his tirade while we rocked and looked out at the nature he talked about. "That place down the road is owned by my buddy Gannon Hart. He feels the same way you do. Built a place for families to camp and get out in nature."

"Yeah, I seen him. He's got a dog."

I smiled, thinking of Meatball. That mutt was just the kind of dog I wanted to get once I had my own place. Twirling a finger through the air, I finally got straight to the point.

"Gannon wants to buy some of this land. Expand his glamp-ground. Get more families camping and visiting your lake. You ever think about selling off a portion? Riding out your retirement with money in the bank?"

Pete threw his head back and laughed, which ended in a fit of coughing. When he'd composed himself, he shot me a look, humor shining out of those soft blue eyes. "What the sam hill would I ever do with a stack of cash?"

I shrugged. "I don't know, Pete. Buy all the whiskey you can drink? Maybe a cushion for this hard-as-a-rock rocking chair?"

He just shook his head and laughed again. "You're too much."

As I sat there in silence, wondering what I could possibly offer the guy to get him to think about the deal, I felt him studying me.

"What?"

He smashed his lips together. "You want me to sell, don't you?"

"Not all of it. Not even half of it. Just a few acres so the glamp-ground can expand and Gannon can hire me to do that. Seems like the best job for me. I'd be outside, not around people, making a place safe for campers."

Pete smacked the whiskey glass on the wobbly wood table between us and hefted himself out of the rocking chair to glare down at me. "Why didn't you say so?"

I spread my hands. "I didn't know if you had any intention to ever sell. When Gannon said something yesterday, I figured it wouldn't hurt to ask you."

Pete began to pace the porch and I felt bad for getting him upset. Obviously, he didn't want to sell and I'd have to come up with some other way to get a job in Blueball while getting back in the good graces of my sister. He didn't need to stress over it.

Pete kicked my boot to get my attention, his hands on his bony hips. "I'll sell a couple acres that include the lake on one condition. You have to get a date to join you for a rustic getaway at the cabin on the top of my mountain. My wife and I honeymooned there." He lifted a finger in the air. "And you have to set things right with your sister."

I blinked, wondering how much whiskey he'd had before I got here. "That's ridiculous."

Pete grinned so wide I saw where his dentures ended. "So is love but you can't go your whole life without experiencing it. You don't want to be a lonely old man like me, trust me, Tank."

My mouth dropped open. He was serious.

"A date?"

He nodded, still grinning like a loon. "And...?"

"And I make things right with my sister."

Pete did a little jig right there on the porch while I groaned.

This was why I didn't like people. They made you consider doing ridiculous things just so you can have the peace you think you want. By the time I left Pete's cabin, I was thoroughly convinced that I was screwed. There was no way I could swindle a woman into taking a weekend vacation with me to a remote location. Maybe next year once I'd been here long enough to meet some actual women, but now? Hell, who was I kidding? Even next year would be a long shot. I wasn't what you'd call social.

And Pete fucking knew it.

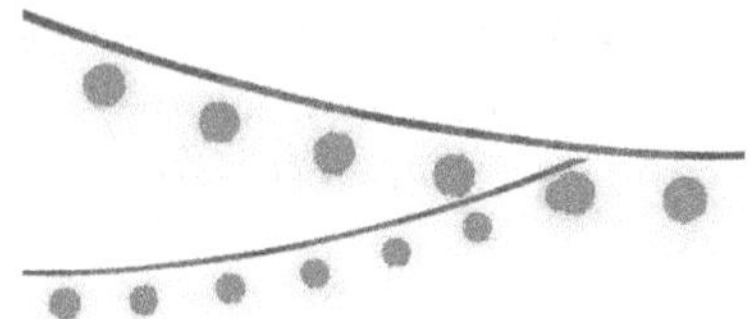

I lay back in my truck bed parked on Pete's property, stretching my back out. I probably should have found somewhere to live that included actual walls and a front door, but until I knew where I'd be working, I didn't want to waste a down payment on a rental too far away. Plus I knew Pete didn't care if I camped out here and I had cell reception. What more did a guy need?

Pulling my phone out of my back pocket, I pulled up Audrey's contact information. Just the sight of her name was enough to have me tightening, remembering the way she went wild in my arms. She'd smiled so brightly up at me, trust shining through the playfulness. She didn't look put off by my size or distrustful of my motives.

She sure as hell looked distrustful when she'd showed up at Glamper's Paradise this morning and saw my ugly mug.

Me: Got boots and a flannel instead of another ridiculous dress?

It didn't take long for the bubble to appear that told me she was writing back.

Audrey the Realtor: Dresses are not ridiculous. They are standard uniform for realtors.

I snorted into the silent night. The woman who'd swung her hips so seductively at the bar couldn't possibly be the same woman who had her nose in the air and her panties in a perpetual wedgy.

> Me: Not practical for seeing the owner about that land. Let's go see him tomorrow morning.

> Audrey the Realtor: I'm sure you're not familiar with how these things are done, but I've spent the day at city hall doing some research. The owner's name is Peter Williams the Third. Single owner. Total of fifty acres. I'd like to work up a proposal tomorrow and get that in the mail.

I rolled my eyes. She spent the day doing research? That wasn't going to get Pete to sell the land. He valued research about as much as if I'd lectured him on not drinking whiskey before noon.

> Me: Not necessary.

> Audrey the Realtor: Definitely necessary. If you want input into what goes in the proposal, you can meet me for coffee tomorrow and state your case. Otherwise, I'll mail it tomorrow afternoon.

Jesus. This woman was a know-it-all when she didn't know a damn thing. I must have given her the impression that because I didn't know how to dance, that I didn't know how to do anything. All she had to remember was the orgasm I'd given her without even taking a single article of clothing off. I was masterful at a lot of things.

And that was when the idea hit me.

> Me: You're a woman.

> Audrey the Realtor: Congrats. You passed
> kindergarten.

I ran a hand over my face. Audrey was a woman. Audrey also wanted this deal to go through. Technically, I could bring Audrey to the cabin up on the mountain and that would look like a date. Pete would be happy, Audrey would be happy, and I'd make Gannon and Lincoln happy with a deal delivered to their doorstep. A happy Lincoln made for a happy Annabel. Boom. All my problems solved.

> Me: Coffee tomorrow. What time?

> Audrey the Realtor: Ten at Crazy Beans.

> Audrey the Realtor: And it's about time you quit
> ordering me around.

I laughed, the sound big and happy despite how alone I was out here in the forest.

> Me: I'll quit ordering you around when I know
> you're a professional.

That was a bald-faced lie. I'd never quit ordering her around, just so I could see her lose her shit.

> Audrey the Realtor: I've been professional the
> whole time! You're the one in flannel barking
> orders like a Neanderthal.

> Me: The whole time? You sure about that?

> Me: Because I distinctly remember the heat of
> you rubbing yourself against my leg.

> Me: Audrey?

Me: Oh, now whose silence is rude??

CHAPTER SIX

Audrey

THE FLUTTER in my chest had to be from the caffeine. Or the sugar. Lord knew I doctored my fancy coffees with plenty of both. Incidentally, I also caught sight of Boston outside Crazy Beans' wide window. I was early, as was professional of a realtor who really wanted the job, which gave me the perfect vantage point to see Boston step down from his truck, all large and manly in his jeans and boots.

And no shirt.

"What the hell?" I mumbled to my forgotten coffee.

It had to be just barely cresting fifty degrees outside this time of year. I'd opted for a light sweater over my dress today, but there was Boston, shirtless on the street corner like it was the middle of fucking July.

He reached back inside his truck and pulled a dark blue shirt over his head, smoothing it down over his impressive chest and abs. The poor cotton was stretched to its limits and so were my nerves. I was here for an important business meeting and all I could focus on was that moment in the hallway of The Tavern when Boston had his big hands all over me and his thick thigh wedged between my legs. I'd had that gorgeous chest pressed up against me. I swiped across my suddenly sweaty upper lip and gave myself a stern lecture.

I was here for business.

I would not be eye-fucking my best friend's brother.

I definitely would never again dry hump his leg like a stray dog in heat.

The little bell over the door rang out, making me jump. I pushed the coffee further away from me on the scarred tabletop. More caffeine was the last thing I needed. Boston's dark head swiveled right and left before settling his even darker eyes on me. He instantly turned in my direction and headed over, the sight of him approaching giving my heart a thousand flapping hummingbird wings.

His hand grabbed the back of the chair on the opposite side of the small table and he scraped it back, folding himself into it and making the damn thing look cartoonish in size underneath him. I smirked, wondering if I should place bets on the chair cracking under his weight.

"Good to see you own a shirt, beast."

Well, shit. That wasn't professional at all.

His lips tilted to the side, a faint hint at a dimple buried in the smirk. "Sorry to cover up, lusty lady."

My nipples perked up, recognizing a challenge when they heard one. Boston looked like the giant, silent type, but behind all that brawn was wit.

I pointed to his empty side of the table. "Customarily, when joining someone for coffee, you should actually order coffee."

I didn't know what it was about this man that brought out my bitchy side, but it was alive and well and not ready for me to wrangle it back in any time soon. Maybe it was the slight burn of shame I felt at having made out with him in a dark corner of a bar when I didn't know who he was. I kept telling myself I'd put my wild and young ways aside in the last year or two and yet I kept finding myself in situations that could only be described as reckless.

"Save my seat," Boston grumbled, lumbering out of the chair and swaggering over to the short line by the cash register.

Straightening my spine, I forced my gaze away from his equally impressive backside. Instead, I booted up my laptop and scanned the letter I'd already written for Mr. Williams. It was good. Approachable, but professional. Encouraging, yet not threatening. I'd run the letter by Jason late last night and he'd been enthusiastic about this deal. He suggested we appeal to Mr. Williams's nature-loving side by promising the land would be used for more families to enjoy the great outdoors. I thought that approach was brilliant.

"Happy now?" Boston plunked a cup of black steaming coffee on the table and sat back in the chair across from me.

I spun the laptop around and gazed at his chin. Shit. Even his chin was hot. It was attached to a strong jaw and lips that promised the best kiss of your life. And I knew that they knew how to kiss. I cleared my throat.

"Here's the letter."

Boston pulled the laptop closer to him, pausing only a second before one beefy finger smacked down on the keyboard. I frowned, leaning over to see what he'd done. The whole damn letter was gone, leaving only my desktop picture of my brothers and me.

"What did you do?" I snapped.

Boston lifted his massive shoulders and let them drop. "We don't need a letter."

"You deleted my letter?" The hummingbird wings burned to a crisp in fiery dragon's breath. My brain was scrambling to think about how to retrieve it. Certainly it was just in a deleted folder, right?

I reached for my laptop, but Boston put his hands on mine, stopping me. "Relax. I have a better plan."

I pulled my hands away from his and sat up straight, putting on my best haughty expression when what I wanted to do was smack that smirk right off his handsome face.

"I'm the professional here. I really think a letter is a good way to introduce ourselves and what we want. Non-threatening."

Boston shook his head and my irritation grew. "No need. I already know Pete."

I gaped. "Pete?" He was already on a first-name basis with the guy I'd spent all day yesterday researching?

Boston nodded, a lock of hair coming out of the knot at the back of his head. "He is willing to sell."

My chest swelled. I could literally feel that commission check in my hands. "Okay!"

Boston held up his palm. "Under certain conditions."

I deflated. "He wants way too much for it, doesn't he?"

Gannon's business was doing well, but I knew he didn't have enough to pay over the true value of the land. He and Paisley just had a baby. Lincoln and Keva were due with their second in a few months. They had to think about raising their families, not wasting money expanding the business when it was overpriced.

"No."

I waited but Boston didn't give me more. The man was exasperating.

"Well, gosh. I can't wait for you to tell me more, beast," I said brightly, my tone tinged with irritation.

There went his lips again, pulling to the side and distracting me from the topic at hand. "He requires I take you to the cabin on the top of the hill for the weekend. And I have to make up with my sister."

The sounds of the coffee shop faded away as I stared at this man. He looked sheepish, not meeting my gaze and hiding behind that lock of hair. I cleared my throat and pulled the sweater tighter over my chest.

"Why?"

Boston's gaze flitted back to me and I found I couldn't

breathe. He had the most intense eyes of anyone I'd ever met. "He wants to see me with a date."

I was already shaking my head before he finished. "Oh, I'm not going to date you."

Boston picked up the cup of coffee, his hand covering the logo and most of the white cup, and took a sip. "I know, LL. This would be a fake date."

I blinked. "LL?"

Boston set his cup down and grinned. My heart tripped over itself. "Lusty lady."

I rolled my eyes, but struggled to keep the smile tugging on my face contained. The guy was ridiculous, but then again, I'd started it by calling him beast.

"This sounds like a terrible plan. How about you get someone else to fake date you for the weekend?"

Boston lost the grin. "I don't know any other women."

"This does not surprise me," I deadpanned.

He shot me a look so heated I had to recross my legs to dull the ache he stirred up.

"Look. Just pretend to be my date when Pete is around, which will be for approximately ten minutes before we hike up the mountain. Once there, you can do your own thing and I'll do mine."

I stared at him. Hard. I felt like I was standing on the edge of that cliff in Hell where all the teens jump into the ocean. I did not have the coordination to make that cliff dive successfully without giving myself a wedgie so painful I couldn't sit for days, so I'd never done it. But this morning, I felt like I was standing with my toes gripping the edge, determined to make a poor decision despite myself.

Boston sat back, folding his hands over his flat belly. He gave a noncommittal shrug that instantly irritated me. "You either want the commission or you don't, LL."

"Quit calling me that," I hissed, reaching up to play with the dainty diamond that slid across the even daintier chain around my neck. It was a gift from my father when I graduated high school. At the time, I'd treasured it. For a guy who barely remembered he had a daughter, I'd thought it was a touching gift. Sadly, I'd since learned it was a bribe, a way to earn my affection even when details of his double life came out and I wanted nothing to do with him. I still wore it as a reminder to never be anything like him.

Boston sat forward suddenly, the coffee sloshing dangerously in their cups as the table dipped. "You act all professional in those heels and that dress and that goddamn sweater, but you forget I know what you sound like when you orgasm."

I gritted my teeth, refusing to let him see the shock on my face. Or the humiliation. "What do you have against sweaters?"

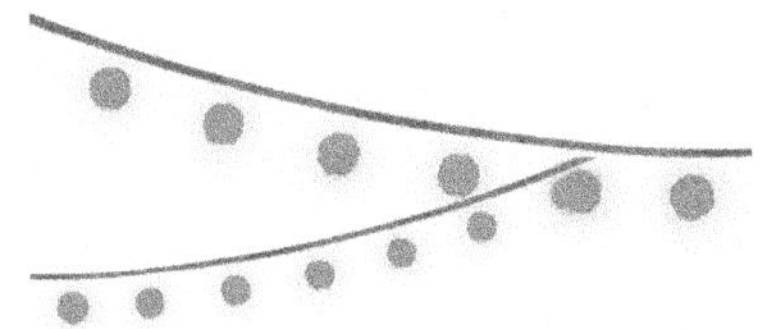

Glamper's Paradise was just ahead. The ride over here in Boston's truck had been strained to say the least. We'd barely said a word to each other and that was fine with me. I happened not to like anything that came out of the man's mouth anyway.

"So, we're doing this?" Boston grumbled right before he pulled into a parking space and put the truck in park.

I unbuckled my seat belt. "We're doing this alright. And God willing we won't kill each other before the weekend's over."

I put my hand on the door to get out, but Boston grunted and put his hand on my arm to keep me in place. He hopped out of the truck and came around the hood, pulling my door open and giving me his palm. I slid out of the truck, keeping my skirt mostly around my legs the best I could from this high up and ignored his hand. My heels landed in the gravel and I had to reach back for the truck to keep me steady. Boston let out a low growl, but I turned away and waved to Keva, who was coming up the brick walkway with a box.

"Morning!" I trilled, a little too high pitched to be normal. I hadn't done anything wrong, but I felt like I'd taken the side of Boston over my best friend just by being in his presence.

"Hey." Keva stopped and put down her box before giving me a hug and giving side eye to her brother. "What are you two doing here?"

"Just talking to Gannon and Linc one more time before we approach Mr. Williams about the sale of his land. Exciting times!" Shit, I needed to dial down the cheerfulness. Keva was looking at me like I'd sprouted a unicorn horn.

"Okay," she said slowly.

"Actually, I'm glad we ran into you, Annabel. Pete has some stipulations before he'll sell his land. Audrey and I will be staying up in his cabin for the weekend."

Keva's eyes narrowed. She stared at Boston and then at me, and back to Boston. "What?"

"Obviously as a fake date," Boston muttered.

"Obviously!" I trilled again, unable to get my voice back down to a normal pitch to save my life.

Keva's face split into a grin. She pointed between us, her grin growing with each passing second. "You two? Dating?" She hitched at the waist and burst into laughter. She rubbed her belly but couldn't stop the cascade of chuckles that had my manic smile faltering.

Why was it so hard to imagine? Were Boston and I really that funny? I mean, the whole dating thing would be fake and just for the one weekend, but why was the idea so hilarious?

Boston looked at me over Keva's head, his expression unreadable.

"Could you...imagine?" Keva huffed between laughs. She pointed at Boston and then dropped her hand to slap her knee. "I'm married to your best friend. You'd be dating my best friend? Ridiculous!" She peeled off another round of laughter that had my gut clenching.

I swallowed down the nausea when flickers of that night at the bar pressed to the front of my brain. Boston looked just as uncomfortable. He stooped down to pick up the box Keva had rested at her feet.

"Let me help you," he muttered, turning his back to me and walking over to Keva's car.

Keva ran after him, still laughing as she tossed over her shoulder, "Have fun this weekend, but not too much fun!"

I smiled weakly and waved her off. Then I spun on my heels and hightailed it to Gannon and Paisley's house. Gannon answered right away, Elise up on his shoulders and pulling on his hair.

"Aunt Audey!" Elise shrieked, making Gannon wince. He slid her off his shoulders and into my arms where I kissed her cute cheeks before setting her on her feet.

"Hey, sweet girl," I said, wishing I had time to play with her and her little brother today. I looked up at Gannon. "Looks like this sale might happen. We better talk about what price you're willing to pay before I go see Mr. Williams."

I felt, more than saw, Boston behind me, his shadow darkening the doorstep.

"Who's you?" Elise asked, pointing up at the big man.

"I'm Boston, Ann—Keva's brother." Boston crouched down and held out his hand. Elise shook his hand like a big girl. I ignored how adorable the two looked together.

"You're big."

Boston grinned. "You are too. What are you? Sixteen?"

Elise cracked up. "No, silly. If I was sixteen, you wouldn't even see me."

"What do you mean?" Boston frowned.

Elise put her hand on an imaginary steering wheel. "I'd be driving to the beach to meet boys!"

"Oh dear Lord," Gannon muttered, putting his hands on Elise's shoulders and steering her back into the house. "Give me a second with Aunt Audrey, okay?"

Gannon stepped out of the house and closed the door. "Think long and hard before having kids."

My face went hot and I desperately did not want to be having this conversation in front of Boston. "No worries there, G-man. Now tell me how much you're willing to pay so I can negotiate that number lower."

Gannon and I chatted for a bit before we settled on a couple price points: what he hoped to pay, what he'd be willing to pay, and what was definitely out of his price range. I shook his hand and promised him I'd do my best to get him a good deal. That was the part I loved about being a realtor. I was helping my clients, my friends, get a good deal on building their dreams.

As we headed back to the truck, Boston put his hand on my lower back. I walked quicker to escape his touch, but I didn't miss his huff of laughter. When he tried to help me up in the truck, I looked up at him.

"Just in case my text wasn't clear, we can never tell Keva. About...you know."

He nodded, looking away. "Agreed."

I grabbed the handle on the truck and hoisted myself up, probably flashing Boston in the process, but that couldn't be helped when you were barely past five feet tall and the truck was lifted.

"But I won't forget it," he muttered before closing the door on my gasp.

CHAPTER SEVEN

oston

"Damn, boy, you work quick!"

Pete smiled at me, his face crinkling into a thousand wrinkles. I hoped he hadn't been nipping off the whiskey quite yet this morning, but then again, he seemed to thrive off the stuff.

I shrugged, letting myself act cocky when I knew my flirting skills had nothing to do with this sudden date for the weekend. I had a niggle of feeling guilty about lying to him. Then I remembered the ridiculous stipulations in order for him to sell and I didn't feel so bad anymore. Besides, I wasn't lying about my attraction to Audrey.

"She's heading over here shortly, but I wanted to stop by and see if I need anything for the cabin beyond food and firewood."

We'd have to pack in everything we'd need for the weekend, which meant I spent all of last night collecting food, water, sheets, and a single bundle of firewood. I assumed if Pete invited us to stay at his cabin, that it was structurally sound. When I glanced around his current living situation, I realized the error of assuming. I wasn't worried about me. I'd lived in horrific conditions before, but I was worried for the woman who wore dresses and inappropriate footwear. Audrey didn't seem the "roughing it" type.

Pete jumped in the air, surprisingly high for someone his age. He hustled back inside his cabin, throwing over his shoulder, "I need to get cleaned up!"

I sighed and sat back in the rocking chair to wait him out. It didn't take long for him to come back out with his white hair damp and combed, his faded shirt traded out for a bright blue flannel and Wranglers that still had a crease down the leg. I let out a whistle.

"You trying to steal my date, Pete?"

"Oh..." he groused, swiping his hand through the air before sitting in his rocking chair next to me. "Don't get much visitors around here."

"Which means the cabin up on the mountain doesn't either. Are you sure it's safe for us to stay there?"

Pete rocked faster. "It's fine. I check it every year and the roof is good. Probably dusty, but you're not the man I think you are if you let a little dust get in the way of a weekend alone with your woman."

I opened my mouth to dispute the claim over Audrey and thought better of it. "So, we'll head up there today and hike back down Sunday afternoon. If you don't hear from us by sundown Sunday, call the police."

Just then a car came cruising up the long gravel driveway to park behind my truck. I'd offered to pick her up via text, but she'd declined. The woman was far more stubborn than she'd seemed that night at The Tavern.

I stood up and Pete followed suit. I came down the stairs of the porch and opened Audrey's door. She got out, dressed appropriately in hiking boots, jeans, and a sweatshirt. Her hair was pulled back into a bouncy ponytail and her face was free of makeup. She was gorgeous.

"Good morning," she said shyly.

When Pete clattered down the stairs, I jolted, realizing he was watching us and I was already messing up this fake date. I leaned down and kissed Audrey's cheek, inhaling the fruity scent of her. She stiffened, but I whispered in her ear. "Act like you like me."

She pulled back, beaming up at me like a crazy woman. "Hey, handsome!"

I bit my lip and moved to the back seat of her car to get the backpack that sat there. Looked like I wasn't the only one who was bad at this fake dating thing. I threw her backpack over my shoulder and closed the door. Putting my hand on her low back, I turned her toward Pete.

"Pete, this is Audrey Hellman. Audrey, this is Pete Williams."

Audrey stepped away from my hand and shook Pete's. "I'm so happy to meet you! Boston has told me wonderful things about you."

My eyes must have deceived me because it looked like ol' Pete was blushing.

"Well, it's lovely to meet any young woman who is special to Tank here." Pete kept his hand on hers, tapping the back of her hand like he just couldn't bear to let her go.

Audrey beamed at him. "I keep forgetting he's called Tank. I call him beast. Both nicknames kind of fit, right?"

Pete spared me a quick glance before turning his besotted eyes back to Audrey. "Oh yes. He is a bit of a beast too. He's a good one though, as I'm sure you know."

Audrey lifted her eyes to me, something twinkling in them that set my veins on fire. "Oh yes, he's very good," she answered quietly, her gaze drilling into mine.

"Okay, we have to go if we want to get there in time to get settled before it gets dark." I put my arm around Audrey's waist and pulled her from Pete. The bastard just chuckled, like he knew I was eager to be alone with her. I wasn't. Not really. But I was nervous, and when I got nervous, I needed to move to burn off that energy.

I stopped by my truck and picked up the huge pack I'd stuffed to the brim last night. With a wink at Audrey, I pulled my T-shirt over my head and stuffed it into the back of my jeans before pulling on the pack and adjusting it across my bare chest. The bundle of firewood was digging into my low back, but that couldn't be helped. Audrey rolled her eyes at my lack of shirt, but I noticed she purposely avoided looking at me. Like my chest was lava, and if her gaze settled on it, she'd be burned.

"Have fun, kids!" Pete hollered, waving us off.

Audrey stooped to pick up her backpack, but I grabbed it and swung it onto my shoulder before she could. "Hey! I can carry my own backpack."

"I know." I grabbed her hand and held it firmly, even when she tried to tug it away initially.

"Let's go, lusty lady," I said with a smirk, the best I could do on the way to the smile I knew I should have been giving her.

The trail up the mountainside was easily marked down here, the underbrush hacked away and the ground mostly packed dirt. The pine trees surrounding us give off a heavenly scent. Audrey let me hold her hand until we were out of sight of the cabin. Then she snatched it back and huffed.

"It's like fifty degrees out here. Do you have a no-shirt policy or something?"

I grinned at the trees ahead of me. This was more like it. I'd been waiting for her to grouse at me. "I do. I typically overheat, so I save the shirt and just go shirtless whenever I can."

"Huh," was her reply.

The crunch of our steps was the only sound to break up the warbles of the birds overhead and the whistle of wind through the tops of the trees. I'd always loved getting lost in nature. Hiking all day and camping out at night. I felt at peace in the great outdoors. I'd been told more than once that I'm a loner, a name I didn't disagree with. It's just that nature follows rules and patterns. People often didn't. And I found that exhausting.

"So, tell me about yourself, Boston Tank Mooney." Audrey's voice cut into my thoughts. I turned back to her and chastised myself silently. As much as I wanted to be out here alone, I was not. I should at least try to be social so that these next forty-eight hours weren't torturous.

I slowed my pace so that she was next to me on the path. She was breathing hard, but not panting. I hadn't bothered to ask if she was used to hiking, which was unlike me.

"Well, I'm thirty years old, recently out of the Army, and I'm hoping to make a home here in Blueball."

Audrey kept her gaze on where she stepped. "Thirty years of life and you can boil it down to one sentence?"

I shrugged. "Maybe I'm not that interesting."

Audrey scoffed. "I find that hard to believe."

Something about that comment warmed my chest far more than the way I overheated every day. "Are you saying you like me, lusty lady?"

Audrey sighed. "I really hate that nickname."

"Yeah, I get it," I agreed, nodding. "How about lusty *wench*?"

Her hand zinged through the air right before it smacked me on the bicep. I grabbed my arm in fake pain while she shot daggers from her warm brown eyes.

"Would it hurt you to be nice and actually try to get to know someone?"

We kept hiking while I thought about that. It sounded painful to actually get to know someone, but maybe not so painful if that someone was Audrey. I already knew she kissed like an angel flirting with the devil on her shoulder.

"Okay, fine. How many times have you orgasmed in the back of The Tavern with a stranger?"

Audrey sucked in an angry breath. "Once, thank you very much!"

"Ah. So I'm special."

Audrey marched ahead of me, clearly pissed off at me based on the way she let out a growl before giving me the beautiful view of her backside hiking up this mountain.

"Are we done sharing?" I called after her, unable to contain the laughter.

She was a quick hiker when she was pissed. I learned another thing about this fake date of mine: she's stubborn as hell. I only caught up to her when we got to a dilapidated wood bridge over a healthy stream a good twenty feet below. Audrey stood there looking at it like it was a snake, ready to strike.

"What's going on?" I asked, looking at her, then the bridge, and back to her. Her face looked pale and her eyes had gone hazy, unfocused. It hit me then that she might be afraid of heights.

I looked back at the bridge and calculated how to get across on the most sturdy parts of it. I slid my hand into Audrey's and took a tentative step forward, but she didn't budge. She remained rooted to the dirt path like some of those tall pines we hiked through.

"How is it you've grown up in Blueball around all these mountains and are scared of heights?" I taunted her.

Her head whipped up and her eyes narrow. At least they look focused again. Perhaps my strategy could work.

"Doesn't Paisley climb electrical poles for a living?" I scoffed. "And you can't cross a bridge."

"You're such an asshole," Audrey hissed, and then turned to light into me further. "I'm here to help you out, you know. You don't have to be a jerk the entire time."

I took a few steps forward, still holding her hand and holding my breath when she followed me, unconcerned with the bridge or the twenty-foot drop if this thing didn't hold us.

"Oh, you're here to help *me* out?" I egged her on. "Pretty sure you're here to collect that fat commission check, LL."

"Oh, because making a living is something to be ashamed

about? Please. You're the one sticking your nose into someone else's business just to get back into Keva's good graces."

I frowned, forgetting this whole argument was just to get her across the bridge. "You don't know anything about Keva and me."

"I certainly do, beast! You think Keva hasn't spilled to us about the bullshit disappearing act you pulled on your own sister?"

Our feet hit the dirt on the other side of the bridge, and I should have counted it as a victory, but all I wanted to do was take off in a run. Leave this woman behind and all the shame that came with my situation with Keva.

I glared at her, towering over her and liking when she shrunk back just an inch from my glower. "You don't know what you're talking about."

And then it was me taking off on the trail and leaving her behind. It took a good twenty minutes of me steaming to realize that this was insanity. I couldn't let this woman derail my plans here in Blueball. I couldn't storm ahead and leave her behind when I knew she didn't have the skills to survive out here. In fact, it was as I worked off the angry energy enough to have a cool head, I realized a colder wind had picked up. I frowned, stopping and pulling the packs off my back to rummage through for the snack bars I'd packed. Audrey wandered up the trail ten minutes later, breathing heavy.

"How about a quick break? We're halfway to the cabin." I held out the snack bar as a peace offering.

Audrey hesitated for just a second before taking the snack from my hands and sitting down on a nearby rock. The sigh she let out made me realize that I should have offered a break before now. Normally, I would have remembered that others didn't necessarily have the same stamina I did, or the same leg length that allowed more ground to be covered. If I hadn't let her get under my skin, I would have realized it quicker.

I chewed on my own snack bar in silence, pulling out the

map Pete had drawn on a piece of notebook paper this morning. I actually thought we might be more than halfway there by now.

A horrible racket of incongruent notes had my head snapping up. Audrey had finished her snack and was sitting on the rock with her hands cupped over her mouth. It took a few more ear-piercing squawks before I realized she was playing a harmonica.

"What the fuck?" I murmured.

Audrey let out a squeaked note and pulled the harmonica from her mouth to glare at me. "What? It's good to have hobbies, yes?"

My mouth fell open, and when she went back to screeching out a harmony not even the drunkest songbird could recognize, I started laughing. This woman was certifiably insane. Grouchy one second, stubborn the next, and then doing the most random shit right after.

Something about that combo did it for me though.

I packed up our trash, helped her off the rock, and stayed by her side the rest of the way to the cabin. I didn't even say anything to piss her off, which had to be a record.

CHAPTER EIGHT

udrey

I SHOULD HAVE BROUGHT a blindfold instead of a harmonica. I already knew Boston was hot, but heavy breathing up a mountain next to him half naked was creating a restlessness inside of me that no amount of hiking could burn through. Some men just looked hotter in nature and Boston was definitely one of them. I, on the other hand, had hair sticking to my neck and face, enough dirt covering my jeans to officially change their color from blue to brown, and a bright smudge of Fruit Roll-Ups on my sweatshirt from when we stopped for another snack. Yes, I thought flattened, dried fruit would make for a good snack for hiking, a notion Boston quickly dashed when he made me aware of the amount of sugar in the product. Pardon me for not knowing the best wilderness food. I was more of a charcuterie-board girl with a glass of white wine, but that seemed impractical in my tiny backpack.

I hazarded a glance over at Boston, confirming yet again that he was hotter than Thor with the hair pulled back, chest heaving, and a light sheen of sweat coating his tan skin. It was so unfair. I looked like an overheated pig on a death hike while he looked like he belonged on the front of an REI product catalog. I wasn't even carrying a pack and I couldn't feel my legs. They'd gone past intense burning to a numbness that spelled trouble for tomorrow.

"We about there?" I panted.

Boston developed the most annoying smirk when he looked at me, but then he pointed straight ahead and delivered such good news I was willing to overlook his judgement of me.

"The cabin is right after that bend."

My euphoria was short-lived however. When the cabin came into view, it didn't look anything like a resort or a fun little cabin in the woods where I could lie in bed all day and listen to the birds chirp. The entire cabin was leaning to the left.

"Is it just me or..."

I tilted my head, wondering if maybe I was just experiencing dehydration on top of exhaustion. When Boston tilted his head alongside me, I knew we were in trouble. I heard him suck in a deep breath and let it out slowly.

"Okay, you check the back of the cabin for firewood and I'll make sure the structure is sound."

Boston clapped his hands and walked away, like his word was gospel or something. Then again, if that cabin collapsed the second we unlocked the door, I wanted it to fall on his head, not mine. So I gave my legs their thousandth pep talk of the day and headed around back. There was a stack of wood under a blue tarp next to an overturned bucket and a shovel. I looked just long enough to confirm it before letting the tarp fall back in place. There were long strings of cobwebs between the pile and the back wall of the cabin. And where there were cobwebs, there were spiders. And probably snakes.

"Damn, look at me being all outdoorsy and shit," I said to myself, walking back to the front to see if we could go inside.

The front door was open, so I went in too, my gaze taking in the meager furnishings. The whole cabin was just one giant room under an A-frame roof. The wood stove was along the back wall. A sink and one cabinet were next to a stove that might have been from the early 1900s. Given that my stomach gave another loud growl, I should have looked longer at the amenities in the kitchen, but my entire focus was pulled to the single bed in the middle of the room.

Boston was cleaning out the wood stove, both of our packs resting next to a tiny wood table with two chairs that most definitely would not hold Boston's weight.

"I know where I'm sleeping tonight," I said with all the enthusiasm I had left in my weary body. "But where are *you* sleeping?"

Boston twisted around and barely spared me a second glance before he shoved more wood in the stove. "I thought you'd be more upset about the lack of a bathroom."

I gasped, gaze frantically taking in every corner of the tiny place. He was right. No toilet. No shower. Just a tiny porcelain bathtub shoved in one corner that was currently holding a stack of blankets that looked as comfortable as burlap sacks.

"But...where...my bladder..." I couldn't even form a coherent sentence. This whole situation was just so far south of the weekend in the woods that had been in my head. I'd pictured drinking my mug of coffee on the deck of a luxury log cabin with the hot tub just a few steps away. Multiple bedrooms and a fully stocked kitchen. Places to hide from the beast and pretend that he didn't drive me absolutely crazy.

But sharing a bed? Peeing outside? This was the stuff of nightmares for a city girl. Sure, I lived in a small town, but I didn't come from a camping family. I was not made for the great outdoors any more than our family Yorkie would hold up in the wild without her fancy gluten-free biscuits.

Boston swept past me and it took me a second to realize that I no longer saw my breath inside the cabin. The wood stove in the corner was pumping out enough heat I could take my dirty sweatshirt off. I was that weird combination of hot from hiking, but starting to get cold because my clothes were sweaty. Boston walked by me again, his arms full of blue tarp.

"Oh God. Are there spiders on that thing?"

Boston didn't even spare me a glance. He unfurled the tarp and began looping a rope through the end of the tarp. "I shook it out. Unpack my bag in the kitchen."

I stuck my tongue out at the back of his head. I really did not like his drill sergeant commands. Then again, I was just standing here like an idiot while he MacGyvered his way through the cabin like some sort of survivalist. Before I could turn and empty his pack, he had a shower curtain of sorts hung from the ceiling and blocking off the view of the bathtub.

"You'd be perfect for that reality show where they go in the wild and have to survive for thirty days." I could see it now. He'd be the master of the jungle with very little clothing and all the social skills of an angry hippopotamus. Now that I thought about it, he actually resembled a giant-sized Tarzan.

"Food. Pack. Kitchen," he called from behind the curtain.

"You Tarzan, me Jane," I muttered sarcastically, walking over to the pack and unzipping the top pocket. When his shirt tumbled out, smelling exactly like pine trees and soap, I closed my eyes and willed myself not to pull the material up to my nose to get a good whiff. He'd smelled good in that hallway of the bar and now I knew it wasn't because of some magnificent cologne. Boston just smelled like the outdoors.

"What did you say?"

I twisted to see Boston standing near me, his hands on his hips, his impressive chest like a walking billboard for creatine and bench-pressing. I shoved his shirt back in the pack and turned back around to pull out cans of beans, tuna, and corn. Jesus. It was a recipe for guaranteed gastrointestinal pain.

"Did you pack any hot dogs?" I asked hopefully, sure that if I just dug a little further, I'd find the ingredients for s'mores. Who the hell went to a cabin for the weekend and didn't pack graham crackers and marshmallows?

"It's getting colder than it should. I need to get more firewood in here just in case. Can you handle getting some food heating up?"

The seriousness of his voice made me pause. He was mostly always serious, except when he was teasing me, but this tone had a tinge of worry that had me doubly worried.

"Colder than it should?"

Boston looked out one of the only two windows in the cabin. "The weather didn't call for a storm, but you never know this time of year. I'd rather be safe than sorry."

I nodded. I'd actually checked the weather too. There'd been no mention of a storm, so maybe it was just colder at this elevation? "I'd rather be safe than sorry too, so I'm going to just heat up the beans. Save the corn for tomorrow."

Boston grunted and walked out of the cabin, which in Boston-speak certainly meant *great, good job, I appreciate your team effort, Audrey.*

I stood with two cans of beans. "You're so welcome, Boston. I really like how we're communicating and not just ordering each other around."

Yes, I was talking to myself while studying a stove that had knobs with no numbers or directions. I put the cans down and twisted one knob, then the second. Only one burner actually began to heat, but I only needed one burner for our simple meal. There was exactly one pot to choose from on the tiny countertop, and after I rinsed it out with questionable water from the tap, I poured in the beans and set them on the working burner.

Boston came back in several times with armloads of firewood, dumping them in the corner of the cabin. The beans were almost done when he came in with a bucket of water and set it down to peer over my shoulder at our dinner.

"You head to the bath and I'll heat some water so you can get cleaned up."

I held up the spoon I'd been stirring the beans with. "You just want to eat all my beans. Well, don't come crying to me when your tummy hurts tonight."

Boston looked at me like I was a forest animal that had snuck into the cabin, speaking a foreign language. "Audrey?"

I brightened, surprised he was using my name. Perhaps he was willing to be civil now that we'd arrived at the cabin. "Yes, Boston?"

He hefted the bucket of water into his hand. "Get in the fucking bathtub."

I pointed at him with the spoon, eyes narrowed. "You're rude."

"And you stink."

I gasped, throwing the spoon at him. It hit him square in the chest and fell to the dirty wood floor. Twirling around, I nearly fell when my tired legs didn't follow the abrupt motion. I righted myself, ignored his snicker, and marched over to the curtain, ripping it aside and stepping inside this makeshift bathroom. I was grumbling under my breath about this being the hardest commission I'd ever make while I got the blankets—scratchy as sandpaper, I confirmed—out of the bathtub and climbed in.

"Do not come in here," I warned. I pulled my shirt and sports bra over my head, sighing in relief to have those sweaty clothes off. My jeans peeled off next with mud falling into the tub. I may have fallen once when Boston had marched up ahead of me on the hike, a fact I would never be sharing with him. My socks were last, and when I was blissfully naked, I realized I had no towel and no water.

"Water's hot." Boston's voice came from just inches away on the other side of the tarp curtain.

I yelped and nearly slipped in the tub. "Just leave it there."

"You're not going to be able to lift it." His beefy hand came around and looked like it was going to yank the curtain aside.

I covered myself as well as a girl with C-cups can and hollered, "Close your eyes at least, beast!"

His exasperated sigh was annoying but at least his eyes were closed when he appeared, bucket of water in hand. "I can't see the damn tub, Audrey."

I guided his hand until the bucket was directly over my tub. "Okay, dump now and then get out."

He did, the warm water flowing over my feet and instantly turning my bones to mush. "Oh my God, yes," I moaned.

Boston jerked back and spun, getting caught up in the tarp and nearly ripping the whole thing down before he got free from it. I sank into the tub and my laugh died on my lips. The heat melted away my tired muscles. The sweat and grime floated away from my skin. This was the heaven I'd been anticipating this weekend.

A towel came sailing over the curtain to land on the floor by the tub. I could have thanked him but I was currently in a state of bliss that left no room for conversation with that Neanderthal. Clanks and curses came from the other side of the curtain, but I stayed until the water went cold and I began to shiver. Climbing out and groaning again at my muscles protesting, I grabbed the towel and wrapped it around myself. When I was sure all the goods were tucked away, I came out from behind the curtain.

Boston set two bowls down on the table, looking like he was purposely looking away from me. "Food's ready."

"Thanks," I mumbled, too relaxed from the bath to remember to be pissed off at him. I fumbled through my bag, squatting carefully so I wouldn't flash my cabin-mate. I pulled out the sweatpants and tank top I normally slept in, wondering belatedly if that would be warm enough for this place. I went back behind the curtain to change, coming out feeling like a new woman.

Boston had already tucked into his beans, but I couldn't blame him. He'd carried both our packs and his was substantially heavier than mine. Plus he was at least double my size and all he ate was fruit and protein bars on the trail. Who can live on that shit?

We were silent throughout the meal. By the time I slid my spoon back into my empty bowl, my eyelids were weighing heavy.

"I'm so tired," I moaned.

Boston did that thing where he laughed but it was only through his nose. "Get in bed. I'll clean up."

My eyes opened wide, remembering the original dilemma. "But where are you going to sleep?"

His jaw tightened. "In the same damn bed, Audrey. Don't worry. I won't touch you."

I aimed a finger at him. "You better not."

That was the last thing I said to him before I slid between the covers and laid my head down on the pillow. The mattress was surprisingly comfortable, or perhaps I was just so tired it didn't matter, but I was out within seconds.

The next thing I knew I was cuddling with a giant warm bear with an erection pressing into my body. It was the strangest dream. Especially when I ground my hips against the bear and I made him moan.

CHAPTER NINE

I DIDN'T SLIP into bed for another hour, pacing the cabin and staring out the windows up at the sky. My cell phone didn't work up here, which didn't surprise me. I figured we'd be cut off, but I didn't figure on a storm rolling through when all the weather apps didn't call for one. But I always followed my gut and my gut was telling me that cold wind blowing in while I gathered more firewood was not normal. The conclusion was that there was nothing I could do. It was dark, the storm would either blow through or not, and we'd have to wait it out here in the cabin.

I tossed and turned, not finding a comfortable spot when my feet were hanging off the bed and I was trying not to touch Audrey, who had her arms splayed out to the side and took up more than half the bed. Every time I closed my eyes, I envisioned the outline of her body behind that damn tarp turned curtain. The sun had been setting through the window behind her and I'd seen every tantalizing curve I wanted to get my hands on again, even though the woman irritated me to no end.

Sleep must have found me at some point because I woke up to all those curves lying on top of me and a swath of hair across my face that smelled like citrus. It was when Audrey rolled her hips, grinding against the erection I couldn't control any more than the way my breathing had picked up at the first realization of her body pressed against me, that I let out a moan. My hands flew to her hips and I held her there for a long moment. Then the hair lifted off my face, and in the dark of the night I saw Audrey's wide eyes staring down at me. I could have been dreaming, but then she let out a full-body shiver and slid off me, ending what would have been the best dream I'd had in years.

Audrey groaned and rolled to her side of the bed. "Freezing in here!" Her voice was high pitched and exactly like the voice that had called out for God when I gave her that orgasm at the bar.

I blinked rapidly, reaching down to grab my dick and inform him that playtime was over. He had no plans to listen. I sat up in bed, alarm finally piercing the fog of sleep and denied sexual tension. It was cold in here. I huffed and could have sworn I saw my breath. Swinging my legs out of bed, I shoved my feet in my boots and grabbed the flashlight I'd laid there the night before, heading for the wood stove to add a few more logs to the small glowing embers that were left. With that taken care of, I went to the front window and peered outside. White flakes drifted down from the sky.

"Shit," I said. My voice carried like a shotgun in total silence.

"What's wrong?" Audrey sounded wide awake now.

I winced, a to-do list already forming in my head. The storm I was hoping wasn't brewing overnight definitely had. I hadn't said a word to Audrey when we got to the cabin, figuring she wasn't prepared to rough it out here in the cabin on a good weekend, let alone through a storm that dumped snow. I didn't need to add her panic to my list of things to deal with right now.

"Just a little snow," I grumbled back, trying to peer out and see how much was sticking to the ground. I'd need to monitor our firewood usage, audit how much food I'd brought and make it last a few days longer if this thing dumped more snow than a dusting, and figure out a way to dig out a path to the outhouse behind the house. Or we'd be using a bucket and I had a feeling Audrey would be highly resistant to that idea.

"I have to pee," Audrey said from right behind me. "I hate to ask, but can you show me where that outhouse is?"

I spun around to see Audrey dressed in sweatpants, a sweatshirt, and a green knit hat that looked like a child made it. While drunk. And possibly blind. Her feet must be frozen inside a pair of socks with dancing pineapples on them. I didn't get a chance to tease her about her outfit choices before her gaze darted behind me and she gasped.

"Is it snowing?" Audrey barreled into me to get to the window, her nose smashing against it and creating a circle of condensation when she breathed. Despite her discordant outfit, she looked cute. Like a city girl playing at roughing it out in nature.

"Yeah. Bit of a storm is blowing through." I didn't like the amount of white that was falling like a thick blanket from the heavens. "Can you pee in the tub for now?"

Audrey whirled around, her face set in a grimace that was made scarier by the shadows my flashlight cast in the dark cabin. "The tub??"

I shrugged and reached out to tug her away from the window. There was a draft coming through that wouldn't help the situation. "Just squat and aim for the drain, LL."

"Do not talk about peeing in a tub and call me LL," she snapped, her legs finally working enough to let me drag her to said tub.

"Sorry," I grumbled, pulling the tarp aside to let her get to the tub. "I keep forgetting you prefer wench."

Audrey growled and the sound woke up the erection that had finally gone down. Which was why I snapped at her.

"Get in so I can go back to bed and not freeze to death."

Audrey lifted her nose in the air like a queen and stepped into the tub. "I always run hot," she said, her tone deep and cartoonish and quite clearly a mockery of me.

It was my turn to growl, which made Audrey laugh as I let the curtain fall back into place. Worries slammed into my brain and I knew I was the only one that had the skills to get us through a freak winter storm with very little supplies, but even that didn't stop my brain from envisioning Audrey pulling down her pants and squatting. There was literally nothing sexy about peeing, and even so, my brain went there. I was clearly not well in the head.

"I can't pee with you right there, beast." Audrey's voice floated over the curtain.

I jolted, realizing I was standing right there next to the flimsy curtain that separated us like an absolute creep. Instead of continuing to be the beast she called me, I walked away and assessed the small stack of firewood I'd brought in last night. I'd feel better if the stack was bigger, but I'd trusted the weather reports instead of my gut. That was my first fail. Second was bringing Audrey with me when I hadn't even assessed the cabin first. I'd have to dig out in the first light of day and see if I could rescue more firewood from behind the cabin before it became soaked.

"Well, that wasn't what I had on my bingo card for the weekend," Audrey drawled just as I heard the curtain being pushed aside.

I spun around and tried to calm my spiraling thoughts. There was nothing I could do since it was still dark. I put enough wood in the stove to last us until morning. Then I could assess and figure out a plan. What I needed right now was to get some sleep so I could execute on that plan tomorrow.

"The stove should keep it reasonably warm in here."

Audrey walked over to the bed and crawled back in, pulling the covers up to her chin. "I think you and I have different definitions of 'reasonably warm,' beast." Her teeth were literally chattering.

I sat down on my side of the bed and pulled my boots off. Contrary to her teasing, I did run warm and I forgot that other people didn't. If I felt comfortable in here, Audrey was probably still freezing. Clicking the flashlight off and plunging us into total darkness again, I lay down and stared up at the ceiling, hoping that roof held like Pete had promised it would.

"You'll probably call me a beast again, but sharing body heat is a good idea when you're cold."

I waited for her to rip me a new one, but she stayed eerily quiet. When she still didn't respond after several seconds ticked by, I lifted onto my elbow and peered down at her. She looked hilariously beautiful with all that blonde hair flowing out from the stupid hat. Even with no makeup, the woman was stunning. Soft, smooth, pale skin with a thick fringe of dark eyelashes that nearly touched her cheeks with her eyes closed. I could have stared at her for hours which was why I chose to tease her instead.

"Already dead of frostbite?"

Her eyes blinked open and she glared at me. "No. Just contemplating snuggling. I'm cold enough to consider it."

I shot her a cocky look that I knew would heat her from the inside. "I didn't suggest cuddling. Just sharing body heat."

"And just how do you share body heat, beast?"

The grin intensified. "Spooning."

Audrey scoffed but rolled over, giving me her backside. "Spooning. Snuggling. Same thing."

I lay back down and threw my arm around her waist and pulled her into me. She yelped and I smiled into the night at the feel of her ass right up against where I wanted her most. I would absolutely be getting no sleep tonight.

"Spooning sounds better," I said quietly. I was not a snuggler. No fucking way.

"As long as we aren't forking," Audrey said with a bubble of laughter in her tone.

I barked out a surprised laugh. For being such a grump in my presence since the night at the bar, the woman was funny when she let herself. I kept my hands away from her body, even as we were pressed up against each other from chest to toes. I had a feeling if I copped a feel, this woman would spring out of the bed and find a way to shoot me. The woman who'd let me bring her to orgasm in the bar had disappeared once she knew my relationship to Annabel.

Audrey's breathing evened out after awhile, but I still couldn't get my body nor my mind to settle. I'd been so desperate to find a way into my sister's good graces, I hadn't spared a thought to this trip being potentially dangerous for Audrey. And that made me the asshole Audrey already thought I was.

"What's going to happen if it keeps snowing?" Audrey whispered, voice sleepy and barely audible.

My arm tightened around her. "I won't let anything happen to you." It was the truth. I wouldn't let harm come to anyone who was with me, but especially her.

"But you hate me."

I shook my head, settling my nose further into her curtain of hair and giving myself a second to inhale her scent. "I don't hate you, Audrey."

She made a noise that was neither agreement nor argument with my statement and the sound lessened the grip of anxiety that currently strangled my throat. "Good thing I brought my harmonica. If we get stuck here, I'll have plenty of time to practice."

I groaned, and this time it had nothing to do with sexual tension or being irritated at the woman in my arms. A long time later, I remembered that I brought earplugs in my backpack and that lucky fact allowed me to finally drift into sleep.

CHAPTER TEN

udrey

I WOKE up at the crack of dawn the next morning in a delightful dream about being hugged by a space heater. That heater turned out to be Boston, once my eyes blinked open and I saw the huge forearm that lay atop my waist. His tan skin was lined with a smattering of medium-brown hair and his hands were nicely shaped. Because of course they were. The man was built like a Greek god from head to toe. Couldn't a girl hope for a misshapen toe or two to make herself feel better?

Far as I'd seen, there was nothing misshapen about Boston. Especially not the steel pipe that was currently digging into my backside. If I didn't already have firsthand knowledge of the size of that thing, I would have sworn he snuck a log of firewood down his pants while we slept. And sadly, I wasn't irritated at all that his dick was currently cozy with my ass cheeks. In fact, I quite liked it based on the ache that came from between my legs and the instant restlessness that had me itching to reach back and grab ahold of that appendage and fuck the consequences.

Which was the exact thought that had me rolling out from under his arm and off the bed like there were fire ants attacking. Boston was all wrong for me. Even beyond his relationship with my best friend, he was not the kind of guy I was looking for. I was ready to meet Mr. Right. The one I'd settle down with and fill a three-bedroom, two-bath house with kids.

My socks hit the wood floor and my legs decided to do a Bambi impression. My knees buckled and my thighs shook as they screamed bloody murder. I went down, hands flailing wildly for the bed. All I got was a handful of sheet that slid off the bed and covered me as I lay in a heap on the floor. Pain slid through me and I may have begged for my mommy out loud.

The mattress creaked, and to my horror, Boston leaned over the side, his long hair adorably mussed and his eyes crinkling at the corners as he stared down at me.

"What the hell, lusty?"

I stared right back at him, brought too low physically to even consider fighting back verbally. "I think my legs are a lost cause."

He grinned so wide I saw a glimpse of his slightly crooked teeth on the bottom row. He wasn't wearing a shirt, which was ridiculous considering I was covered from head to toe and was still freezing. The sight of his broad shoulders had that ache between my legs coming back, and quite frankly, I was too achy everywhere to deal with more.

"I'm glad my recent disability makes you happy," I snapped.

That made him disappear from view as he flopped back on the bed, but I heard the howl of laughter. It was the kind of deep belly laugh that automatically made your lips tilt up in a smile, even if you didn't understand the punchline.

I knew exactly two concrete things about Boston: he could make a tree trunk orgasm just looking at him and he had the best laugh I'd ever heard. All the other details were just that: details that didn't matter.

"Could use a hand over here," I said dryly, rolling my eyes when that sent him into another round of belly laughs.

Boston eventually rolled off his side of the bed and came around to help me up. He manhandled me in a way that I should have hated on principle yet didn't. Not at all. With one swift yank, he lifted me bodily off the floor and onto my feet. He kept his hands on my hips until we were both confident my knees wouldn't buckle.

"You want to use the bathtub and I'll go heat some more water? I think a warm bath might help your legs loosen up."

I looked up at him to see concern on his face. Maybe the beast did have a kind bone in his body after all. "That sounds great. Thanks."

I hobbled to the makeshift curtain and pulled it back, climbing into the tub to do my business. Never in all the months I studied for my realtor's license did I think I'd go to these lengths to earn a commission. I was peeing in a bathtub for fuck's sake.

"Ready for water?" Boston called out.

When I was undressed and I made him promise to keep his eyes averted, he poured a bucket of water in the tub and went back to heat another. By the time the tub was full and I was feeling limp and pain-free, Boston announced he was heading out to assess the situation.

"I left a Pop-Tart heating on the wood stove for you when you're done," he rumbled in that deep voice of his.

My eyes sprang open. "Sugar? You're purposely feeding me sugar?"

I barely heard his grumble before the loud scrape of the door being opened cut him off. "Seems to be all you run on."

I grinned, leaning my head back on the porcelain tub and appreciating the hot bath. For as much of a grump as Boston was, I couldn't deny that he was taking good care of me. He was dealing with the wood situation to keep us warm and he'd packed in food for both of us. Those were nice gestures that didn't fit his constant stormy glower.

I'd pulled on a pair of ski pants and a clean sweatshirt, sitting down to eat my perfectly roasted Pop-Tart when Boston came through the door again. A gust of cold, wintery air came with him, making me shiver. He was covered in snow, the sight of which made my stomach tighten with anxiety.

"Do we need to call a snow plow?" I asked.

Boston stomped his feet and then shed a few of his outer layers by the door. He ran a hand through his hair and then pulled it back into a knot on the back of his head. He still didn't answer when he came to sit in the rickety chair across from me.

"No snow plow."

I smiled. "Oh good. You think most of it will have melted by tomorrow morning?"

Boston looked at me and then his gaze dropped to the scarred tabletop. "Uh, no. I was able to see down the mountain enough to know the bridge is mostly washed out and we got about a foot of snow. Maybe less lower on the mountain."

The food in my mouth tasted like chalk. "A foot?"

Boston's jaw clenched and he brought his gaze back to me. "We can't hike out in a foot of snow. And with the bridge uncertainty, there's no way we can get back without help."

The pastry fell from my hand and broke apart on the table. "I'm sorry. I was hallucinating and thought you just said there's no way we can get back."

Boston put his hand on mine, smothering it with heat. "We can and we will get back. It just won't be tomorrow."

My mouth dropped open. This was not part of the plan. I wasn't a wilderness girl. I couldn't pee in a bathtub for longer than a day or two without surely losing my mind. I was built for afternoon coffee dates, and girls' night at a bar, and dinner "al fresco" in my world meant eating out on the patio right on Main Street where cars driven by friends honked at you to say hello.

I snapped my mouth shut and stood so quickly the wooden chair fell over backwards, clattering to the floor. "I'll call my brothers. They can get us out of here."

Ace was a fireman. Blaze was a retired stuntman with a kennel of support dogs that could track us down. Callan was an EMT. Daxon built custom log homes with his bare hands. Ethan…well, Ethan was all around a handy guy and exactly who I'd go to if I fell apart emotionally and I'd eat my damn hat if I wasn't already halfway to a complete meltdown. If they couldn't get me out, no one could.

Boston stood up too, reaching for me. His hands held my arms steady when what I wanted to do was run for my phone and power it up.

"No cell service up here."

I reached up and smacked him on the chest. He didn't even flinch. I could have been a fly landing on his T-shirt for all my fists affected him. Physically assaulting people wasn't normally my reaction to bad news, but I could feel my heart rate climbing with no end in sight. The four walls seemed to close in around us.

"Could you at least try sugarcoating it first?"

Boston's thumb began to sweep up and down my arm. His eyes warmed but his jaw never unclenched. "I won't sugarcoat the situation, Audrey. I'll always tell you the honest truth, even if you don't like it. What I'll also do is get us out of here. You can count on that."

"When?" Hope latched on to his words like a lifeline.

"Multiple people know where we are. They also know the storm rolled through and I'm sure they guess that we're stuck. It'll just take some time for them to get some help to reinforce what's left of the bridge and we can cross."

I used my hands to grip his T-shirt. It was either that or hit him again. "When, Boston?"

He shrugged. The irritatingly calm oaf *shrugged*. "Maybe a few days?"

I wrenched my arms out of his grip and spun around, beginning to pace the cabin. "I can't believe this is happening."

"It's honestly fine. I brought enough food to last if we ration it. And there's firewood out back that I can bring in to start drying. We should be fine."

I glanced at the stack of firewood Boston had brought in last night only to find two measly logs. Two logs did not make a stack. "Where's all the dry firewood?" I spun back around, suddenly feeling like the temperature had dropped another few degrees in here while he'd been gone.

Boston wasn't holding my gaze. "We went through it overnight and this morning."

"Oh my God, we're going to freeze to death!"

Later, I'd probably look back at this moment and wonder when I'd gotten so bad at handling a crisis, but at the moment, all I could do was try to breathe without passing out from anxiety.

Boston spun around and grabbed the chair he'd been sitting on. He picked it up and held it above his head and for a split second I thought he was going to throw it at me like some kind of WWE wrestling match, wilderness edition. I wouldn't blame him either. I was overreacting and I knew it in the back of my head, but I couldn't seem to stop my panic from overflowing. In the next moment, he brought the chair down on his raised knee, the whole thing splintering into a pile of sticks.

"Boom. Firewood," Boston deadpanned.

We both stared at the stack of wood at his feet. That was when the hysteria took over. I threw back my head to stare up at the wood ceiling planks and began to laugh an unhinged laugh. The kind that makes others cringe and small animals run for cover. If this was a movie, I was the villain, losing my mind and letting everyone know it.

Boston already had half the chair fed into the wood stove before I was able to collect myself enough to speak. "Pete's going to be so mad at you."

Boston smirked, though I didn't miss the way his gaze flickered over mine first to make sure I hadn't completely lost my mind. "I'll buy him a new table and chairs. In the meantime, I'll bring in the wet firewood and get it drying out while we burn that hideous set."

I looked at the poor table and single chair, knowing its fate was sealed. "It's not hideous really. Just rustic."

Boston swept past me to the front door, pulling on his boots again. He shook his head, his gaze lighting on the dining set like it'd personally affronted him. "The chairs are made for children."

That brought the laughter back. Boston was adorable when he pouted. The giggles kept coming the whole time I ate the forgotten Pop-Tart off the table before it got burned in the wood stove along with everything else. The stack of firewood grew, covering a third of the floor space in this cabin. Then I heated up a Pop-Tart for Boston. After all, he was doing all the work.

When he was satisfied with the firewood situation and the table and chairs were no more, he took all the scratchy blankets from the corner and threw them on the bed.

"Now what?" I asked, genuinely curious as to what the game plan was.

Boston spread his arms wide. "Now we sit and watch the snow fall."

I raised an eyebrow. "In bed?"

His spreading grin made my stomach swoop. "Yes, lusty. In bed."

CHAPTER ELEVEN

oston

"DID you ever build blanket forts when you were a kid?" Audrey asked, her knit hat askew on her head, her eyes alight with levity now that it was warmer in here.

I grinned, thinking back on building forts with Annabel...er, Keva. Damn. It would take me some time to remember she wanted to be called Keva. In my head, she'd always be Princess Annabel, dressed in a Disney princess ball gown and her little nose in the air. But she was grown up and married now. If she wanted to be called Keva, I needed to at least try to respect her wishes.

"Hell, yeah. I think every little kid does at least once or twice."

I lifted a blanket off the bed and draped it over the headboard. Audrey ducked her head and scooted back, now under the makeshift tent of blankets. I tried to get in on the other side, but the entirety of my legs stuck out and my head kept the blanket impossibly high on my side. Audrey rolled her lips in and then burst into laughter, falling over and slapping her hand on my thigh.

"Goddamn blanket isn't big enough," I grumbled, climbing back out to find a bigger one.

The situation wasn't dire. I knew this and yet my worries about Audrey's comfort kept me on edge. If I'd been on my own, I wouldn't have had a single worry. I'd have dealt with the cold and dried enough firewood to make it two freaking weeks up here. The panic on Audrey's face when I told her the bridge was washed out had hit me like an icicle right through the chest. It didn't take a psychologist for me to understand that my guilt over not taking care of my little sister when she needed me most was running amuck in this situation. I couldn't fail yet another vulnerable female.

"My sister and I would make them and then we'd have to tear them down before my father got home because he hated the mess."

I grimaced. "Sounds like a gem."

Audrey snorted, then immediately smiled and clapped when I found a bigger blanket to drape over the headboard. "Don't get me started. I need alcohol before I talk about my family."

Once the blanket made a decent tent, I rooted around in my pack before coming back to the bed and sliding in. This time, I ducked lower. My feet were still out of the blanket fort, but my head wasn't threatening to punch a hole in the top this way.

I shook the glass bottle of whiskey. "Did you say alcohol?"

Audrey's face lit up and she wiggled her fingers at me to hand it over. "Bless you, Boston Mooney. You're quite civilized for a beast."

She took a swig of whiskey and then hissed after she swallowed, handing it back to me. Audrey really was pretty. Smiling more than anyone I ever knew. Even when she was mad at me, her face was so expressive I just wanted to stare at her.

I waited until we'd both had a few sips before asking the question. "So, tell me about your family."

Audrey sighed and scooted down to lean her head on my shoulder. I froze, not wanting to jostle her or give her any excuse to move away. "It's a long story, but just a few years ago my mom, sister, and I found out that my father had been married before. Did you see the woman I was with at The Tavern?"

I tsked. "Audrey. We aren't talking about that, remember?"

She grabbed for the whiskey bottle and tugged it out of my hand. "Only in front of Keva."

"Oh, gotcha. I didn't understand the rules." I found myself grinning. "And yes, I saw her. She looks like quite a character."

Audrey swallowed another sip, her voice getting raspier the more she drank. "She is. I love her so much. That's my father's ex-wife. Or she would have been his ex if he'd actually divorced her before getting involved with my mom and having me and my sister."

Anger filled every crevice of my body. What kind of man treated women and his own children like that? The unfairness of it all hit me. Why did my parents, who were good, honest, loving parents, have to die while men like Audrey's dad live a thousand more days just to hurt more people?

My hand lifted from my lap and hovered over her thigh. I finally placed it there, the breath whooshing out of my body when she didn't bat me away. "I'm sorry, Audrey. That man doesn't deserve to have the title of father."

Audrey squeaked. "That's what I said! But my sister didn't seem to care. She just wanted Dad to keep funding her college lifestyle and who cares about who he's hurt." Audrey shook her head, her blonde hair flying around her shoulders. "I don't under-stand that. No amount of money or support is worth letting that kind of behavior slide."

I thought about her story, understanding dawning as to why she was so prickly with me. She didn't let me get away with a goddamn thing and it was obvious why.

"What about your mom?"

Audrey's leg tightened under my grip. I could feel the anger vibrating off of her. "She stayed with him for a whole year after we all found out. I mean, my dad basically was living a double life, having a wife and five kids in the neighboring town while we never even knew. Come to find out, my parents' marriage wasn't even legal." Audrey slumped against me, her head coming back to my shoulder.

"Damn." I felt terrible for her, but I also really liked her curled up next to me.

"I know, right? Mom finally kicked him out, but I'd already lost all respect for her. She and I still have a strained relationship. She doesn't understand why I like hanging out with my half brothers and my father's ex-wife." Audrey threw her hands up and then let them fall, one of them lying atop my hand on her thigh. We weren't exactly holding hands, but damn close. "They have the same trauma as me. A shared grief. The same anger and disappointment in the same man."

I nodded. "I get it. Grief and trauma bond people more than anything else sometimes. I think that's why I'm so close to Lincoln. We bonded in the military and nothing will shake that."

Audrey's head nodded on my shoulder. "And Keva?"

The familiar guilt stirs up at the mention of her name. "We should have bonded tight when our parents died. But I ran away to the military and left her behind."

I shifted, unable to sit with the feeling. Audrey lifted her head and I could feel her studying the side of my face. I was about to climb out of the blanket fort with some kind of ridiculous task I didn't actually need to do, just to get her to stop studying me when she laced her fingers where they lay on mine. Audrey gave them a squeeze and I hazarded a glance over at her.

Her eyes were soft. Compassionate. Understanding. And I didn't want any of that. Didn't deserve it. I abandoned my sister. I should be hanged for that level of cowardness.

"People react a million different ways to grief. While your reaction wasn't great for Keva, it was a perfectly natural reaction.

Keva won't harbor ill will forever. She just wants you to be there for her now."

I growled and flung her hand off, getting out of the blanket tent and pacing the cabin. Audrey crawled out too, pulling her hat off and tossing it on the bed. I couldn't even look at her. I felt like my skin had shrunk, and I wanted to claw it off of me.

"I don't deserve her forgiveness," I rasped, finally coming to a stop and staring out the window. My hands were clenched into fists, and if I didn't think it would scare her, I'd have slammed one against the wood log of our cabin wall just to have something that would hurt worse than this feeling in my chest.

The scent of Audrey hit right before her soft body pressed against my side. I looked down at her, ready to bark at her to leave me alone. Her hands came up and squished my cheeks, startling me. Then she stepped up on to the overturned bucket I'd been using to heat water for her baths. The extra foot put her almost eye to eye with me. I opened my mouth and suddenly her lips were crashing down on mine, stealing my breath and chasing away any coherent thought. Her tongue darted inside and suddenly my fists were no more. My palms skimmed over her curvy hips and I was sinking into the kiss, as helpless as a newborn kitten.

Audrey pulled away far too soon, but even so my heart was pounding and my lungs were pumping oxygen in and out in a rapid fashion. Her eyes were sparkling and I couldn't even fucking remember what we'd been talking about. She patted my cheeks.

"And there's the beast antidote."

"Huh?" My brain cells hadn't come back online. My hands flexed, getting a better grip on Audrey's body, not understanding the kiss was over.

Audrey grinned and let go of my face. "I had a feeling kissing you would turn off the beast mode."

I grimaced, hating that term. "Beast mode?"

"Yeah. When you go all growly and pissed off. You pace like a giant beast, ready to tear down walls and rearrange faces. It's impressive. Really. I was terrified." She waggled a finger at me, clearly having some fun at my expense. "But I know your secret. Your kryptonite is a kiss."

My eyes narrowed. "From you," I clarified. If she was going to peel back my layers, she better get it fucking right.

Audrey's eyes went wide for a split second and then she was shrugging, stepping down from the bucket. The damn thing tipped and she went sprawling. I caught her, of course, pulling her into my chest and steadying her. She looked up at me, brown eyes trusting me more than I deserved.

"I never thanked you properly, but thanks for the orgasm the other night."

I was hard simply from her kissing me, so hearing those words from her while she was in my arms just made the situation in my pants all the more dire. And then the long list of reasons we couldn't be together again like that flooded through my brain.

"You're just so damn prim and proper in your dresses," I said gruffly, forcing my hands to let her go. "I want to mess you up."

Audrey scoffed, tucking hair behind her ear. "I wasn't wearing a dress at The Tavern."

I grunted, not agreeing that my logic didn't hold up. I did want to mess her up when I saw her in dresses, but it was so much more than that. I was physically attracted to her, for sure. And yet even when she was mouthing off and wearing baggy sweatpants I still wanted her. It was all messed up. *I* was all messed up.

"I wear business attire when appropriate, but I'm not prim and proper," Audrey was still arguing with me.

I couldn't help the sound that escaped my mouth. "I know. You made out with a stranger in a bar. Ain't nothing prim and proper about that."

Audrey straightened her spine, as if she was a queen in this backwoods cabin. "And you like me, even though you always bark orders at me."

"No, I don't." That was the last thing I needed. A crush on my little sister's best friend.

"Yes, you do."

I opened my mouth to argue but Audrey cut me off with a devilish gleam in her eyes.

"You forget I've felt your erection twice now. You like me."

Done with the taunting, I grunted my displeasure. I spun around and fed another log into the stove. I would not continue this ridiculous thread of conversation. Nothing good could come of it. I either denied I liked her, which we both knew wasn't true, or I agreed and then we had a situation on our hands that felt like a ticking time bomb. Neither was a desirable outcome, so I chose to walk away.

Sadly, Audrey chose to walk away just far enough to sit on the bed and put her harmonica up to her mouth. The first note split my eardrum. The second stabbed at my brain like a barbed ice pick. I grunted again and Audrey only played louder.

"This is going to be a long couple of days until we're rescued," I grumbled.

"Same, beast, same," was all she said before going back to the harmonica.

CHAPTER TWELVE

Audrey

LATER THAT NIGHT, after we both put down the whiskey and fell asleep in the same bed, I woke to find myself nearly completely covered by the man lying behind me. Even I could admit that kissing him was probably the wrong move. It had shut down his panic, but it was like striking a match in a room with five industrial stoves pumping out gas. There would most definitely be an explosion, but I had a feeling it wouldn't be the kind I was hoping for.

I hadn't realized just how much Boston wanted to make things right with Keva. I'd only heard Keva's side of things over the years, which wasn't fair. Now that I could see and feel the anguished guilt pumping off of him, I understood just how desperate he was to patch things up with her. If he and I let this powder keg of lust between us explode, it would hurt his chances with Keva and I couldn't be responsible for that. Besides, I'd already put one-night stands behind me.

When the first of the morning light streamed through the

windows and hit my eyelids, the furnace of heat at my back was gone. I rolled over to see an indent in Boston's pillow, but no Boston. I didn't panic when I didn't see him in the cabin. He wouldn't leave me. For all his grumbliness and irritable nature, he was a caretaker at heart. He wouldn't abandon me here.

Rolling out of bed, I got dressed in the last clean outfit I brought with me: a pair of pink sweatpants, a crop top I loved to work out in because of what it did for my boobs, and another gray knit cap I'd made when I was in my knitting phase a few years ago. I brushed my hair, but it was a bit of a disaster from the snow, the bath, and no hair dryer, so I pulled it into a low braid on either side. The sweatshirt I brought wouldn't hold up well against the snow, but I had no plans to be out in the elements any longer than I had to to find Boston.

Thankfully, I didn't have to go very far. I found him only a few yards from the front door of the cabin, shoveling snow. I looked up into the sky to see more flakes falling, albeit at a much slower pace than yesterday. He hadn't heard me coming with his back to me and the way he was mumbling to himself as he attacked the snow like it personally offended him. The man really was a specimen. Why were all the ones who looked like Captain America and Aquaman had a baby lacking in basic personality?

"Hey, beast! It's still snowing. What the hell are you doing?" I mean, come on. The snow was settling on the path he'd just cleared and yet he kept attacking the snow pile like he could singlehandedly clear this whole mountaintop.

Boston straightened for just a moment, looking over his shoulder at me, his gaze not even meeting mine. Then he spun back around, looked at the foot-plus of snow in front of him and threw the shovel like an Olympic javelin thrower. He spun back around and marched back up the path like I wasn't even there. If I hadn't stepped to the side, he might have just barreled right through me.

Well, shit. Boston was in a mood.

I grinned and chased after him. I had to see this up close and personal. He threw open the front door and ducked his head to step inside. I followed and closed the door, watching him take off each offending layer and throw the article of clothing as far as he could. This was like watching a six-foot-four toddler have a tantrum, and I was fascinated.

"Is everything okay?" I asked quietly.

Boston ripped his sweatshirt over his head and tossed it to the ground. My mouth went dry taking in the sweaty T-shirt, molded to his torso and showing off the rippling muscles.

"I've got to do something to get us back," he finally said, pacing the cabin like a trapped bear.

I shook my head, not understanding why he was in a panic to get back now when yesterday he was so calm about the situation. "You're that concerned with getting back to Keva and settling things?"

Boston shrugged, then reached for his hair with both hands and ripped the leather cord out that held it back. He looked like he was ready to pull his hair out with his bare hands.

"Yeah, that's part of it."

He finally stopped pacing and just stared out the window. Instead of staring at his backside and lusting over the broad shoulders, muscled waist, and the ass that defied gravity, I walked over to my backpack and took out my dirty clothes. My plan was to ask him if he'd fill the bucket for me so I could wash the clothes and lay them out by the wood stove. Look at me, being all outdoorsy and shit again.

I ducked my head to see into my backpack, pretty sure I had all the articles of clothing on the floor. "What's the other part?" I asked over my shoulder.

Boston's gaze had zeroed in on my lace panties on the floor. I snatched them up and put them under the pants I wore yesterday, but it was too late. He threw his hands in the air and began to pace again.

"Fucking Blueballs town. Stuck. Of all the. One bed." He was mumbling and I only caught snippets here and there.

I stood, clothes bundled in my arms. If he was going to have a freak-out, he needed to at least rant correctly. "Dude, it's actually just Blueball. Singular. If you're going to live here now, you gotta get the town name right."

Boston moved so fast I dropped my clothes. He grabbed me by the shoulders, shoved me against the dusty wall of the cabin, and crowded me, ducking down until we were nose to nose. His warm body felt like cuddling with a giant teddy bear, the kind you win at a fair and don't have room for but keep anyway because it's so damn adorable. His breath was coming in pants, but after I swallowed hard and got my bearings, I realized I was the one panting. His hands were braced on the wall above my head and his hips kept me pinned.

And there it was: the erection that told me just how much Boston Mooney liked me after all.

My tongue darted out to lick my lips and his gaze followed the motion. The tension was thick between us, that powder keg of repressed desire just ready to blow.

"I was talking about my own blue balls, and I got two of them, lusty."

Then his mouth was on mine, his lips coaxing me open. I didn't need much encouragement. The ho side of me was alive and well, ready to get back to where we'd left off at The Tavern. My hands gripped his biceps and the fact I couldn't get anywhere close to grabbing the whole circumference of his arms made me melt a little more. His body pressed me into the wall, but the flick of his tongue made me forget about those solid wood logs digging into me. When I countered, my tongue thrusting into his mouth, his hands slammed down on my hips and suddenly I was yanked from the wall.

"Jump, baby," he ordered against my lips.

I did, my legs coming around his waist. I tried to lock my feet, but his wide body spread my thighs too far for that. He ground against me, his erection finding just the right spot as he brought my back to the wall again. I let go of his arms long enough to rip my sweatshirt over my head. The second Boston saw what I was wearing underneath, he groaned, dipping his head to kiss the top side of my breasts that threatened to spill out.

The fire between us licked at my heels, threatening to explode. I tilted my head back as he thrust his hips against me, my eyes rolling back and shutting. Then I gasped as Boston pulled one strap of my shirt down and pulled my breast out. His jaw went hard and the rumble I felt in his chest made me feel like a beauty queen despite being pressed against a wall with a boob out and my hair in unwashed braids. He bent down even further and latched his mouth onto my breast, his tongue flicking my aching nipple. The heat of his tongue against my wet flesh made goose bumps pop up all over my skin. I began to thrash, needing more of his mouth. His cock. His hands. All of it. I needed all of it right now.

I grappled with his shirt, hearing threads snapping before he finally took his mouth off my breast to let me pull it up and over his head. My fingernails dragged over his scalp as I dug my fingers into his hair. He looked at me like a wild animal about to eat a snack. And I fucking loved it.

"I knew you liked me shirtless, lusty," he grumbled, giving me a cocky grin before kissing me again. His hand came up to cup my breast, his fingers tweaking my nipple. Hard. Then he thrust his thick cock against my center and I could feel the beginnings of an orgasm sneaking up my spine.

"Oh God," I panted, pulling my lips from Boston's. I was shaking, a leaf tossed in the wind and pushed left and right by a force more powerful.

The fire popped suddenly in the wood stove right next to us and we both froze. Boston stared into my eyes, his own hazy with lust, but also a creeping awareness that spelled death to my orgasm. His thick bottom lip was wet and I had the insane desire to bite it. To do something, anything, to get him to stop the thoughts that I knew were running through his head right now. He was listing off all the reasons this was wrong. Or maybe that was just me.

Instead of egging him on, I released his hair and pushed against his chest. He didn't budge an inch, but he backed up enough to let my legs slide down his body. I covered my bare breast and got it tucked back into my top. Boston cleared his throat and adjusted himself, stepping away and checking the stove.

I couldn't let him give me yet another fully clothed orgasm. The man was insufferable as it was. And we had no future. Except as friends, which couldn't happen if we kept tearing the clothes off each other. Keva was my best friend and I knew exactly how much Boston had hurt her when he left her behind. She had no other living family. She deserved to have her brother in her life and not have everything be awkward when he and I were in the same room. Boston and I messing around was just not smart.

I turned toward my clothes, picking them back up off the floor. With tight control over my voice, I tried to act like nothing had happened.

"Put some fucking clothes on, would you?" I snapped.

I heard the rapid thud of his boots on the hardwood floor right before he tackled me.

CHAPTER THIRTEEN

oston

AUDREY WAS DRIVING me batshit crazy.

These four walls were not big enough to give me the space I needed to get myself under control. She pressed her gorgeous ass up against me all night long, like she liked feeling what she did to me. If I didn't get some fucking sleep soon, I was going to lose my shit. Then she was poking at me during the day with her sharp retorts and teasing nature. I didn't even have a goddamn shower to rub one out and get myself even slightly sated before I had to deal with her yet again. I kept trying to push her away and exhaust myself with physical activity, but stuck in this tiny cabin, there was nowhere to escape.

I found myself running across the floor, ready to give her a piece of my mind for snapping at me to put on some clothes when *she'd* been the one to rip them off me. Lust and frustration built to such a height that I couldn't see straight. Which was the only explanation for why I didn't stop. I just barreled right into her and we both landed on the bed, the frame hitting the wall with a crunch that spelled trouble for the integrity of the bed. I'd have to buy Pete an entire cabin of new furniture before we got rescued.

Audrey yelled and then her voice cut off as my body pinned her to the bed and forced the air from her lungs. Her cheeks were red and it made me joyous to see her pissed. *Join the club, honey.*

She flailed for all of two seconds before stilling and staring up at me. Our bodies were pressed together from chest to shin, both of our lungs pumping heavy breaths in and out. Her hair poked out of the braids she'd put it in. The hideous hat she wore earlier had fallen off when I yanked her sweatshirt off, thank fuck. She was dressed like a street person, yet she looked absolutely stunning without a single swipe of makeup on her face. Her eyes bore into mine, the brown heating to a melted chocolate.

I fucking wanted her.

"How about we make a deal?" I found myself saying, dick already too engaged in this conversation to make wearing pants comfortable.

Audrey blinked once. "Huh?"

I was desperate to find a way to make this work. And I was pretty sure I wasn't thinking with my brain any longer. "I think it's clear we're driving each other crazy. I say we have sex. Purely platonically."

Audrey's forehead made a crease that was fucking adorable, and I was a guy who had never found anything adorable in my life thus far. "That's the opposite of what platonically means, beast."

Now I was frowning. Audrey's breasts were pressed up against me, tighter with each rapid breath she took. I wasn't good with women. I could admit that. But I wasn't an idiot when it came to reading people. Audrey wanted me, maybe as much as I wanted her.

"I know what it means, but it's coming out wrong. I just mean a temporary fake relationship with benefits."

Audrey pursed her lips and it took all my strength not to dip my head and take advantage of them. Who was I kidding? The only thing that actually held me back was the slight chance she might say yes to my ridiculous offer and I'd get so much more than just a kiss.

"That's quite a mouthful," she finally said. Then her gaze dropped and so did all my hopes. "I told myself after The Tavern that I'd quit random hookups. I'm not looking for that, Boston." Her gaze lifted and I could see the plea in her eyes. "Despite my family troubles, or perhaps because of, I want commitment, marriage, a family. I want it all."

My stomach clenched and all the doors of possibility with Audrey slammed shut. I couldn't even get my sister to talk to me, let alone offer this woman all the things she wanted. And Audrey deserved them all. After telling me about the despicable things her father did, of all the people in the world who deserved to have their dreams of white picket fences come true, it was Audrey.

I couldn't offer her a one-night stand. She'd already bent to accommodate my fake dating weekend in the cabin. I wouldn't be the asshole who asked her to compromise her dreams even more. The whole point of coming to Blueball was for me to stop being the asshole who ran away from his family problems.

Instead of claiming her lips like I'd wanted to, I bent my head and kissed her cheek before pushing my body away from hers and rolling off of the bed. As I stood there looking down at her, I let myself feel the full weight of regret. Had I been a different person, at a different point in my life, with a different background, I would have promised all the things Audrey wanted.

But I wasn't that guy. I couldn't promise her anything when I had no home, no job, and no family that would speak to me.

"You should have that, Audrey. Every single thing you want and more."

The words felt like sandpaper scraping along my throat.

Audrey sat up, her shoulders slumped but an intense light burning in her eyes. "And that's not you?"

I straightened my shoulders as if standing at attention. I would face this punch to the gut like a man. I was many things, but I wasn't a liar or someone who shied away from the truth. "I don't think I'm capable of the things you want."

When the light died in her eyes, I turned, mumbling something about needing more water for baths today. Audrey let me go, unusually quiet as she went about gathering her clothes again.

I couldn't provide her with the big dreams she had in mind, but I could take care of her while we were stuck on the top of this mountain. It was a paltry offering, but it was all I had.

We didn't say a word as the day went on, just moving about each other like wounded animals who just wanted to survive the day. She washed her clothes and I helped her hang them on the top of the curtain by the bathtub. She used the outhouse, traipsing over the pathway I'd tried to clear this morning. I counted the minutes until she came back, anxious about her safety when she was out of my sight.

We both took baths, somehow moving in sync without words. I had told her the truth and that was that. I should have been able to push all thoughts of her away. Sadly, all our conversation did was make me even more highly attuned to her every move. I heard the plunk of the water as she stepped into the tub. The soft sigh that fell from her lips when she lowered herself into the warm water. The steady drips rolling off her body when she stood up and grabbed the towel off the floor to dry off. I drilled my fingers into my ears to block it out and then went outside to kick some logs and growl at the sky. Anything to get out of that cabin and away from pure temptation.

At some point in the afternoon, the snow quit falling and the sun came out. Ironic, really. I felt like absolute shit and yet nature was showing off her beauty, turning the landscape into some kind of wilderness wonderland. If the sunny weather held up, most of the snow would be melted off in a day or two. By then our friends would be looking for us and we could deal with the washed-out bridge together. All in all, things were looking up.

And I'd never felt worse.

CHAPTER FOURTEEN

udrey

I HAD a lot of thoughts running through my head that day during the silence between me and Boston. Like, why did I have to choose today, of all days, to stand firm behind my principles? Or, would guaranteed orgasms from a hot beast of a man be so bad while I was waiting for Mr. Right to find me? And, holy shit, I'd felt Boston's erection multiple times now and at what point was it totally understandable and forgivable that a girl would fling her principles out the window for guaranteed excellent dick?

My brain was wrestling this alligator of a problem to the point of exhaustion. I threw my useless phone back in my backpack, wishing like crazy that I could text my friends and they'd give me their honest advice. I could clearly envision it. Paisley would tell me to go for it if it felt right. Keva would absolutely vomit if she knew it was her brother I was hung up on, but if she didn't know, she'd be all-caps yelling at me to use a condom. Marlo would make some deadpan quip about embracing orgasms before we were all dead and buried six feet under. The consensus, no matter how varied or morbid, would be to go for it.

I crawled in bed as soon as the sun went down and tried not to listen to Boston taking a bath behind that flimsy curtain. I grinned up at the ceiling imagining him trying to fold his huge body into that tub. There was a heavy thump not long after, followed by a growl. I had to slap both hands over my mouth to stop the laugh. Boston went on to curse under his breath at least a dozen more times, so I tried to divert my attention to all the reasons why I didn't want a casual hookup.

Mostly, I just didn't want to end up leading the same kind of life my father did: deceiving people and breaking hearts. I tried to fluff my pillow as sleep would not come. Hell, nothing was coming around here.

I huffed, letting my brain go where I wouldn't usually let it go. All the silence in the cabin and the lack of light left me with too much thinking time on my hands. My daddy issues were why I wanted a husband and family. A sense of normalcy I hadn't had for a few years. And there was nothing wrong with that. Except for one thing.

If I let my father's bad behavior dictate how or when I hooked up with men, then I was letting that behavior control me. Even after I'd removed myself from his life, he was still controlling me.

And I was not okay with that.

The curtain yanked back and Boston emerged. Even in the dim light of the moon and the one battery-operated lantern in the kitchen area, I could clearly make out his form. He was naked, save for a towel wrapped around his waist that didn't quite cover him completely. Every step showed his thick thigh coming through the split of the towel. He halted on his side of the bed.

"Turn around," he said gruffly, returning to barking orders at me.

I huffed again and made a hasty decision that felt damn right. "No."

Boston stared down at me, wet hair dripping onto his chest.

I propped myself up on my elbows and shot him a flirty smile. "Do they drug test in the military?"

Boston grunted.

"Have you always been this big? Because you look like you got into some anabolic steroids and maybe even some beaver tranquilizers."

Boston stood there blinking the water out of his narrowed eyes, not saying a word. He was probably confused. I stared right back, a cocky little grin on my face. I was headed to orgasm town once I told him I changed my mind. All that muscle was about to be pressed against me. *Fuck yes, come to mama.*

"You know, I was thinking," I began, sitting up and flipping my freshly washed hair over my shoulder. "Would it really hurt to have a cabin-only temporary fake relationship with benefits?"

I'd barely gotten the last word out of my mouth before Boston reached down to the roll of the towel and whipped the material off of him. I got the first sight of Boston's naked cock and all the spit dried in my mouth before flooding back with a vengeance. I was most certainly drooling. Feeling that thing pressed against me was nothing compared to looking at it directly. Could a woman be blinded from gazing upon dick perfection?

"COTFRWB is my favorite kind of sex," Boston grumbled.

It took me a few seconds to understand what he was saying, mostly because I'd been struck dumb by the sight of Boston bared before me. All my other senses had gone mute, giving all my attention to my eyeballs. Boston made the statue of David look like a middle school boy who hit puberty late.

"Are you sure, Audrey?" Boston's rumble of a voice brought my attention back to his face. He'd pulled his hair out of the way, fastening it with the leather strap he always wore on his wrist when it wasn't in his hair.

If my friends—other than Keva of course, that would just be gross—got an eyeful of Boston right now, they'd be screaming at me to take advantage of the situation. I'd be a fool not to, and Audrey Hellman was a fool no longer. Keva would never have to know. This was cabin only, baby.

"Fuck yes," I said clearly, watching his cocky grin turn to a wolfish smile.

"Then you're wearing too many clothes." Boston emphasized this statement by wrapping his big hand around his perfectly curved dick and giving it a rough tug.

I swallowed hard to combat all the saliva that was trying to drown me and whipped my sweatshirt and tank top over my head in one move. It landed somewhere behind me, but could have landed in the wood stove for all I cared. Boston's eyes dipped immediately, latching on to my bare breasts.

"Fuck," he murmured, hand tugging again on his dick.

I licked my lips and went on all fours to crawl across the bed, now eye level with his beautiful dick. "Can I?" I asked reverently.

Boston grunted but took his hand off his dick to give the two of us a moment alone together. "I always knew you were lusty."

I flipped him off and watched his face morph into an angry frown. Then I opened my lips and sucked just the head of him into my mouth, flicking his smooth skin with my tongue. Boston's strangled groan was all the answer I needed. My hands came up to wrap around his cock. There was no way I could encircle it with just one hand. I relaxed my jaw and let him slide further inside, the saliva finally being put to good use.

His hands found my hair, his fingers sifting through the strands to then grip me in his fists. I looked up at him, stilling my movements on his cock and sliding my hands around to the muscled globes of his ass. This had to be the hottest thing I'd ever seen. The clench of Boston's teeth, the ache in my jaw, the view of his gorgeous body from down here, the heat in his eyes gazing down at me like I was also the hottest thing he'd ever seen. And then now, as I gave him full control, I could have come just from the anticipation.

I knew the moment Boston understood what I was giving to him. His cock grew impossibly larger in my mouth and his hips jerked, like he couldn't control himself. His chest rumbled and then he was moving, his hands pushing on the back of my head to slide him further inside my mouth. Just when I thought I might choke, he tugged on my hair and slid back out.

"Fuck, Audrey."

I would have smiled like a satisfied cat, but my lips were stretched far too wide for that. Instead, I gripped his ass and let my nails dig into his skin. He hissed and pushed my head back down, sliding to the back of my throat and holding there for a long moment.

"Fuck, fuck, fuck," Boston chanted, pulling back out. His thick chest was heaving as I focused on pulling air in through my nose. "Just a little longer, baby."

I'd give him all night. I was getting just as much enjoyment out of this as he was. As he pushed back inside my mouth and pulled back, I felt spit slide down my chin. Which pretty much matched what was happening between my legs right now.

Boston let out a holler, pulling so hard on my hair it stung. He slipped out of my mouth and I would have fallen over if his hands hadn't come to my shoulders to steady me as he stepped back.

"Fuck, Audrey, that's enough."

I swiped at my chin and watched the way he tried to get himself back in control. This was the part of sex that I loved. The power that filled my chest, knowing I'd made a big, strong man lose control. In every other situation, this man would overpower me, but not here. This was my domain and I intended to wield my power for good.

And then a thought occurred to dampen my mood. "Oh shit. Do you have a condom?"

Boston shook his head, like he was having a hard time

clearing his thoughts. "Yeah. In my wallet." He spun in a full circle, looking for his pack.

I lay back on the bed while he fetched it, relieved we didn't have to cut things short. I enjoyed having him in my mouth, for sure, but I desperately wanted him to fill my other holes. I giggled at the thought, happy I'd changed my mind about all this.

"Is something funny?" Boston muttered, rolling a condom on and stepping back over to the bed.

"Nope. Just dick drunk I guess."

That made Boston give me a lopsided grin. "Come here."

I sat up and crawled back over to the side of the bed. "Where do you want me?" I asked coyly.

Boston's eyes closed briefly, and when he opened them again, there was most certainly a fire burning in them. "Flip over, feet on the ground, hands on the bed."

I obeyed, getting in position and wiggling my ass for him just to hear that growl. His hands held my hips but I realized quickly my ass only came up to mid-thigh on him. The first trickle of anxiety hit. I craned my neck to see him behind me.

"How do things fit when you're a giant and I'm petite size?"

Boston's thumbs stroked the tops of my ass. "We go slow and you trust me."

"I do, you know," I said honestly. "Trust you."

Boston bent in half, placing a kiss on the middle of my back. "I'll make it good for you, I promise," he whispered against my skin.

I shivered and dropped my head, turning off my brain and just letting myself feel him. He kissed his way to each cheek before kneeling between my legs and parting me. I sucked in a breath and then lost it when his mouth and tongue attacked my flesh. My thighs began to shake. My arms gave out and my moans were swallowed by the bed. He pulled back and stood before I orgasmed though. His quiet chuckle followed my moan of protest.

"Keep your face in the mattress and brace with your arms."

I didn't have a chance to ask questions before he notched his cock at my dripping opening and fed an inch of himself inside me. It was a tight fit, but not painful in any way. Then he put his hands back on my hips and suddenly my feet no longer touched the floor. I yelped, but quickly forgot about my position in relation to the earth when he slid inside another inch. He had to work himself in, pausing to let me adjust.

"Good?" he grunted.

There was a sting now, but the feeling of being filled to the brim was too wonderful to tell him to slow down. "Yes," I breathed, breathing slow and long to make myself relax. His grip on me stayed steady as if he wasn't working hard at all to hold my lower half in the air.

"Hold on, baby," he whispered, right before pushing impossibly further, his thighs now pressed against the back of mine.

I moaned into the mattress, the sound half pleasure, half pain. Boston held still, his fingers digging into my hips now. I could feel a tremor in his legs, but I couldn't worry about him just now. I needed all my attention on surviving what would surely be the biggest orgasm of my life. Tendrils of pleasure skated up and around my spine already and I needed more. I squeezed my inner muscles, pleased when he grunted in response.

"Ready?"

I loved how he checked in with me. He was destroying me. But with impeccable manners.

I lifted my head for a brief moment. "Show me what you got, beast."

Boston took me seriously, pulling almost all the way out before slamming back in. I shouted and his grip only got harder. The beast was unleashed and I was along for the ride. His cock glided in and out in an increasing rhythm, bottoming out inside me each time. Organs were rearranged and somehow my body accommodated the attack. The tendrils became a tsunami, threatening to break me. I felt sweat drip down my neck and onto the bed. My thighs were shaking so hard I had to wrap my feet around the back of his calves to have some sense of being tethered to this world.

"Oh God, oh shit, Boston!" I chanted, wishing I could contribute in some way but finding I was completely at his mercy. My body seemed to like the situation, ramping up into an orgasm faster than ever before. Lightning hit my spinal cord and I lost all coordination. My brain went offline and my eyes squeezed tightly shut. My whole body jolted in his hands and suddenly I was pressed down into the bed, shaking violently as Boston rutted behind me, his movements short and desperate. He shouted long and loudly in my ear, his body shaking above me and pinning me to the bed in the most uncomfortable position.

And I didn't give a fuck.

I was a dead woman.

Here lies Audrey Hellman. Death by out-of-this-world sex.

I'd been dicked down and dicked to death.

My friends would laugh their asses off that I'd passed from this world in such a manner. I didn't have one damn regret though. I just closed my eyes, rode out the aftershocks, and smiled my way into the afterlife.

$\mathscr{B}$oston

I WOKE UP EARLY, the first bright light of dawn creeping through the windows like even Mother Nature knew to be happy today. Being with Audrey had just about blown my mind last night. Not to toot my own horn, but I wasn't a small guy. Especially *that* part of me. Audrey, barely coming up to my chest, had taken all of me, letting me manhandle her without a single complaint. Then afterward she curled up into my arms and fell asleep like she trusted me implicitly. Of course, now her ass was pressed up against my morning wood and I really, really wanted a repeat of last night.

Could a man become addicted to one pussy after a single amazing encounter?

Lincoln would give me shit for days if I told him what was running through my brain. He and I had solidified our friendship in the military when we were on leave at eighteen and had a wild night that we didn't entirely remember. He didn't seem like the settling-down type either, but now look at him and my sister. Married, a son, and another baby on the way.

Not that I was looking for any of that. Audrey and I had an expiration date. COTFRWB didn't leave room for feelings or future plans. As I lay there with her hair tickling my face, I could at least admit that this didn't feel like a cold, calculated one-night stand. This felt like more than that, probably because we were stuck up here in this cabin. There wasn't an immediate exit strategy, and above all else, I hoped we'd be friends. Otherwise things would be awkward around the tiny town of Blueball if I stayed and put down roots here.

"Hey," Audrey said sleepily, turning in my arms and smiling up at me. There was a pillow crease across her cheek but it only made her prettier. The sheet hid her boobs, which was probably a good thing. Who knew what I'd do if I got my eyeballs and hands on those babies again.

"Morning," I grumbled back, running my hand down her hip and away from anything that might tempt me. Funny thing was, even the smooth skin on the back of her knee was turning me on. Better to focus on getting out of here. "Sun's out. Might be able to hike out if you're up for some manual labor."

Audrey's eyes lit up but she made no move to get out of bed. "I'm in the mood for breakfast first, beast."

I grinned. "The last Pop-Tart or a bowl of corn?"

She groaned and my dick took notice. "I can't wait to eat a big ol' plate of eggs and bacon and pancakes when we get out of here." Then she rolled to her back, stretching her arms and legs. She winced.

"Sore?"

"Mmm. Yeah. You kind of did a number on me last night." She wagged her eyebrows so she didn't seem too mad about it. "I think my hips are bruised in the shape of your hands."

Horrified, I whipped the sheet off of her. She yelped, but I was focused on her hip bones where there were indeed some bruises beginning to form. I lightly ran a finger over them before leaning down to kiss them. It wouldn't help them heal, but I felt like I owed her some care that I hadn't shown last night. Her answering moan had me lingering though. The scent of her filled my head and then I was groaning, burying my face in her thigh. Fuck, I wanted her again.

"Let me make it up to you, then," I murmured, parting her legs and settling there. She was bared to me, gloriously pink and wet and literally the most perfect pussy I'd ever had the pleasure to view. Audrey's hand came down to push the hair away from my face, her bottom lip caught by her teeth. She didn't say no.

I swiped my tongue upward, letting the taste of her bloom in my mouth. I couldn't seem to get enough of her. I should have done this longer last night instead of being the beast she affectionately called me. I could feast on her and her alone for days. Audrey's hips shifted with a soft moan. I made sure to be gentle, to keep my tongue laving her soft folds and giving her pleasure without the rough invasion of last night.

It didn't take long before her head began thrashing back and forth on the pillow, her hips wild and uncoordinated. I placed my palm against her soft stomach and kept her where I wanted her, not letting up for one second. My tongue and mouth and teeth were simply thanking her for last night. Every muscle in her body went tight when I sucked her clit in my mouth. Then she whimpered long and ragged, the sound music to my ears. Her thighs trembled and she coated my tongue. When she finally went limp, she let go of my hair and began to giggle up at the ceiling. I kissed her thighs and made my way up her body to kiss her good morning.

Definitely not one-night-stand behavior, but I couldn't help myself. I wanted to taste her joy too.

Her arms wound around my neck, a pretty blush to her cheeks. "That definitely does not motivate me to go out in the cold and shovel snow."

I shook my head. "I'll do the shoveling. You just stand there and look pretty."

She made a face. "I'm not a helpless female, you know."

"Oh, I know, but you've got five brothers. I'd rather get you off the mountain without blisters on your hands."

A single eyebrow lifted on her forehead. "You'll ruin my pussy but not my hands?"

Now it felt like I was blushing. Boston "Tank" Mooney didn't blush. I pushed off her warm body and rolled to my feet beside the bed. Audrey's gaze instantly fell to my cock, who was fully erect and thinking it was his turn now.

"I'll get breakfast going and then we'll head outside." I turned, finding my pants and pulling them on before I got any stupid ideas. I heard rustling behind me as Audrey got dressed too. I let her have the Pop-Tart while I took the can of corn. The smile she gave me was worth it.

"I don't know, Boston. It still looks pretty thick out there." Audrey licked the frosting off her fingers and looked out the window. "I think we may need one more day of sun to melt some more of it."

My brain instantly went to what activities we could get up to if we spent one more night in this cabin. I'd take no food and feast on Audrey instead. "There's more snow on the ground than I'd like, but we could probably make it to the bridge today."

Audrey turned around. "Yeah, but the bridge is out, so we'd have to camp there until someone could rescue us and it's still pretty cold. I think we stay here another night."

If I'd been by myself, I would have left immediately. But I had Audrey to consider. I couldn't see her camping out in the snow by the bridge. Besides, if we didn't show up tonight as expected, Pete would call Gannon and Lincoln. Better to head out tomorrow and hope they'd meet us on the other side of the washed-out bridge. We could use all the hands available to get across safely.

I put the bowl in the sink. "Okay. We stay."

Audrey cheered and ran to get her hat. "Snow day!"

I rolled my eyes but couldn't help the grin that tugged at my lips at her enthusiasm. We got our boots on and I got to shoveling the path to the outhouse and then began clearing snow down the trail in preparation for tomorrow. I didn't know what Audrey was up to until a burst of snow hit me square on the back. I turned, getting a snowball to the face this time.

"What the fuck?" I swiped the snow from my face to see Audrey laughing her ass off just twenty yards away. She had an entire pile of snowballs at her feet.

"Better run, beast!" she hollered, picking up two more snowballs.

I growled my displeasure, but didn't waste any time running to get around the side of the cabin. There was no doubt in my mind that Audrey would pelt me with every single motherfucking snowball she had in her arsenal. Two could play that game though and I was trained for this shit. Well, not for snowballs, but I'd take those over bullets and bombs any day. I heard a snowball whizz past me and land harmlessly on the ground. Sliding around the back corner of the cabin, I stooped to make a few of my own snowballs.

The woman could have had a bell tied around her neck and she would have been quieter than the laughing, stomping-boots mess that followed me around to the back of the cabin. I let loose the first snowball the second she came into view. I got her right in the chest, causing her to drop one of her snowballs and yelp out a curse word far worse than I used in the military. That made me laugh, of course, which just pissed her off more. She came running for me and I didn't have the heart to pelt her in the face. Instead, I dodged her lame snowballs and ducked low to tackle her around the knees.

We went down in a flurry of arms and legs and snowballs. She called me a cuntlicker, which was a little too on the nose given this morning's activities, but was also pretty funny coming from her lips. We ended up both laughing, lying on our backs and gazing up at the snow-covered pine trees.

"I've always wanted to make snow angels. Scoot over, beast."

"You scoot over," I shot back, but defied my own words by scooting over to give her room.

I watched her swing her arms and legs in the snow, her face lit up with giddy delight. She was stuck in a cabin without a toilet and barely running water, but Audrey was happy.

When she stood, admiring her snow angel, she held a hand out to me. I took it, though I didn't need her help getting up off the ground. She held my hand and swung our arms as we walked back to the front of the cabin.

"Let's go for a walk."

We headed down the path I'd cleared, then crunched over some snow in the area I hadn't shoveled. She kept up a steady stream of conversation, telling me about her new career, her friends, and ending with the subject of Keva.

"I think you need a plan."

I pulled her to a stop by tugging on our conjoined hands. "A plan for what?"

She looked at me like I was as dumb as the tree stump next to me. "A plan to win over Keva. Duh." She let go of my hand and started gesturing wildly. "I'm a peacemaker by nature. I can help. I say we set her up for an intervention of sorts. We'll force her to listen to you. You plead your case, you promise to be there for her going forward, and then you hit her where it hurts."

I didn't like one damn thing about this. "Where it hurts?"

"Yeah! There's no one who can get through to Keva quite like Lucas. You use that. Tell her you want Lucas to have an uncle in his life. That'll get her, I know it will."

I was already shaking my head. "No. Absolutely not." I backed away and Audrey reached for me. "I will not manipulate my own sister."

"No! That's not what I meant at all. You're merely showing her what having you in her life will be like." Audrey grabbed my flannel and pulled me in close, looking up at me with earnest eyes. "You're a good man, Boston. Sometimes Keva has to be hit over the head—metaphorically, of course—to get the message. She's wonderfully stubborn that way."

I shook my head again. "I appreciate your help, but I have to do this my way."

"But..." Audrey's lips pursed, the pout so damn cute I almost caved. "I can't fix my own family. At least let me help fix yours."

My ribs squeezed as understanding dawned. Despite the smile and usual enthusiasm for life that she displayed, Audrey held a lot of hurts inside. I brought my hands up to skim her hips before sliding around her waist and pulling her close. I leaned down and plucked a kiss from her pouting lips.

"I really do appreciate it, Audrey, but I made this problem and I need to be the one to fix it. And I think part of that fix is simply time and continued commitment to being in her life."

Audrey seemed to reluctantly come around to my decision, but as we walked back to the cabin, she drilled a finger into my gut.

"Fine, but if you need help, you just have to ask, okay?"

I squeezed her fingers where they were laced with mine. "Will do."

CHAPTER SIXTEEN

udrey

"YOU SHOULD COME in this bath with me," I shouted from behind the curtain, sinking further into the hot water Boston had poured in. His answering snort made me smile. Somehow in the space of three days, all his irritating mannerisms and grunted answers now made me smile instead of want to punch him in his gorgeous face.

"I can barely fit by myself, let alone with you in there." I heard a splash from the kitchenette. He'd said a sponge bath was just as good, but that was a flat-out lie. Nothing was better than a hot bath after playing in the snow.

He was right, but after a day spent talking and playing and touching, I just felt this insane need to keep him close to me. I splashed water onto my face and tried to rein in my feelings. This would hopefully be our last night here stuck in this cabin. I should have felt relieved, even excited, to get back home. And I did, but I also felt anticipatory sadness. I would miss this time in the woods. More specifically, this time with Boston.

He'd made me feel completely protected and cared for, a remarkable feat for a girl who'd had her whole world crashed in by the very people who should have loved her unconditionally. Not that Boston loved me or I him. It was more of an affection that came out of nowhere and that I wasn't ready to let go of.

With that in mind, I stepped out of the bath before the water turned cold, ready to get in bed for one more amazing night. I toweled off quickly and stepped around the curtain. Boston was stark naked in the kitchenette area, dumping a bucket of water down the sink drain. His naked backside was a thing of glory. Huge boulders for shoulders, bubbled muscles dotting his back, and all that football-god goodness leading down to a thick waist. And then there was his ass. Two muscular globes that I wanted to sink my teeth into. It should be illegal for this man to wear pants. His legs, the kind rugby players develop, were moderately hairy. Just enough to rasp against my skin and highlight the differences between us.

I pulled off my towel and wound it up as I approached on tiptoe, snapping it against his ass. Boston jumped, dropping the bucket in the sink and spinning around. His hair was loose, the tips wet around his collarbone. He looked like a fierce warrior about to take down a predator with his bare hands. He was impressive, but I wasn't scared.

"You better run, lusty," he growled.

When I didn't move, he brought his hands up like claws. I let out a screech that was half laugh, spinning on my heels and running. To where, I had no idea. There was no escaping him in a tiny cabin. I rounded the bed and put it between us, hands on the mattress, eyes wide. The fire in his dark eyes made my heart race. Then he began to smile and my heart was a goner.

"Whatcha gonna do if you catch me?" I asked breathlessly.

"Keep you up all night, screaming my name," he answered smoothly.

I froze for a second, considering my options. It wasn't a choice really. I jumped and landed on my back on the bed, my arms out to the side in surrender. Boston chuckled at my antics. He put a knee on the mattress and loomed over me. His cock saluted me, bobbing there between us.

"One slight problem. I don't have another condom."

I gave it less than a half a second of thought. "I'm on birth control."

Boston put his fist in the bed by my face, his knee pushing my legs apart as if his rightful place was between them. "I haven't been with anyone since my last physical, which was clean."

I reached up and pushed the hair out of his face. "And I haven't been with someone in over two years, so I think we're good. I'm okay with it if you're okay with it."

He didn't answer me but the wolfish grin said it all. He moved south quickly, parting me with his fingers and working me over with his tongue. He didn't let me come, despite the hair that I pulled as I held his head against me. He flung my hands off and climbed back over my body.

"Have to be inside you," he whispered. The words sounded desperate. Like maybe he was anticipating missing this time together too.

I bent my knees further, wrapping them around his waist. With a hand between us, he lined us up and then he was giving me an inch of himself at a time, letting me adjust. It didn't burn this time, but that overwhelming sense of being stuffed to maximum capacity was still there.

"Boston," I whispered, arching my neck and breathing through it.

He stilled his hips and leaned down to kiss my neck, his teeth and tongue getting in on the action. It wasn't long before he moved downward, putting his mouth on my breasts. I loved the time and attention he spent there, even as I got antsy. I lifted my hips, desperate for more of him. He tsked at me, looking up with humor in his eyes, even as his mouth latched on my nipple. He let it pop out of his mouth and then he sat back on his haunches.

"Have to see you taking my cock."

I moaned, pussy clenching at the thought. He flattened my knees out to the side and his hands held on to my hips. He looked down between us, jaw clenching hard at the sight of him disappearing into me.

"Fuck, Audrey."

He pulled out slowly, then thrust back in, moving my entire lower body up onto his thighs. I wasn't even slightly in control yet again and I fucking loved it. I reached behind my head and held on to the headboard. Each time he thrust inside, the bed creaked dangerously. I didn't care. The whole cabin could burn down and I'd scream at Boston to keep going.

"You feel fucking perfect," Boston ground out between clenched teeth.

"Same, beast."

His pace increased and my thighs began to ache. My arms burned from trying to hold on. He wasn't hitting as deep this time, but it almost felt better. I could relax into the sensation rather than worry about him impaling important organs.

"I don't know what to look at. You taking my cock or your breasts bouncing each time I bury myself inside you."

Boston wasn't the conversational type. I had to work hard to get long sentences out of him, but now I knew he was just saving all those words for talking dirty during sex. And I was fully on board with it. I'd take his silence if I got this kind of treatment in bed.

"Boston," I moaned, just on the cusp of falling over the edge, but not quite able to reach it.

"Shh. I got you." And he did. Still holding on to my hips, he was able to reach over with his thumb, hovering it right over my clit. Each time he thrust, it meant his thumb hit that little bundle of nerves exactly how I needed it.

My moans got louder and every single nerve ending went offline except the ones between my legs. Then everything exploded in the most pleasurable orgasm I'd ever experienced. I leaned my head to the side and buried my face in my arm to stifle the screams. The pleasure built so high it bordered on pain. Or perhaps that was from the way Boston went absolutely feral.

His hands tightened on my skin. His heavy breathing turned to grunts and then the bed was rocking into the wall so hard I thought I might have to be rescued from the rubble. There was no other way to describe it except for rutting. Fucking. In the very best primal way. By the time he roared out his own pleasure and finally stilled, we were both sweaty and shaking, limbs and hair askew as we both just collapsed.

Long minutes later, he reached over and pushed the hair out of my face. "Did I hurt you?"

I lifted my head in proof of life. "No, beast."

He made a noise. "If I had any strength left, I'd spank you for that nickname."

My body perked up and I told that ho to sit back down. "How about we take a quick cat nap first?"

His rumble of laughter shook the bed, but he eventually rolled me over and tucked me under his chin, my back to his front. I was the little spoon to a much, much larger spoon. We fell asleep that way, but he did wake me up at some point in the night to slide back inside me as we lay there. It was slow, half-asleep lovemaking that was just as lovely as the other two times.

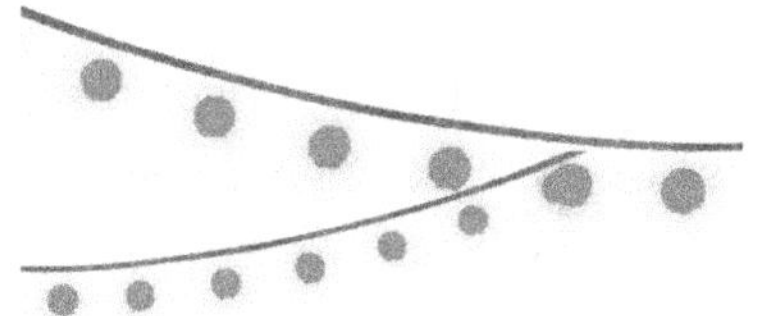

"Wake up, sleepyhead."

Boston's usual bossy order was softened a bit this morning with a kiss to the forehead, but it still woke me up. He was dressed and had his pack on already. I sat up and took in the cabin. He'd already packed everything and put things back to the way they'd been when we came here. Minus the missing furniture. He threw my backpack on the bed.

"No more Pop-Tarts but I'll split the last can of beans with you."

I grimaced and got out of bed. Boston's gaze snagged on my naked body, but then he snapped his head to the side, staring out the window.

"I might gag eating it, but I'll try." I knew I'd need the energy to make it down the mountain. I would also try to ignore the way my chest was beginning to ache. Things already felt different between us. I knew it had to be that way, but it didn't mean it didn't hurt.

"The snow looks almost gone, so we should be able to get to the bridge quickly. I imagine Pete will have called in help, so we should be back home by tonight."

With my back to Boston, I pulled on my clothes before sitting on the side of the bed to eat the bowl of beans. When I ate as much of it as I could stand, I washed the bowl out, dried it, and put it back in the stuffed cabinet above the stove.

"Okay. Ready to go!" I tried to infuse some enthusiasm in my voice, but I think we both knew it was fake.

Boston waited patiently while I used the outhouse one last time and then we were off, hiking down the pathway side by side. I was conscious of the foot of space between us, but I tried to take in the beauty of the trees around us instead. It really was beautiful. Tall pine trees still covered in just a dusting of snow. Birds chirping and rustling in the bushes. Nature had made it through a storm and come out the other end more alive than ever. I latched on to that life analogy with everything I had.

"We'll have to play the part if Pete is there at the bridge," Boston said half an hour into our hike.

I gave him a forced smile. "No problem."

Boston grunted and kept right on hiking. I had to move fast to keep up with his long legs. As the silence stretched out, I realized that maybe we'd been wrong about our abilities to compartmentalize things. Or at least I'd been wrong about myself. Boston seemed to have reverted back to his silent, grunting self just fine. Me, on the other hand, could have cried at the drop of a hat.

COTFRWB was the stupidest idea ever.

We were nowhere near the cabin now and our relationship was as fake as ever, but now those benefits we'd indulged in had roped in my heart and left me feeling sad afterward. I didn't want to just be friends, but I'd take friends over this awkward silence.

I finally mustered up the nerve to discuss things with Boston like two grown adults when we came around a corner and voices greeted us. Heads popped up at the crunch of our boots and everyone began shouting at once. Pete, Gannon, Paisley, Lincoln, Keva, Lucy, Bain, Marlo, and all five of my brothers and their wives were standing on the other side of the washed-out bridge.

The cavalry had arrived.

CHAPTER SEVENTEEN

oston

"OH, THANK GOD." Pete's hair stood on end and he looked like he hadn't slept all weekend. "Never would have forgiven myself."

"We're fine, Pete. Just had a few snow days." I didn't want the guy worrying himself about us. I'd kept us safe. I put my arm around Audrey's shoulders. She stiffened but didn't pull away.

"Although we can't say the same for your table," Audrey muttered out the side of her mouth, loud enough for only me to hear.

I squeezed her shoulder to shut her up. We needed to get over this bridge first. Then we could address the furniture that had become our firewood. As I saw it, the table and chairs were the price Pete had to pay for sending us up to a primitive cabin in a storm.

"You okay, Audrey?" hollered one of the tall brothers on the other side of the bridge.

Audrey seemed to bloom in the presence of her brothers, her muscles loosening and a smile breaking out on her face. "I'm fine, Callan! I'd like to get across sometime today though so I can officially hang up my camping gear for good."

A dark-haired brother, who seemed like he was in charge based on the way he belted out orders—which made me like the guy, not gonna lie—grabbed a long ladder. "We hiked up here early this morning and saw the washed-out bridge. We went back and got more people and equipment. The boys and I will get the ladder across and Gannon and Lincoln have been working on some knots. When they throw them over, get them around your waist and cinch them tight, okay?"

My gaze kept going to Annabel—dammit, *Keva*—taking in the way she went from absently rubbing her belly to wringing her hands. If I wasn't reading her completely wrong, my sister was worried about us. And fuck if that didn't feel good.

The guys got busy with the ladder and I released Audrey to catch it as it landed on our side of the bridge. It wasn't a long bridge by any means, but it was a steep drop if the ladder failed us. The thing looked solid though, which helped relieve some of my nerves.

"Nice ladder," I said to the dark-haired guy.

He stood and wiped off his hands. "We don't mess around with our equipment on the Auburn Hill Fire Department. Not like Blueball and their monkey business equipment held together by duct tape."

Audrey snorted. "Blueball has the same shit you do, Ace."

The siblings all talked at once, proving that town pride was strong on both sides of the fence. Or bridge, as it were. Gannon whistled to get my attention, throwing over the first of the safety ropes. I put it over Audrey's head and somehow managed to get past her flailing arms to cinch it around her waist.

I put both hands on her cheeks and got right in her face, my body effectively blocking off her communication with her brothers. She sucked in a breath and suddenly no one else was there. It was just us again.

"You're going to crawl across first, lusty, while they hold the ladder and I hold your rope. Go slow and do not look down. Look at your brothers and just put one hand in front of the other. Can you do that for me?"

Audrey's eyes went wide and she stared deep into my eyes. All the memories we made in that cabin flashed across my vision. The way she trusted me so completely, giving her body to me and making me laugh more than I've laughed in years. Then she blinked and she was back to the girl I met before this extended weekend. Smiling and happy, covering up everything below the surface.

"Of course I got this! Just call me a ninja." She let out a giggle and then pulled away to step around me. "Y'all better record this. I'm gonna go viral with how quickly I get across."

She dropped to her knees as I grabbed the end of her rope, wrapping it around my hands and finding a good spot to hunker down. I braced my feet against a rock and held on like Audrey's life depended on it. I couldn't give her the white picket fence, but I'd give her my life to make sure she kept hers. She deserved to walk away from this weekend unscathed. To go find a man who'd give her the house and the kids. I'd be a distant memory and I'd be okay with that, knowing I'd kept her safe so she could pursue her dreams.

Audrey started crawling across the rungs. I had to clench my jaw and force myself to breathe evenly. She followed my instructions, keeping her head up and her gaze on her brothers on the other side. One of the quiet brothers was on the other end of the ladder, holding it in place even as it began to sway the tiniest bit with her movements. Ace huddled over him, coaxing her across with calm instructions and encouragement.

She made it across several years later, or so it seemed to me. By the time her brothers and their wives pulled her into a crushing group hug, I'd lost all feeling in my hands. I unwound the rope and tried to get feeling back.

"Here, brother." Gannon tossed me my rope and I tossed him Audrey's.

Lincoln stepped forward and wrapped the end of my rope around his hands. "Remember that one day at Fort Jackson? The one we swore we'd never talk about?"

Keva looked at her husband quizzically and then over at me. I knew the day he meant and didn't really want to get into it in front of all these people. I gave him the barest of nods as I tightened the rope around my waist.

Lincoln looked me right in the eye. "I had your back then. I have it now. You got me?"

We'd been through a lot together and climbing a rickety ladder over a steep ravine was the tamest of them all. I shot him a grin and kneeled down at the end of the ladder.

"Today's a good day to mess some shit up, yeah?" I started crawling, trusting that Lincoln had me. The ladder let out way more groans and creaks than when Audrey had climbed over, but I knew it would hold me. Even if it didn't, I was now close enough to the other side to make a grab for it. And if the worst happened, and I fell to the bottom of the ravine, I was pretty sure I'd just break a few bones, not die from it.

There was far less fanfare when I made it to the other side, but I did get some high fives, fist bumps, and slaps on the back. With a fake smile, Audrey came over and snuggled against my side, like a real couple would. A pang of something I couldn't identify made a headache bloom.

Pete clapped his hand on my shoulder, wagging his bushy eyebrows. "Well, the storm wasn't planned and the bridge didn't hold, but I hope you two lovebirds enjoyed the bed up there."

Keva gagged, then covered it up with an unconvincing cough. All five heads belonging to Audrey's brothers spun in my direction. I didn't look at any of them, not needing to see their glares firsthand to know they were aimed at my head.

I simply nodded, giving the old man the words he wanted. "Yeah, Pete. The comfortable bed was the most perfect part of the weekend."

Audrey was pulled away from my side by her friends before it got any more awkward. Gannon, Lincoln, myself, and all five of Audrey's brothers cleaned up the equipment, each of us carrying some of it as the group began to go back down the mountain. To their credit, Audrey's brothers asked questions and seemed cautiously friendly. As far as I knew, Audrey hadn't filled them in on our fake relationship status, but perhaps Gannon and Lincoln had. Either way, they didn't find a way to kill me and bury my body out there in the forest, so I considered that a win.

When the cars at the bottom of the trail finally came into view, Audrey let out a whoop that echoed off the trees. "I can't wait to take a long hot shower!"

Everyone laughed, except me because I was mostly just trying to keep my brain from envisioning her in the hot shower. I couldn't walk around with a boner in front of her brothers. I should have had my brain focused on where I'd be staying tonight. I could always just camp out in my tent somewhere, but if I was going to try to make a home here in Blueball, I'd need to look for an apartment or a house to rent sooner rather than later.

The men loaded up the trucks with the ladder and ropes. I handed Audrey's backpack to her as she stood by her car saying goodbye to her friends. They were already making plans for a girls' night once she was rested up. Pete was watching us all curiously, probably overwhelmed by all the people on his property.

Audrey's gaze went to Pete and quickly flicked back to me as she took the backpack. "You'll follow me home? After that hot shower, I was hoping for some snuggle time on the couch with real food. Nothing canned!" She leaned against my side, putting her head on my arm.

She was flirting with me, but I could tell it was forced. Knowing we had an audience, I couldn't tell her to cut the crap. "Yeah. That sounds great."

Annabel, with her back to Pete, rolled her eyes. I put my hand on her shoulder, gently, though I still startled her. "Do you have this weekend off work?"

She eyed me wearily. "Yeah."

I nodded. "Great. Would you be up for some baby shopping followed by lunch? I'm sure this new baby needs a few things that aren't hand-me-downs, right?"

I felt Audrey's hand come up to rub my back in circles before she quickly dropped it and moved to climb in her car.

"Um, sure. That would be great." Annabel didn't look convinced that anything about that plan would be great, but she'd agreed.

I took my pack off and stowed it in the back of my truck. Climbing in, I hollered to Pete that I'd come by tomorrow to chat. Then I sat there waiting for Audrey to finish hugging everyone goodbye. For a woman who said her family blew apart recently, she sure seemed to have a lot of people who cared about her. It did not escape my notice that Gannon and Lincoln were the only ones to say goodbye to me. And that somehow added to the ache in my chest that I couldn't identify.

Eventually, we all left and I kept a close eye on Audrey's car, following her back to her house. As I pulled up to the curb and she parked in the driveway, I saw that the place was small, but nicely kept. The houses on her street were close together and barely had a front yard. Then again, I slept in a tent, so the place looked spacious to me and something to be proud of.

Audrey was back to looking either at my chest or over my left ear as she let me into her house. The inside looked warm and inviting with throw blankets over the couch and pictures on the bookshelves next to the fireplace. The kitchen looked fairly up to date and quite luxurious compared to the cabin. I didn't walk any further into the house, knowing she didn't want me there and we no longer had an audience, so there was no reason for us to keep up this charade.

"I'll go ahead back to my tent. Thanks for keeping things up in front of Pete." I edged toward the door, car keys still in hand.

Audrey dropped her backpack to the floor by the kitchen

table and spun around. "A tent? Ew. No. You can stay here, at least for tonight. I'm sure my roommate won't mind."

Then she held up an object in her hand, the silver on the side of it catching the light from above the table. It was her saucy grin that held my attention though. I was a sucker for a genuine smile from Audrey. "Besides, I have to practice my harmonica and I know you don't want to miss that."

I groaned, despite the weight on my shoulders feeling lighter now that she was back to joking around with me. As horrific as her harmonica playing was, I would miss hearing her butcher every song I'd learned in kindergarten. "Maybe you should go back to knitting."

Audrey grimaced. "No way. Did you not see how bad my beanies were?"

We grinned at each other, and just like that, I had a place to stay for the night.

CHAPTER EIGHTEEN

udrey

"WHAT IS THIS? A lumberjack in our midst?"

Madi's high-pitched voice snapped me out of whatever was going on between Boston and I. We shouldn't be gazing into each other's eyes anyway. His eyes were dangerous territory. I tended to get lost in them and forget all about the plans I had for my future. Madi swept into the room, another new hat on her head that I could have sworn I saw on a celebrity on social media last week.

I shot her a smile and returned her hug, caught up in the layers of jacket she was wearing. Or was it a shirt? A caftan? Despite our rent issues, I was happy to see her. I was happy to see our shared house too. I was just happy to be rescued with the promise of a hot shower and real food.

"I always thought he was more of a rugby player," I replied, pulling back from the hug. Both of us turned our attention to Boston, who stood there looking uncomfortable. Although he did look exactly like a lumberjack in that dirty flannel, the hiking boots covered in mud by his feet where he'd taken them off, and the four-day-old beard.

Madi gave him an exaggerated once-over that made my skin prickle with unease. "Oh, I don't know. Maybe a lumberjack and a rugby player had a baby? Hello, handsome." Madi may have been talking to me, but her gaze was locked on Boston. "Where the hell have you been hiding this man?"

Madi sauntered over to him, her hand reaching out to run her fingers down his arm. Boston did a head nod instead of a smile or greeting. I would have recognized his unease right away if I wasn't dealing with a serious case of jealousy.

"We, uh, got snowed in up on the mountain," I said, coming over quickly to stand by Boston. "Remember we were going up to that cabin this weekend?"

I gave Madi a look that should have had her backing off. I went up to a cabin for a romantic weekend with a man. Why was she now flirting with him in front of me? Girl code said back the fuck off.

Ignoring girl code entirely, Madi now walked her fingers up Boston's arm and then ran her hand down his chest. I wanted to smack it off, hopefully breaking a finger or two. Boston shifted back just enough so she was no longer touching him.

"Were you headed out?" he finally said, no trace of warmth in his tone.

"I'm off to a party in the city. You should come. They would adore you."

Call me a green-eyed monster, I didn't care. I was done. I looped my arm through Boston's, a careful smile frozen on my face. "We're actually exhausted from the weekend. Shower, food, and then bed. Right, beast?"

Boston nodded, catching on to my annoyance. For all his brawn, this beast also had a brain. He turned a blinding smile on me, right before he bent and picked me up, princess-style.

"I get to soap you up first," he growled.

I saw Madi's mouth drop open from the periphery of my

vision. But then Boston locked gazes with me and I didn't fight it. I was happily lost in those dark eyes while he held me so carefully against his chest. All I could think about was his hands sliding over my body, soap bubbles and goose bumps in his wake.

"Wow. Okay. I'll be sure to wear earplugs when I get back. Have fun, you two!" Madi hollered after us.

Boston already had us down the hallway. "Where's the bathroom?" I pointed the way, but my stomach chose that moment to let out an embarrassing growl. Boston glanced down and grinned. "I should feed you first."

I put my hand on my stomach and hoped it would shut up. "Pssh. Who needs food? I liked the soaping-me-up plan."

Boston put me down at the doorway to my bathroom, his hands on my hips to steady me. "I'll go call for delivery. Wait. Do they do that in Blueball?"

"Yes! Gannon convinced Diego at Grass to do delivery when they opened. First restaurant in Blueball to do that and they made a killing. Now a few others have followed suit, but I love Grass."

Boston frowned. "I do not like grass."

I laughed. "No. The restaurant is called Grass, but they have tons of grass-fed meats and salads and sides. You'll love it, I promise. Maybe get the meat lovers special and I'll take the steak salad?"

"Okay. You shower. I'll get food." Boston was already reaching for his phone in his back pocket. My grand dreams of being soaped up popped.

"But you'll stay?"

Boston lifted his head. "Yeah. I'm staying." And then he was smiling at me and those eyes were doing their thing and I was lost, just staring back and leaning against the doorframe in a daze.

When he swatted my backside and spun to leave, I jolted back to reality. I got busy in the bathroom, shaking my head at myself. Just a few days ago, him spanking me would have had me biting his head off. Now I had to squeeze my thighs together to stop the ache there from making me crazy.

I stripped out of the clothes I'd worn at the cabin, happy to finally see them go. The hot shower with my fancy soap was almost better than sex. A-week-ago me would have said way better than sex, but then I'd experienced sex with Boston and I could no longer agree. I rushed through the shower, salivating over the food coming and another night spent in Boston's company.

The food had just arrived when I came out of the bathroom, hair wet and pajamas on. I'd chosen my sexiest pair, the ones I rarely slept in because the top was too skimpy for keeping my boobs in place while I slept. My ass cheeks peeked out the bottom of the shorts too, which was just an added bonus I hoped Boston would like.

Boston turned around with the food bags in hand. His eyes widened when he saw me, a reaction that was good for a woman's soul, you know? He put the bags on the little table where Madi and I usually ate and sat down, busy unpacking our dinner while studiously ignoring me.

"Madi left a hundred-dollar bill on the table with a note," he said, shoving a container to my side of the table. I sat down and glanced at the money. The note was short and not-so-sweet: More coming, promise!

"What's that about?" Boston grumbled, opening his container and digging in.

I put the first bite of steak and salad in my mouth. The burst of lemon vinaigrette and blue cheese and the most perfectly cooked steak hit my tongue and I had a mini mouth-gasm. My eyes slid closed and I needed a moment to myself to ride out the pleasure of freshly cooked food not from a can or box. When I could open my eyes again and swallow, I saw Boston frozen with a fork halfway to his mouth, his dark gaze as hot as lava.

"What? Isn't it good?" I gestured to his meal.

His face clouded over like a thunderstorm. "You keep

groaning like that and I won't let you finish your damn meal." He shoved the bite in his mouth and glared at me.

I was too happy to be home and still with Boston to get pissed off about his need to constantly order me around. "I enjoy simple pleasures. So sue me."

"Tell me about the money from Madi."

More orders. I rolled my eyes, but answered around another bite of food. We were too hungry to be polite and swallow first. "She hasn't had her half of the rent the last few months. I've covered for her and she's paying me back. Slowly."

Boston dropped his fist on the table with a bang. I jumped in my chair. If looks could kill and all that...

"What? Why is she going out partying when she owes you money?"

I would not want to be on Boston's bad side. The man looked absolutely feral on my behalf. I put my hand on his, trying to loosen up his fingers. "Don't break my table, beast. It's okay."

Boston wouldn't let me open up his fist. "It's not okay, Audrey." He shoved his chair back and stood. I gaped at him. "I'll go find her and get that money. She could probably sell her clothes and pay you back just from that."

I jumped up too, incensed. "You can't just jump into my private business, Boston! I told you I have it handled."

Boston folded his arms across his chest and I was shocked he could even do it. I wouldn't have been surprised at all if I heard a seam or two rip. "You were about to jump right in with a damn intervention when it came to Annabel."

I opened my mouth to argue, but then my brain caught up. He was right. I'd stuck my nose in for sure. "I just want to help you. Somehow, some way, I actually like you, beast."

Boston dropped his arms. "I like you too, despite the stupid dresses you wear."

I scoffed. "They're not stupid! They're professional!"

His lips wobbled. "You're missing the point."

I flopped back in my chair. "No, I know the point. We want

to see the other person happy, so we try to jump in and help. I get it. Which is why I think we need to discuss a cabin-plus-house temporary fake relationship with benefits."

Boston sat down too, leaning his elbows on the table and making the wood creak under his weight. I made the mistake of looking into his eyes and now I was trapped.

"CPHTFRWB?" he whispered, the sound like logs snapping in a bonfire.

I grimaced. I also had to squeeze my legs together again to keep from begging. "That's getting to be a mouthful."

The side of Boston's mouth hitched up. "I'll give you a mouthful."

It physically hurt to hold in the laugh. "Did you just flirt with me?"

"Get the fuck over here." Boston shoved back from the table.

That was one command I could happily follow. I jumped out of my chair and rounded the table, stepping one foot to the side of him and lifting my other leg like I was mounting a horse. His hands grabbed for my ass, squeezing my flesh like he'd just been counting down the seconds until he got to touch me again. When I sat down on his lap, I knew for sure he wanted me just as badly. My hands landed on his massive shoulders. I leaned in and caught a whiff of firewood and dirt and sweat.

"You stink, beast."

Boston grinned. "Most beasts do. But for you, I'll shower."

He stood up from the chair and I whooped at the sudden change in elevation. My legs wrapped around his waist and he began to walk us back to my bedroom and bathroom like he didn't have an entire person clinging to his front side. In my bedroom, he lifted me off of him and placed me on my bed.

"I'll be right back." He backed away, still looking down at me. "I love those pajamas. You better take them off before I get back."

I gave him a saucy grin. "Why's that?"

He unbuttoned his flannel before ripping it and his T-shirt

over his head. My mouth went dry taking in his naked torso. The man really was ridiculously good looking. Nature should have spread out the gift of muscle to a few other males. It was just unfair, honestly, to pile it all on one man.

Boston's hand went to the buckle of his belt. "Because I'll tear them off your body and you won't be able to wear them again for me."

The man winked at me and disappeared into the bathroom, leaving me groaning in anticipation on my bed. I had no idea what we were doing, but I wasn't going to question it when it felt so damn right. I'd worry about Keva and all that later. Right now, I just wanted one more night with Boston before reality set in.

CHAPTER NINETEEN

oston

THE CHAIR LET out a dangerous creak. This was not an uncommon occurrence in my life.

"Why do you keep it if it's from your father?" As much as I wanted inside Audrey's body right this second, I also wanted inside her head. The shower and the full meal had given me new life. I had plans to keep Audrey up all night.

Audrey sat up on the bed and eyed me in the dainty antique chair that sat in the corner of her room with a towel slung over the back. She shrugged. "Just because my father's an ass doesn't mean his entire lineage is. Seemed a shame to let Mom throw away an antique even if the sight of it makes me angry."

I fisted my cock, letting myself simply enjoy the moment when her gaze dropped. The way she bit her lower lip and her eyelids drooped. I could visually see the tension dropping from her shoulders. I liked that I could do that for her. "What if we gave you a new memory about this chair?"

Audrey stood up from the bed, her lip popping away from her teeth as she smiled flirtatiously. I could have sworn her hips were shifting more dramatically than normal as she walked over to me real slow.

"What kind of memory?" Her hands came up to push her hair behind her shoulders, thrusting her breasts out even more. Her nipples were already beaded and ready for my mouth. I loved how responsive her body was to me.

I spread my legs wide and gave a good tug on my dick. Shit, I could come right here just watching her walk. "Whatever memory you want to make, baby. If you're asking my opinion, I think you should start on your knees and work your way up from there."

Audrey came to a stop between my feet. I held my breath. I wanted her so badly she could ask me to bend all the rules and keep her a dirty secret for years. My one goal in coming to Blueball had been to reconcile with my sister. I was shocked to find out that a slight blonde with daddy issues and a knack for falling into terrible hobbies could make me toss out my mission so easily.

The breath whooshed out of my lungs as she knelt at my feet. She looked so pretty kneeling there, her big brown eyes looking up at me with nothing but trust and affection. It was a look a man could get used to. Audrey was the quintessential girl next door with wholesome good looks that made every man with any sense in his head look her way. But I knew her secret. My wholesome girl liked her sex sweaty and dirty.

Audrey's hands dragged up my calves, and my brain quit thinking about anything. She massaged the tops of my thighs, and I couldn't remember when a woman had taken the time to make me feel good. Sex in the past had been quick encounters with a race to the finish line. That was not the case with us.

"How's this working for you?" Audrey asked on a whisper.

I had to keep my eyes from rolling back in my head when she

cupped my balls and gave them a gentle squeeze. "I have the very best memories of this fucking chair."

She grinned, as I knew she would. "I better give you some more, then, because every time you groan, you give me good memories too."

She came up on her knees and licked up my shaft from root to tip. My upper body jackknifed up and the chair groaned in protest. Audrey put one finger in my chest and pushed. It took a deep inhale, but I was able to rest back on the chair. I was rewarded by her taking me in her hands and her gloriously hot mouth. The woman worked me over like she knew all the right moves to have me exploding in her mouth.

When sweat began to bead up on my brow and my breastbone from holding back, I lifted my hands from where they'd been gripping the underside of the chair and cupped her cheeks, pulling her off me.

"I can't, baby. Come climb up on my lap instead."

Audrey pouted, her lips red and slick. She was a fucking wet dream there at my feet. "One of these days I will taste you. Swallow you down. Choke on you."

I squeezed my eyes shut. "Fuck, lusty. Please quit talking."

Her tinkling laughter had me opening my eyes again. She stood, then turned around, sitting on my lap and leaning back against me. My dick pulsed under her. She reached down and grabbed the tip of me from between her legs.

"I want you to do that thing you do," she whispered.

I moved her hair aside and kissed a line from her neck to the middle of her shoulder blades. There wasn't one inch of her body that wasn't sexy as hell. "What's that?"

"Manhandle me. Take control of my body so all I have to do is feel you destroying me and putting me back together again."

The growl from my chest wasn't planned, but I couldn't act like I wasn't affected by the things that came out of her mouth. Audrey was giving me her complete trust and it did something to me. I wanted to be the one she turned to and trusted for everything. I didn't know how that would work, given our restrictions, but I wanted to at least give her this.

I kissed my way back up her neck and lightly bit her earlobe. "Wrap your feet around my legs. Hands on my knees." She instantly obeyed, her position now spreading her thighs wide and pushing her ass back against me.

Putting my hands on her hips, I lifted her in the air easily. My dick swung back up, ready to go. I placed a kiss on the little indent low on her back and then slowly lowered her to my tip. I held her there, letting the first inch of me stretch her out like I knew she needed. When Audrey began to squirm in my hands and arch her back, I gave her another few inches. The little mewls and groans falling from her lips made me crazy. A bead of sweat slid down the side of my forehead.

"Hold on tight, baby."

That was all the warning I gave her before I slammed her down on me, making her take my full length. She cried out but tossed her head back like she liked it. I lifted her almost completely off of me again and let her slam back down. The chair groaned almost as loud as my girl. I kept her lifting and dropping at a rapid pace, her body completely at my mercy.

I was about to lose my shit. Pretty sure there was blood on my lip from where I'd been biting it, trying to hold back. Audrey's fingernails dug into my knees and then she was shaking like a leaf, crying out a garbled version of my name. I felt her body lock around my cock like a vise, and I was done for. My balls contracted and an electric shock shot up my spine. I came so hard I wasn't sure I'd survive it. I kept pumping into her, needing to be deeper inside her so that she'd never leave me.

Even the aftershocks stole my breath. My body lay over Audrey's, bending her practically in half. It couldn't have been comfortable, but I couldn't seem to move. My dick began to soften and still I held her with an arm banded around her waist. I didn't want to separate from her. And more importantly, I didn't want to explore why that was the case. Pretty sure I wouldn't like the answer.

We did eventually make it to the bed, but I held good on my intentions, keeping her up into the early hours of the morning. When I heard her roommate return, I made sure Audrey's orgasm that round was particularly loud. If it made me a bastard, then so be it. We finally fell asleep, a sweaty mess of limbs and smiles on our faces.

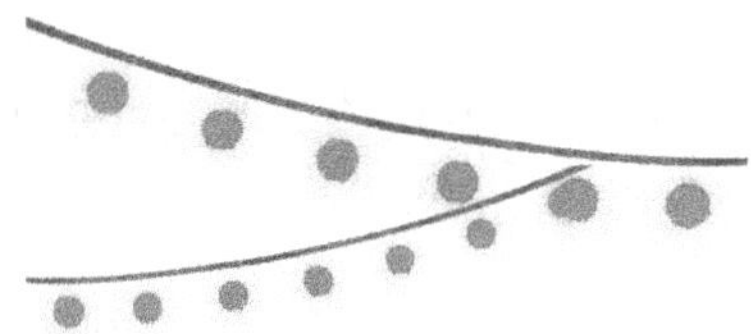

"You're a sneaky bastard, you know that, beast?"

I spun around, heart in my throat. I had one foot inside my truck, but Audrey had somehow woken up and followed me outside. The sun had just come up and she should still be getting her beauty sleep.

"What are you doing?" I asked, pulling my foot out of the truck and frowning at her. She looked like she'd been ridden hard and well, her hair a tangled mess and puffy eyes. Pretty sure there was even a red spot on the side of her neck that might be the beginnings of a hickey, but I didn't want to point it out. Not when she was storming out the door in another one of those prim little dresses and looked ready to kick me in the nuts.

"I could ask you the same thing. Where the fuck you think you're going?" She stopped right in front of me, steaming mad.

I flicked the ruffle on the sleeve of her slate-gray dress. "Nice dress."

She slapped my hand away which almost made me laugh. But I preferred my nuts intact.

"You're going to Pete's, aren't you?" She didn't give me time to answer. "Which, as the Glamper's Paradise realtor, I should be there for, don't you think?"

"Uh, I mean, I guess."

That was apparently not the right answer as her eyes nearly bugged out of her pretty head. She let out a frustrated sound and walked around the hood of my truck. It took her a couple tries, but she made it up into the passenger seat, tugging her dress down to her knees.

I looked up at the morning sky. Sadly, no answers appeared and I was left to figure out this woman on my own. I climbed in behind the wheel and started driving out to Pete's place. Audrey finger-combed her hair and pulled down the visor mirror to run her fingers below her eyes.

I smirked. She looked prettier than any girl in Blueball, so I didn't know why I felt the need to poke the hornet's nest instead of telling her the truth. "You still look like you got fucked good and long last night."

Audrey gasped, slapping the visor back up and staring out the windshield with a haughty glare. She didn't speak again until we pulled into the lane that led to Pete's remote cabin. She waited until she was about to slide out the door, not waiting for me to help her down.

"Good thing no one knows I didn't have time to put on underwear." She turned and gave me a devilish smile. "Then I'd really look like I got fucked, huh?"

The little hellion slid right out of the truck and walked up to Pete's porch like she didn't just drop a bomb on me that left my pants situation inappropriate for getting out of the truck. Pete came out of his cabin and gave her a hug, waving to me and getting Audrey seated in the chair that should have been mine.

Long minutes later, I got out too, purposely keeping me gaze away from Audrey. We told Pete all about our stay and confessed about the table and chairs that had been sacrificed. Thankfully, he laughed his ass off and told us it wouldn't be his problem much longer when he sold that part of land to Gannon. He waited until the end of our visit to ask about my sister.

"Did you patch things up with Keva?"

I scratched my beard, having decided not to shave it last night. It felt weird to have hair on my face, but I kind of liked it. Like this version of me in Blueball was about becoming my true self.

"Didn't have time last night, but that's my plan starting today."

Audrey reached up and held my hand, running her thumb over my skin. I held on, liking her touch way more than I should for something temporary. I liked her comfort. I liked that she cared enough to butt her nose into my business.

We left soon after that, heading for Crazy Beans in downtown Blueball when Audrey said she needed caffeine or she'd simply perish. Considering I was the reason she was lacking sleep, I thought it was my duty to get her the biggest coffee I could find. We parked and Audrey let me help her down from the truck this time. Thank fuck, because she would have flashed the whole downtown if I hadn't grabbed the hem of her dress. She smirked as she brushed past me.

The second we stepped into Crazy Beans, I knew I'd been manipulated.

Lincoln and my sister were sitting at a table, sipping drinks in the corner of the shop. Lincoln lifted his head and saw us, instantly waving.

"Oh look! Keva and Linc are here! Let's go sit with them," Audrey said with a voice too bright to be real.

Great. Yeah. Let's sit with my sister, Audrey's best friend, and pretend we didn't have our mouths and other body parts all over each other last night.

Audrey leaned in and whispered, "Order me a caramel latte, would you?" She shot me a smile that turned my blood cold. "Good thing I didn't do something silly like not wear underwear, right? That would be awkward."

She winked and walked over to their table, leaving me in a place called Blueball, where the roads were paved to hell in frustration.

CHAPTER TWENTY

udrey

I SHOULDN'T HAVE DONE it, but sometimes you have to make your move and apologize later instead of waiting for the permission that will never come. I also knew there'd be a price to pay later for sticking my nose in Boston's business, but I was betting on that punishment being something I'd ultimately enjoy...if you know what I'm saying.

My gaggle of friends and I could always track each other's location. There was no way to be single in this modern world without having a girl squad to keep each other safe. So when I saw Keva's location hovering at Crazy Beans, I had a sudden hankering for caffeine.

"Hey, friends," I said as I hugged Keva and then moved to Lincoln. Being the gentleman that he was, he stood up to give that hug even when I waved at him to stay seated. I couldn't have been happier that these two lovebirds found their way back to each other. I'd never seen Keva happier and I could honestly say she was glowing with this pregnancy.

"Before you start, it's decaf." Keva gave me a look that said not to start shit, so I made the motion of zipping my lips.

Just like tracking locations, we also made sure the procreating members of our squad kept healthy during their pregnancies. Just ask Paisley. We'd made her go on walks in her third trimester when all she wanted to do was lie on the couch and holler at Gannon to bring her food. We also showed up on her doorstep with at least a month of frozen meals when she gave birth to Aster. Paisley believed she could do everything, all while taking care of a newborn and lacking sleep for nights on end, but we had her back anyway.

I had a seat in one of the four chairs around their table. "Mind if we join you?"

Keva shot me a look that she knew I was up to no good. "Looks like you've joined us," she said wryly.

I just smiled back, knowing the sarcasm was born from her strained relationship with Boston, not me.

"We're glad you're here, Audrey." Lincoln gave me a genuine smile, which I appreciated.

I felt Boston's presence before he touched my shoulder. He cleared his throat and reached around to set my coffee in front of me. "Hey, Lincoln. Ann—Keva. Mind if I sit?"

He was so polite he was adorable. My heart squeezed at the uncertainty in his tone. Whenever he talked to me, he belted out orders that were more firm than that ass I could bounce quarters off of, but not with his sister.

"Sure." Keva was curt, but at least she allowed him to join the group.

Boston sat and the chair let out a squeak. Another victim to Boston's bulk. He took a sip of his coffee, gaze darting around the coffee shop, maybe looking for something to talk about. The awkward silence was killing me, and Keva wasn't even my sister.

"Hey, so did you hear Boston had to break apart the table and chairs in the cabin so we'd have dry firewood?" I put my hand on Keva's arm. "I don't know what I would have done without him.

Probably froze to death or died of starvation from forgetting to pack food."

Keva's lips curved in the barest of smiles. "I'm pretty sure you can't starve to death in four days."

I patted her arm. "You clearly don't understand my stomach."

Lincoln laughed, gesturing to Boston, who looked a little embarrassed that I was singing his praises. "You remember that one hike in 2020 when the whole platoon got lost?"

Boston nodded, finally looking comfortable in the conversation. "Yeah, you were sure you were going to be punished for getting us lost. Pretty sure you cried like a girl."

"Fuck off, Tank. I'm telling this story. You packed so much food in your pack that all of us lived off it until the Humvee came for us the next day." Lincoln turned to us. "We'd never seen one guy pack so much food!"

Boston patted his flat stomach. "Gotta feed all these muscles."

We all cracked up. Except Keva. She snorted and it wasn't a cute snort.

"2020, huh? That was Lucas's first birthday. When I was celebrating it alone. No family."

The table got deathly quiet. Inside I was fuming. I didn't know when it had happened, but I was on Boston's side now. How long was Keva going to hold a grudge? She was the ultimate grudge holder, but this was getting ridiculous.

I smacked her arm. Hard. Her jaw dropped but I beat her to it.

"You weren't alone, bitch. I was there. Janice, Paisley, Marlo. Stop being such a hard-ass."

Keva looked ready to blow. We'd had our arguments before, but we usually kept them to one of our houses when we were having a girls' night and needed to clear the air.

Boston leaned over the table, putting his hand between us. "Hey. It's okay, Audrey. I deserve that. And I can fight my own battles."

He and I glared at each other, silently communicating. He desperately wanted me to back off and I just as desperately wanted to shake some sense into my best friend.

Keva shoved away from the table. "I should get to work." She spun on her heel and walked off with barely a wave goodbye to Lincoln.

"Keep trying, bro. She's just feisty without caffeine these days. I'll calm her down." Lincoln put his hand on my shoulder and then he was racing out the door after Keva.

Boston slumped back against the chair, his jaw hard, but his eyes defeated. I was both angry at my friend and feeling like I needed to apologize for her and how badly that had gone. Maybe we needed to approach Keva at her home, where she could vent without our neighbors hearing her private business.

I put my hand on Boston's, relieved when he didn't pull away. "We'll keep trying," I whispered.

He didn't look at me, but he squeezed my fingers tighter.

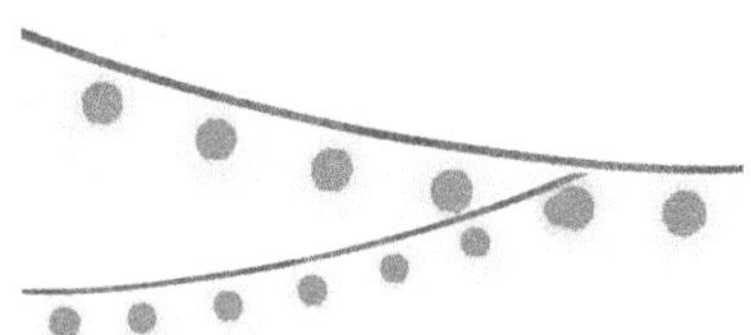

I'd seen Boston grumpy. I've seen him angry. I'd seen him so focused a bomb blast wouldn't have fazed him. But I'd never seen him like this. He'd actually handed me the keys to his truck and told me to drive him around to look at apartments. Then he'd gone totally silent, a shell of the man he normally was. I kept up a steady stream of conversation as I drove around Blueball, but he didn't chime in. I took him to the only two apartment complexes we had, then a few of the houses that I knew were for rent.

Without input from Boston as to what he liked, I had to pull to the side of the road to look at our agency's listings on my phone. There was one cabin for rent about two miles from the entrance to Glamper's Paradise. It was surrounded by trees and fairly primitive inside. Not much better than the cabin we'd been stranded at all weekend.

It was perfect for Boston.

I reached across the truck console and patted his arm. He rolled his head against the headrest to look at me, his gaze finally meeting mine. I could have wept. His dark eyes were shuttered and fractured, sad beyond belief. I was a sucker for sad eyes. Much to my friends' dismay, I gave five dollars I really didn't have every month to a charity because I'd watched a commercial about abandoned dogs. Those poor, scrawny animals had looked at the camera with these big, sad eyes and I'd gotten my credit card out. Boston's were a hundred times worse because I knew him personally. Intimately.

"Let's go check out this cabin and then I'll take you home and run you a bath."

He didn't fight me on my suggestion which told me how low he felt. "Will you wash my hair?"

Shit, I'd wash every inch of him if he just promised to keep talking. "You bet. I'll even blow-dry it with my round brush. You'll look so pretty."

He didn't laugh, but he did look like he'd actually survive the rest of the day, so I counted that as a win. When he saw the dilapidated cabin, he perked up even more. When I got him back to my house and in my bathtub, he leaned his head back as I massaged shampoo into his hair, trusting me with his body like I trusted him. I rinsed the suds out and Boston caught my wrist in his hand. He blinked his eyes open and stared at me.

"You're really good at being a peacemaker. It's not your responsibility to do it, but you're damn good at it."

He didn't have to take care of me so well when we were at the cabin, but he did. Simply because he could. I was just returning the favor. I leaned over and kissed him, telling him with my lips and tongue how much he meant to me. I didn't even protest when he pulled me into the bathtub fully clothed.

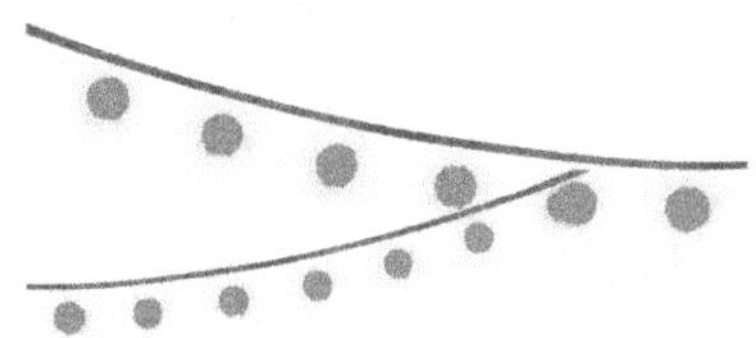

Me: Ladies, we need an intervention.

Marlo: Oh! Who, when, where, and why? I'll bring the brownies.

Paisley: Let me guess. Keva?

Me: Ding, ding, we have a winner.

Marlo: Okay, we got the who. Tell us the why.

Me: She's eviscerating Boston and he's been nothing but sweet and considerate. She needs to give him a chance. Just hear him out.

Paisley: Keva is an expert at using a grudge as a weapon...

Marlo: Do you know she still won't talk to Bob at the deli counter for that lunch meat he sold her like four years ago? One little bout of food poisoning and she glares at him. Poor guy always looks like he's going to cry when she comes in the store.

Me: Boston just wants a chance to talk to her and apologize. I say we come at her from all sides.

Paisley: Sneak attack! I love it.

Marlo: I'm not good at sneaking. Or surprises.

Me: You work on dead people, Marlo. What's more surprising than death?

Marlo: EXACTLY. I don't like surprises because every person I put in a casket was surprised by death that day. I prefer a well-thought-out and planned attack that everyone knows is coming.

Paisley: For fuck's sake. I don't have time for this. I got a baby on the boob and another that wants the crust cut off her sandwich or she won't go to kindergarten. I'll go see Keva at the clinic tomorrow after drop-off and put the screws in her about how important family is with a new baby. That'll get her emotions revved up. Then I'll tell her you're swinging by later, Marlo. That enough planning for you?

Marlo: Yes, thank you. And I'll forgive the snippy tone considering you have a human nipple clamp twenty-four seven.

Me: This conversation has gone horribly awry. Maybe talk about the regrets of dying people or something, Marlo. I'll swing by with Boston after you, so make sure you text me when you've left.

Marlo: You do know the people are dead by the time they come to my mortuary, right? I don't actually talk to them about their regrets. I mean, sometimes I talk to them if they look like good people, but they do not talk back to me. Just to clarify.

Me: Well, thank fuck for clarifying, Marlo.

Paisley: I just jostled Aster from laughing so hard and now she's crying.

Marlo: Switch her to the other nipple. See, this is where a third nipple could come in handy.

Paisley: Huh. I don't think a third nipple is actually functional. Is it?

Me: LADIES. Focus. This needs to work. For Boston's sake and Keva's.

Paisley: And yours. Am I right?

Marlo: You two were adorable when we rescued you. And before you even say it, you've never been a good actor, Audrey, so I don't buy that fake relationship story.

Paisley: True. Audrey had a glow to her.

Me: I'm not pregnant, so shush. And it's all temporary.

Marlo: What's temporary?

Paisley: The sex or the relationship?

Me: I hate you both.

Marlo: No, you don't. You love us and I have a sneaking suspicion you might have similar feelings for the tall, dark, and handsome ex-military lumberjack that is currently sharing your bed.

Me: How do you know he's sharing my bed?

Paisley: I know the look of a woman who's getting good sex...

Marlo: Me too, but the opposite. I'm what a woman looks like when she's not.

Me: Guys, can you keep quiet about this for now? I just don't want to hurt Keva and right now she hates her brother. I can't exactly tell her I might have accidentally developed some feelings for him.

Paisley: Probably for the best. We already discussed how she can hold a grudge. How about we work on getting her to accept Boston? Then we can work on the idea of you two dating.

Marlo: Sigh. So does this mean I'm the only single one of the group??

Me: You gotta find a man who will actually talk back when you chat with him. Preferably not a dead guy.

Marlo: So I'll be single forever, is what you're saying...

CHAPTER TWENTY-ONE

AUDREY TOLD me she had work to do today, so I left when she did, heading for Glamper's Paradise. But not before teasing her about the dress she wore. This one went down past her knees like showing off those joints was scandalous in a business meeting. She gave me the bird which brought the first smile to my face since before yesterday's disastrous meeting with my sister.

I hoped Gannon and Linc had some manual labor that I could do while my life was on pause. When I got there, Gannon informed me that Linc was already working on a backed-up sewer line on one of the trailers. I opted to help Gannon instead.

We hiked along the path that led to Pete's land. Gannon and Linc had already cleared the path in hopes of owning the piece of land one day, but Gannon wanted to discuss the topography and potential for cabins. I appreciated that he included me so readily, like I was already part of the team. I'd built bunkers and temporary shelters many times in my travels with the military, so it wasn't outside of my wheelhouse to know the best spots for a cabin. Once we'd walked it on foot, we stood back and discussed what could be done.

"I think you can get quite a few cabins while maintaining privacy, depending on how many acres Pete is ultimately willing to sell."

Gannon had his hands on his hips, staring out at the land with a look that told me he'd already made them his. At least in his heart.

"And how much it costs," Gannon said wryly.

I put a hand on his shoulder. "Pete's a good guy. He's not looking to make a pile of money off this sale. He wants it to go to good use, which this is. I'm sure, with Audrey's help, we can work out a unique sale that will benefit both parties."

We stood there, looking out at the land, envisioning what it could look like with cabin rentals for families from all over. It wouldn't be fancy and that was exactly the point. The focus would be on wholesome activities that families could do together, creating memories that would last lifetimes.

"Hey, you play any instruments?" Gannon asked out of the blue, turning and slowly walking back to Glamper's Paradise.

I chuckled, remembering hundreds of nights in the military spent playing whatever instrument we had on hand. Coming up with songs and games to pass the time. Storytelling. Bullshitting, was more like it. There was one guy who strapped a banjo over his pack every time we were on the move. We gave him shit for it—and nicknamed him Billy, as in hillbilly—but eventually all of us ended up playing the instrument.

"Yeah, I can actually play the banjo."

Gannon fist-pumped the air. "No shit? The banjo?"

"Yeah. Why are you asking?"

Gannon clapped his hands together. "Well. Linc and I started a band and we need a banjo player."

I frowned. "Since when?" Banjo playing was a bit of a dying

art form, to be honest. It was up there with playing the accordion.

"Since right fuckin' now." Gannon halted abruptly, his expression one I'd seen on his daughter Elise's face the first time I met her and she begged me to put her up on my shoulders so she could pretend she was flying. "Do you sing too??"

Gannon was one crazy motherfucker. I liked him. "More of a backup singer, but I can hold a note most of the time."

Gannon hooted and a few birds flew from the tops of the trees surrounding us. "I'll buy you a banjo and we'll start practices as soon as it comes in."

"Wait. Practices?"

Gannon shook his head like he was disappointed in me. "Duh. For our band. We still need a band name, so put your creative thinking cap on, would you?"

We kept walking, finally making it back to the glamp-site when the sun was high in the sky. I had time to wonder about the ache in my chest. For the first time, it wasn't just from the way things were between my sister and me. Now that ache was softer, more nuanced. And probably stemming from Audrey. She'd defended me yesterday. I hadn't had someone in my corner in a long time. Sure, in the military we'd watched each other's backs but that was mostly because our lives depended on it. It had been years since someone who actually cared for me had stood up for me simply because they wanted to protect me from emotional hurt. Probably not since Mom and Dad died.

And now this thing with Gannon. He'd accepted me into his friend group and his business without question. He didn't find me lacking in any way. In fact, he found me a valuable addition to his life. For a self-proclaimed hermit like me, that acceptance was foreign. And quite frankly, disconcerting. I didn't know what to do with it.

Linc spotted us as we got close to the parking lot, his shirt and jeans covered in questionable muck. "There you guys are. I could have used your help."

Gannon and I shared a look. "Sorry, bro. We were super busy. Looks like you got the sewer line fixed, huh?"

Linc narrowed his eyes. "You fuckers purposely left, didn't you?"

Gannon grinned. "Everyone has to be initiated into their first sewer line backup. I don't make the rules, Lincoln."

I chuckled while making sure I inhaled through my mouth, not my nose. Linc stunk to high heaven. He turned to me, pointing at my chest.

"What are you laughing for, fuck face? You're next."

That shut me up quick.

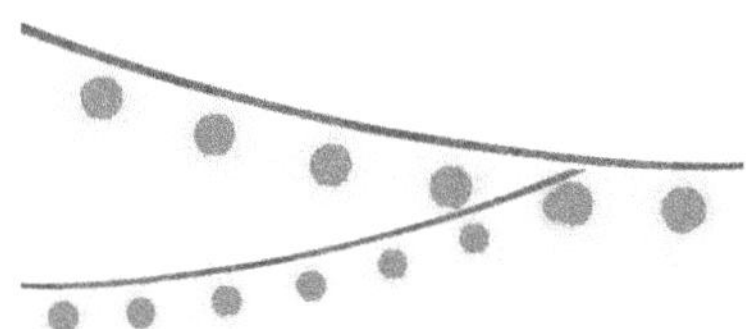

I spent the afternoon filling out the rental application paperwork Audrey emailed me. When she got home some time before four, she rushed inside the house and grabbed me by the hand, yanking on me.

"What are you doing?"

"Come on. Let's go!"

When I didn't move an inch, Audrey's shoulders dropped. "It's Keva. She needs our help."

That got my ass in gear. We were flying down the road in my truck before Audrey got the explanation out. "She was crying earlier and the baby—"

"Why was she crying?" I growled, positively furious. I loved

Linc like the brother I never had, but if he made my sister cry, I was going to pound his face. I'd done it before, I'd do it again.

"Let me finish a goddamn sentence and you'll know, beast." Audrey shot me a reprimanding look, but I was too busy envisioning Linc's black eye. "She was crying, because that's what pregnant women do. But the baby now has hiccups from all the crying."

I frowned, not understanding at all. The military didn't exactly train you to deal with pregnant women. I had to assume you approached one similar to approaching an active explosive, which I did have training on.

"Are hiccups dangerous?"

"Well, no." Audrey's hands were twisting in her lap, which made anxiety cramp in my gut, but I didn't know why we were both worried.

She wasn't making any sense. "Aren't hiccups just an irritation? In which case I shouldn't be going over there at all. I tend to only escalate her irritation."

I pulled up in front of their house, the long driveway and tall pine trees on the front of the lot concealing my truck. Audrey put her hand on my leg, turning big brown eyes on me that spelled trouble.

"Please just come in."

I shook my head, trying to not let her pleading sway me. "Yesterday didn't go so well. I'd rather regroup."

"Do you trust me?"

I stared back at Audrey.

Fucking hell. "Yes."

"Then come in with me." She squeezed my thigh and then got out of the truck. With a growl of frustration aimed at the universe in general, I climbed out too.

Linc opened the door before we even knocked, like he'd been expecting us. He and Audrey shared a look, so clearly they'd been communicating about Keva. It struck me that everyone knew about my sister except me. We followed him into the small living room they'd transformed into a cozy space. She was curled on the couch, a blanket over her lap and a snapping fire in the fireplace. It was the soft sob that had me putting all our differences aside and rushing to the couch.

"What's wrong, Annabel?" I sat down so fast, she rolled into my side, looking up in surprise. "Tell me and I'll fix it."

Tears lined her lashes, turning her eyes into the kind of sad pools that killed a man. The tip of her nose was red and there wasn't a trace of makeup left on her skin. She didn't answer me, but she didn't pull away either.

"Hey." I put my arm around her, silently begging for her to let me be there for her. "Whatever it is, we can fix it. I'm sure of it. Do I need to kick Linc's ass? Because I can do that too."

That got her attention. She let out a watery laugh and slapped my chest. "No, Boston. I'm crying because my friends are little manipulative bitches."

I sat up straighter, still holding her close. "I normally wouldn't fight a female, but I can make their lives miserable. Just say the word."

That got another watery laugh out of her. Then she laid her head on my chest, a move she hadn't done since she was a little kid. I found myself having to swallow hard around the emotion clogging my throat. We used to watch movies together just like this, sharing popcorn before Annabel fell asleep. She never made it to the closing credits, and I'd carry her to bed. I'd been a good big brother for a while there. I knew I could be again.

"I'm crying over you, you big lug," Annabel finally whispered.

Her words had barbs, leaving blood in their wake. I was tired of feeling this way, but more than that, I didn't want my sister to feel this way. To shed tears because of the stupid decisions I'd made when I was old enough to be called an adult but still didn't know shit.

"I'm sorry, Annabel. I'm sorry for leaving you. I'm sorry for keeping you and Linc apart. I'm sorry I wasn't there for you when you were pregnant with Lucas. I was just a stupid teenager who was dealing with a grief so big I thought running away was the answer."

"I was grieving too," she said, voice breaking.

I squeezed my eyes shut. "I know. But back then the grief was so thick I couldn't see that. I could only feel this horrific pain and look for an escape. If I'd been wiser or older or just less of a lughead in general, I would have taken better care of you. I'd have made the decision to stay. That's something I'll forever regret."

Annabel sniffled hard and grabbed a handful of my shirt.

I grimaced, looking down at her. "Did you just use my shirt to wipe your nose?"

Her shoulders trembled, but this time, I thought it might be from laughter. "Seems like the least you could do."

I grinned, leaning my head against the top of hers. "I'd give you all my shirts, Princess Annabel."

She sniffled again at the nickname I'd given her when we were kids, burrowing harder into my side. "My friends told me that if I keep pushing you away, I'll forever be alone."

It might kill me, but if that's what she wanted, I'd give it to her.

"Is that what you want? For me to leave you alone?"

She sat up, pushing away so she could look at me. Her eyes were rimmed with red, but she still looked so much like the little girl she used to be. "No. I really don't. I'm just stubborn."

"Like a mule," Audrey whispered from the doorway to the kitchen, where apparently she and Linc were giving us privacy. Or eavesdropping, more like it.

Annabel grinned. "If you're interested in a little mule for a sister, I'd like you to stay."

Happiness instantly flooded my veins, but my eyes filled with tears. Fuck. I wasn't going to cry. Then Annabel's eyes went shiny again seeing mine. We both cracked up while wiping our eyes.

"I really fucking hate crying," Annabel muttered.

"That's a Mooney trait, I think," I muttered back.

I turned back to her, serious again. "So, I'm forgiven?"

She held her arms out. "Forgiven."

We hugged and over her shoulder I saw Audrey wiping her eyes. Linc was smiling like he'd never been prouder of his wife. I pulled back, serious about my role in her life.

"I have a present in the car. Mind if I go get it?"

Annabel looked confused, but nodded. I hustled outside and grabbed the two gift bags out of the back of the truck where I'd stored them since I drove into Blueball for the first time. Audrey and Linc had joined Annabel in the living room when I got back inside. I handed both bags to my sister and had a seat next to Audrey.

"When did you get these?" Annabel looked at me curiously, but she opened the first one, pulling out an official-looking piece of paper. She and Linc read it, then Annabel gasped. "This is a college fund for Lucas?"

I nodded. "That's a gift for you guys. I'll get Lucas his own gift once we spend some time together and I get to know him." I could only hope our reconciliation meant I got time with Lucas.

"Thanks, man. That's super thoughtful." Linc leaned across to shake my hand.

Annabel opened the second gift bag, pulling out a bigger gift wrapped in tissue paper. Once she got the paper off, she dipped her head and started crying again. Linc took it from her hands and saw what it was. I'd carved out a wooden frame that would hold two pictures. I'd burned in the word *Family* at the top of the frame. The top picture was a simple shot of me, Annabel, and our parents on vacation the summer before they died. We all looked happy, and sunburned, arms slung around each other. I'd kept that photo in my belongings the entire time I was enlisted.

"The second picture will be a family portrait of you guys. I wanted my nieces and nephews to know the family they came from. To know even before they were born, they were loved."

Annabel looked up, tears freely flowing down her cheeks. She gave me a smile that shifted something in my heart. We were okay. More than okay. We had a whole life ahead of us to be a family.

Audrey laid her head on my shoulder and used my T-shirt to wipe her nose.

udrey

"YOU OKAY?" I had to go into the office this morning to help out Jason with one of his clients, but I made the trip as quickly as I could. Boston had been exhausted last night after everything with Keva. Even I'd woken up with swollen eyes from crying and it wasn't my family.

Boston sat on my couch, head in hands, rubbing his temples. His head popped up, and even though he looked as gorgeous as usual, he looked tired.

"Yeah, I'm good. Just finished the paperwork for the cabin rental. I doubt I'll get it though."

I sat down next to him, putting my palm on his back and rubbing in circles. "Why do you say that? They've been trying to find a renter for a couple months already."

Boston sighed, pulling back his hair with one of my black elastics. "I don't have employment yet and I have no history of rentals previously. I look terrible on paper."

"Well, did you put all your military experience on there?

Being a veteran in good standing will look better than all those other details. And you have a job offer from Gannon. If I can get him to put the job offer details in writing, we can attach that to the rental application."

"But the job offer is contingent on Pete selling the land and we haven't secured that yet. That'll take time."

I put my hand over his, where they were clenched together, turning his fingers purple. "Good thing you have a fabulous real estate agent who already contacted Pete about his conditions being met. He said to swing by tomorrow with the offer from Gannon and he'll take a look. So then this most fabulous—and did I mention, gorgeous?—real estate agent then called Gannon who is right now putting together his offer details."

The worry in Boston's eyes leeched out little by little until he was biting back an actual smile. "Damn. Who is this real estate agent? I'd like to meet her."

I let go of his hands to backhand his muscled arm. He didn't even flinch. "I'll do you one better. I'll let you take this real estate agent shopping for furniture and then a celebratory dinner."

"Furniture?"

I stood. "Yes. You're going to need furniture for your cabin. No sleeping in a sleeping bag on the floor, okay? Let me get out of this hideous dress first." I used air quotes so he'd know I didn't agree with his assessment of my professional attire.

Boston hopped to his feet. "Can I watch?"

I looked over my shoulder coyly, making sure I gave my hips an extra shake as I walked away. "You can watch, but you can't touch."

Boston lunged for me and I shrieked, running to the bedroom and trying to slam the door on him. He caught it, of course, and barreled into my room anyway. I backed away and held my hands out.

"Nah-uh. Keep back, you beast. I'm serious about not touching. You need furniture. I refuse to visit you at your new cabin if you don't have somewhere I can sit."

Boston waggled his eyebrows, folded his arms across his chest, and leaned against my doorframe. "You can sit on my lap, lusty lady."

I reached around my back to unzip my dress. "Get your head out of the gutter, Mr. Mooney."

He just shook his head. "Not possible when you're around."

If he was already in the gutter, I might as well keep him there. I turned, giving him quite the show as I let the dress fall to my feet. I bent over to collect the dress and grinned when I heard him groan low and deep in his throat. I'd never considered making a living as a stripper, but I put my imagination to good use, getting dressed as provocatively as possible. By the time I was ready to go, Boston was rock hard behind the fly of his jeans. It was a shame to waste a perfectly good erection, but I was thinking long term. I wanted Boston settled here in Blueball so I could date him for real. Possibly forever.

"Let's go, beast."

He groaned, but followed me out to his truck. There were a thousand more groans as I took him to three different furniture stores, but by the time I called it a day, he had all the items he'd need for the cabin on hold. Once we knew he was approved for the cabin, then we could swing by and pick everything up.

"Can we get to the fun portion of the day?" Boston whined.

I cuddled up to his chest as we stood next to his truck. "You're worse than Lucas when he wants a dinosaur."

Boston dipped his head and laid an open-mouthed kiss on my neck, his warm hands settling on my hips. "I would have whined less if you would have let me touch you earlier instead of just looking."

"Oh, so this is *my* fault?"

Boston lifted his head, his hands sliding over my hips to caress my ass, pulling me tight against him. "No, Audrey. You've been amazing. You've gone way out of your way to help me with everything since I've been in Blueball. I hate doing anything that requires socializing, but I love that you force me to do the things I know I need to do but procrastinate on."

I cupped his face, enjoying the beard that had grown while we'd been up at the cabin. "I'm glad you say that because I want you to take me to Grass for dinner."

He rested his forehead against mine, his dark brown eyes boring into mine and doing a number on my heart. "Do I have to talk to people?"

"Yes, beast. But I know you can do it. I'll be right there with you."

He screwed his eyes shut. "Fine. But only because I like when you're happy."

We held hands in the truck and we held hands walking into Grass. Pete was nowhere around and even though small towns were known for gossip spreading, I didn't mind if there was a rumor about us that could get back to Keva. She'd assume we were acting out the fake relationship we'd already told her about. Plus, I couldn't seem to keep my hands off Boston. Clothed or naked. In public or private.

"Audrey!" Diego bellowed from behind the counter, throwing his hands in the air. He came around the counter and hugged me, eagerly looking at Boston. "You must be the lumberjack I keep hearing the ladies talk about."

The two shook hands, but I could tell Boston was embarrassed. "I don't know about all that, but I'm Boston Mooney. Keva's brother."

"It's good to have you, Boston. We're always looking for good men in Blueball." Diego pointed at him. "I'm thinking a ribeye, the biggest we got, and a baked potato. Can't forget the side of broccoli though. You're mature enough to know that a big man like you still needs his veggies. Am I right?"

Boston grinned, dipping his head in agreement. "Exactly right. Except I always let the lady order first."

Diego smiled so wide I saw his back molars. "Oh, Audrey!

You got yourself a good one!" He cackled, heading behind the counter to take our order officially.

I went to pay, but Boston beat me to it. "And I always pay."

Diego looked like he had hearts in his eyes for my man. "I'm just going to put this out there. Don't freak out, please. But if ever there was a wedding, think of Grass for your caterers."

Heat hit my cheeks and I laughed, trying to diffuse the awkwardness. Boston and I had definitely not discussed anything like that. Way too soon. "Oh my gosh, Diego. Too soon. But thank you though."

We paid and moved to the dining area to claim a table. There was a private one in the corner that I was walking toward when I heard Muriel's voice behind me.

"Holy shit, that one looks like he could drink peanut butter. Let me at him!"

I spun around to find the owner of Gin/Tan/Laundry plastered against Boston's side, her red fingernails creeping up his arm. Boston had frozen, like maybe if he stood still long enough, she'd think he was dead and move on.

"Tell me, handsome. When you do push-ups, do you push the earth downward?"

"Uh..."

I plastered myself to Boston's other side. "Hey, Muriel. I see you've met Boston. Boston, this is Muriel."

"You smell like a campfire, which I can't say doesn't smell good, but I bet we need to wash those clothes. How about you come on by my laundromat and I'll treat you to some of my top-shelf gin while it's on the spin cycle."

I didn't really appreciate Muriel hitting on my man—fake or otherwise—when I was standing right there. Even if the pickup lines were the oddest ones I'd ever heard.

"Actually, this is Keva's brother," I began to explain, but Muriel cut me off, her face lit up like a Christmas tree.

"Oh! I heard about you coming to town. Are you single, sunshine?"

"Yes," Boston answered a millisecond before me.

"No."

Boston and I looked at each other, clearly not on the same page. Irritation won out over jealousy, even though I had no real right to be irritated. I turned my brightest smile on Muriel.

"He's just kidding."

Boston jolted, as if just now coming to life and realizing that if he would open his mouth and talk, he could get himself out of this situation. I knew the man hated to socialize, but Muriel wasn't going to go away without a very strong and clear no.

"We're dating," Boston blurted out. He pulled his arm away from my hands and wrapped it around my shoulders possessively. "Talking about getting engaged, in fact."

I blinked, trying to hold the smile on my face. My stomach decided to sink to the floor, along with all my hopes and dreams. I could have cried if we didn't have an audience. Here I was, in the arms of a man who I was having feelings for despite my best intentions, and he pulled out the engagement card? When this was all fake? When we were hiding from my best friend about it all? It just felt horribly wrong. All the guilt I'd pushed away in favor of a temporary physical relationship that blew my mind and that no one would even find out about, hit me full force.

I loved Boston.

And this was all fake.

Muriel let go of Boston like he'd suddenly burned her. "Sorry, Audrey. I had no idea. I just saw a man who looked like he could clap with one hand and went for it. Us single girls pushing forty don't have time to waste, you know?"

I could feel my cheek muscles failing me. "Yeah, I get it. It's all good, Muriel." It was so *not* good I could barely keep my knees from buckling.

"I got your dinner, guys," Diego's voice came from behind us. "But did I hear you talking about an engagement?"

The people at the table next to him gasped and suddenly every head in the place was swiveling our way. Diego practically threw our plates on the table in the corner and spun in a circle, hands outstretched.

"It's a celebration! To the happy couple!" He lifted his hands in the air and everyone shouted congratulations and cheers.

My nose went numb and all the blood in my body rushed to my head. This had all gone horribly wrong. What were the odds that the one time Boston conversed with a stranger, he'd cause this kind of a reaction?

His arm turned almost painful, holding me to his side. I looked up at him to see a stunned, frozen smile that probably matched mine. "Oh shit," he muttered, looking like a ventriloquist with how little his lips moved.

"Yeah," I answered weakly.

Then he shrugged and let go of my shoulders, spinning me into his chest. "When you can't beat 'em, you join 'em," he said right before tipping me over his arm and kissing the ever-loving hell out of me in front of what felt like the whole town.

The assembled patrons cheered even louder. A few whistles joined in and one particularly crabby old person hollered for us to get a room. It was perfection. The moment every girl dreams of.

Except it was all for show.

Not one bit of it was real.

The kiss spiraled on and I couldn't help but melt into it. When he finally let me up for air and escorted me to our table, I wasn't sure if I could hold back the tears. Eventually, everyone went back to eating their dinners and stopped staring at us. Boston inhaled his dinner while I could barely get a bite down.

"You okay?" he asked quietly, using a napkin to wipe his mouth.

I put down my fork. I didn't want to have this conversation here and I certainly didn't want to have it now, but there was no stopping the words from gushing forth. The dam that I'd built to filter out these kinds of demands was washed away by the kind of hope and yearning and pain that comes from seeing your dreams within grasp but just barely missing them.

"I don't want COTFRWB."

Boston blinked. "I know. That's why we have CPHTFRWB."

I was already shaking my head. He didn't get it. "No. I want EFRRWAB."

Boston screwed his face up. "You lost me."

"Everywhere forever real relationship with all benefits." I straightened my spine. "That's what I want."

CHAPTER TWENTY-THREE

$\mathcal{B}$oston

I HEARD the same line so many times I'd started to roll my eyes at it. Getting out of the military and adjusting to civilian life was hard. I'd always thought that meant PTSD-type situations, which were a real and terrible thing, but it also just meant being bombarded with family and friends, people you'd been able to keep a distance from because you were physically stationed elsewhere for years at a time. But just a few weeks under my belt of civilian life and I was hip deep, slogging through emotions that I wasn't terribly good at in the first place and now even worse at from lack of use. First my sister. Now Audrey.

The car ride home from Grass was quiet. Probably because I'd mumbled something and then scraped my chair back, leaving the restaurant and barely remembering to wait for Audrey. She'd just poured her heart out and part of me wanted to pull her into my arms and give her everything she wanted. The other, bigger, part of me was already running in the opposite direction, wondering how normal people were able to articulate their feelings like that without somehow dying right there on the spot.

Audrey didn't wait for me to open her door when we got back to her place, she just slipped right out of the truck and hustled to the front door of her house. With every step away from me I could literally feel her slipping through my fingers. I'd patched things up with Annabel just to fuck them up with Audrey.

I slammed my truck door shut and ran after her, telling myself that I was made of sterner stuff than this. I'd literally faced death over and over again in the military, yet I couldn't face a heartfelt conversation? Bullshit.

"Audrey! Wait!" I caught up to her in the living room, snagging her arm and spinning her toward me. "Can we talk?"

Her expressive eyes looked shiny in the moonlight and I knew I'd been the one to put the doubt and fear there. I'd heard all about her asshole father, wondering how he could walk away from someone wonderful like her and here I was potentially doing the same damn thing.

My heart grew three sizes just watching the way she lifted her nose, straightened her spine, and met my gaze as she let me have it. "I *was* talking, Boston. Kind of hard to have a conversation though when the other party doesn't speak."

I dropped her arm—hell, I wasn't worthy of even touching her—and looked down at my boots, wondering how in the world I found myself with a woman like Audrey, professing to want to date me. Forever. "I know. And I'm sorry. I'm not good at this."

"Bullshit," Audrey snapped.

I lifted my head to see her practically snapping embers out of her ears in the dark living room.

"You shared lots of personal things with me up in that cabin. I just saw you put your heart on the line for Keva. You can do it, Boston. You just don't want to. With me."

Her voice wobbled, and if I could have done a good job at it,

I'd have punched myself in the face for making her doubt her worth.

"It's absolutely not you. I just always thought I'd be like Pete, alone somewhere in the forest, living out my days a hermit."

"Why?"

I sighed, wishing I could explain it. "I'm emotionally damaged goods, Audrey. My parents died the same day. Just poof. Gone. My whole support system vaporized. I couldn't fathom that level of pain, and when it hit me, I just shut down. I left. I spent years avoiding anything that even had a whiff of emotion attached to it. I did it once, I'll probably do it again. You deserve someone who can handle normal emotions without abandoning you."

Audrey's hand came up to my arm, her fingers freezing cold as they touched my overheated skin. "Those weren't normal emotions. Those were big, overwhelming emotions that anyone would have had a hard time with. You needed therapy. Guidance. Someone who understood what you were going through and could help. You can't blame yourself for your reaction and then think you're somehow damaged."

And that was Audrey in a nutshell. I'd hurt her and here she was defending me. I would give anything to have her keep touching me, but I couldn't let her think I was something I wasn't. "It's taken me twelve years to make things right with my sister. I've never even dated anyone longer than a weekend. That pretty much tells me I suck at relationships."

Audrey sniffled, but then her face cleared. "Okay, listen. I think I came on a bit strong. Take the word forever off the table completely. How about we just talk about dating for real? Do you want to date me, Boston?"

With every fiber of my being. I kept a tight rein on my voice, not ready to let myself hope for too much. "I'd like to try, but not if I'm going to hurt you in the process."

Audrey nodded, sliding her hand down to lace our fingers together. "It's my responsibility to protect myself. And I think we should start with that. We'll just give dating a try and see how it goes. But I'd like to be honest with Keva. No more hiding."

I nodded. "Agreed. I don't want to endanger my newly formed relationship with her, but I agree that we shouldn't lie."

Audrey smiled and the ten-ton rock on my shoulder lifted. "See? Look at that. You're already really good at relationships."

God, she was cute when she was persistent. Which was why she'd be a fabulous real estate agent. She was small but ferocious when she wanted something.

"Know what else I'm good at?" I gave her fingers a squeeze. "Cuddling."

Audrey's eyes lit up. "You are very good at cuddling. I think it's your size. You can wrap your whole body around me, and I'm in this safe cocoon."

I tugged her toward her bedroom. "Come be my butterfly."

She snorted at my cheesy line, but followed me down the hallway. We cuddled even after we both fell asleep. At some point in the night, I got my T-shirt off of her and slid inside her warmth, giving us both a slow, half-asleep orgasm that dragged us back to sleep all tangled together. I wasn't good with words, but I knew her body better than my own. Maybe, just maybe, it would be enough to keep her.

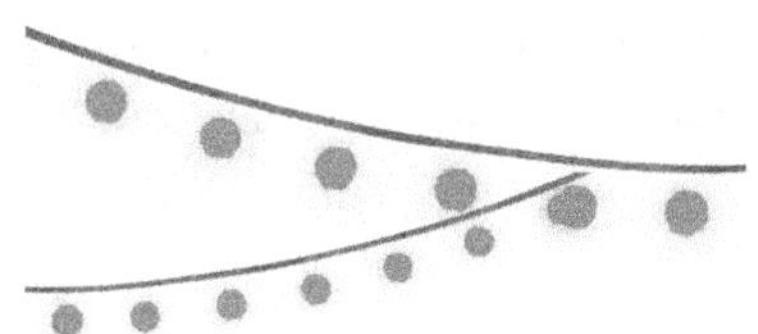

"Wake up, Aud! We're going furniture shopping for Boston!"

Annabel's voice seemed to come from my dream. It wasn't until Audrey's elbow jabbed itself into my gut as she tried to scramble away that I realized it wasn't a dream.

"Shit," Audrey whispered, flailing comically until she managed to get out of bed. Stark naked. She grabbed the first thing she saw and pulled it over her head, running out of the bedroom like her feet were on fire.

I blinked, trying to clear the dream and figure out what was going on. Once my brain realized my sister was here, in Audrey's house, and Audrey had just run out of here naked except for my Army shirt, I groaned and let my head flop back to the pillow.

"What the fuck?" Annabel's voice cut through my morning like a knife.

Yep. My sister was smart. She put two and two together and came up with betrayal. I rolled out of bed and grabbed a pair of jeans off the floor, tugging them on and tucking myself into them before coming out of the bedroom.

Annabel had her hands on her hips, glaring at Audrey. Audrey had her hands in her hair, looking adorably mussed but stressed.

"Look. We literally just said last night that we planned to tell you."

"Planned to tell me? How long has this been going on?" Annabel gasped. "Wait! Has this whole fake thing been real the whole time?"

"Since the cabin," I said, pulling Annabel's gaze from Audrey.

She tilted her head to the side, studying me before rolling her eyes and turning back to Audrey. "Jeez, put a shirt on, would you?" She pointed a finger at Audrey. "Best friends don't do that."

"I know, and I'm sorry. I didn't plan—"

"Hey." I cut Audrey off and got between the girls. "It's my fault. Don't blame her."

Annabel narrowed her eyes. "Did you force her into sleeping with you?"

Audrey huffed behind me. "No! Of course not."

Annabel lifted her eyebrows. "Then it *is* her fault."

I growled out my frustration, grabbed Annabel's arm, and hustled her to the front door. "Let's get out of here and talk this through."

"But you don't have a shirt."

"Just the way I like it," I mumbled back, not concerned about my lack of clothing in the slightest.

"Wait! I'll come with you. Just give me a second." Audrey raced around the house, looking for shorts in the kitchen. She was clearly frazzled.

"No," I called over my shoulder. "Let me talk to my sister. Alone." Audrey was always trying to make things right for everyone else. It was time she didn't have to do that.

The door slammed shut behind me. The cool air felt amazing. What was not amazing was the look Annabel was giving me. A mixture of anger, disgust, and humor. It was the humor that pissed me off, but confirmed what I'd been feeling last night. It was quite humorous to think that I'd be good enough for Audrey.

"I know what you're thinking," I said, steering her toward my truck.

She dug her heels in. "I highly doubt that, big bro. Let's take my car. Wait. Where are we going?"

I shrugged. I didn't care. I just needed to talk to my sister and make sure I hadn't damaged our relationship or her friendship with Audrey. "Coffee?"

Annabel sputtered out a laugh, spinning her keys around her finger. "Not a chance, hotshot. You need a shirt and shoes for that. Audrey might find all this nakedness cute, but I don't. Let's go to my place. Linc should be back after dropping Lucas off at school."

Dutifully, I got in her car, banging my knees on her dash. Annabel just cocked her head back and laughed. "You should see your face. You look like you woke up on the wrong side of bed."

I grunted, going for the handle above the window when she

peeled out of Audrey's driveway. "The bed wakes up on the wrong side of Boston."

Annabel almost had to pull the fucking car over she was laughing so hard. "Goddamn, I've missed you."

She had a smile on her face the whole time we drove to her house, which surprised me. I expected anger. Some snappy comments. Maybe even a rescinding of our newfound peace treaty. Perhaps she intended to direct all her anger at Audrey, a notion I'd have to squash real quick.

Linc came out the front door when we pulled up their drive-way. I hadn't seen their new place in the light of day. It was cute. Homey. Plants in bright containers on the porch. A welcome sign on the door that looked like some shit you'd find on Pinterest. I'd left my sister when she was a kid, but she was a full-grown adult now.

"Did you pick up a stray?" Linc called out, sipping his coffee and hiding his grin.

"Fuck off," I muttered, getting out of the car and approaching the house.

"Did your clothes fall off?" Linc drawled.

Annabel sputtered. "Audrey's clothes fell off too. Found these two shacked up and naked. I might need to bleach my eyeballs, babe."

Linc put his arm around my sister. Watching the two of them together was both odd and the best thing I'd ever seen. I liked that my sister had a partner, someone who'd never leave her side. I was such a dumbass for ever trying to keep them apart. Another example of how I was bad at relationships.

"Listen, Annabel. I didn't intend to start anything with Audrey. You have to know that. But I like her. A lot."

"Just come inside, Boston."

I stood my ground. "No. Not if you're just going to take it out on Audrey. She did nothing wrong. She's been wanting me to tell you the whole time, but we couldn't. Not when we were at the cabin, at least. And then I didn't know she wanted more from me until last night."

"More? As in what? Moving in?" Linc asked.

The idea of moving in together didn't repulse me like I thought it would. I'd always craved being alone. Living in close quarters in the military had always made my skin crawl. I needed my alone time, but suddenly being with Audrey sounded like the very thing I'd been missing my whole life.

I lifted my arms and let them drop to my sides. "I don't know, man. I just know I want more too. Whatever that looks like."

"Do you love her?" Annabel asked, staring me down so hard it felt like an interrogation.

"I—" I stopped, my throat closing on the words I thought I could say. I didn't love her, did I? Love was for other people. People who hadn't been hurt and closed themselves off for over a decade. Right?

"I don't know that I can give her what she needs. What she should most definitely have," I finally said. Love wasn't even at the heart of the matter here. It was irrelevant. If I couldn't give her that happy family life, then what was the point of confessing feelings?

"What does she want?" Linc asked.

Annabel answered for me. "A husband. A happy, conflict-free marriage. Two to three kids. The dream."

I lifted my hand. "See? I'm not made for that stuff."

Annabel grimaced. "Did you get shot in the balls or something? I mean, I would think you'd tell me if you sustained an injury like that, but maybe not."

I screwed up my face while Linc laughed. The fucker. "No, I didn't get shot in the balls."

"Then what the hell is the problem? If you love her, marry her and give her babies. It's not that hard."

It was hard. It was the most daunting thing I'd ever been asked to do. It went against everything I had planned for my life.

The fact that my own sister couldn't understand that was starting to piss me off. "Keva."

"Don't Keva me now, bossy Boston! I'm calling you on your bullshit whether you like it or not." She pulled away from Linc and spun toward the house. "Now get your ass inside or I'm going to be pissed at you for real."

She stepped inside the house, slamming the door behind her. Linc and I stared at each other as the wind whistled through the pine trees. He lifted his eyebrows like there wasn't really an option.

"You heard the woman."

CHAPTER TWENTY-FOUR

udrey

Me: I'm so stupid.

Paisley: Hey! Don't talk about my bestie like that.

Me: Keva barged into my house just a few minutes ago and basically walked in on Boston and me.

Marlo: No fair! Please tell me that man was naked. I think I need to do more barging in on people…

Paisley: I'm sure she'll understand. Did she seem mad?

Me: Keva? Mad? No, of course not. *eye-roll emoji*

Marlo: Don't freak out. It could be worse.

Me: I was naked except for Boston's Army T-shirt. How could it be worse?

Marlo: Sounds exactly how Boston found out about Keva and Linc. Except Linc knocked her up. You aren't pregnant, are you?

Me: Thankfully no.

Paisley: Why don't you come by my place this afternoon. Hopefully Aster will be down for her nap and we can strategize.

Marlo: Do I even need to say it at this point? I'll bring the brownies...

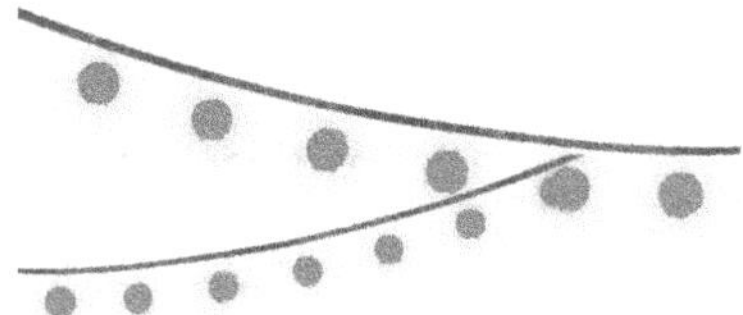

BEFORE I COULD EVEN CONFIRM the get together with my girls, my phone vibrated with an incoming call. Mom's name filled the screen and dread followed quickly. I should have anticipated this. Small-town gossips would have gotten hold of that juicy information at Grass last night and spread it far and wide by breakfast time. I was too wrapped up in Boston—literally—to think straight.

"Hey, Mom."

"Audrey? What's this I hear about you getting married?" Her usual demure voice sounded positively shrill this morning.

I squeezed my eyes shut and flopped back on my bed. The sheets had Boston's pine and earth smell. I just wanted to wrap myself in them and keep out the real world.

"I'm not getting married, Mom. I am dating someone though." At least I thought I was. If Keva put up enough of a stink about us together, would Boston change his mind? The thought made me feel nauseous.

"Oh, well, that sounds better than engaged. Is he a good man? You know I honestly think you should do a background check before you continue to date him."

I sat up, scooting so my back was against my headboard. "Mom, I know Dad was an asshole, but I don't think all men are like him."

Mom sniffed. "I'm not so sure about that. That's exactly what I used to think too. Then your father lied to me for years and took off when his lies were outed publicly. Wouldn't hurt to be overly cautious up front."

My phone vibrated again and I pulled it from my ear to check the caller. "Hey, Mom, I have to go. My boss is calling me and I need to go to work. Talk later?"

"Okay, I'll let you go, but I'll look into doing that background check."

I dropped my head back and cracked my skull on the wall. I had enough doubts in my head about Boston and me as it was. I didn't need her adding to them. "Bye, Mom."

Jason Hellman's call had gone to voicemail, which was just as well. I wasn't sure I could put on a chipper, professional voice right now. Instead, I got dressed and forced myself to eat a piece of toast before heading into town. I needed to stop by the office and then head over to Paisley's. But first...caffeine.

The line for coffee at Crazy Beans wasn't long, probably because I was later than the normal morning rush. I kept my head down like I was reading something extremely important on my phone. If anyone came up to me with congratulations on my supposed engagement, I might burst into tears and horrify them.

"Look what the cat dragged in."

The low voice behind me cut through my mental fog, sending a shiver of revulsion up my spine. I twirled around to see my father standing in line right behind me, his dark hair perfectly styled and his mouth set in the sneer he wore almost every day growing up. Nothing and no one had been good enough for him. Where my little sister, Zoey, bent over backward to get his approval, I went the other way. I wanted nothing to do with him now that I was an adult and especially because he and my mother were no longer together.

"I could say the same thing about you," I drawled. "I didn't know they let you back in Blueball."

His brown eyes, so similar to mine, took in my dress. His look said he wasn't impressed. Sadly, there was still a part of me that wished he'd caught me on a better day. A day when I'd actually taken the time to do my hair and put on makeup. So maybe I was still a bit like my sister after all. I'd have to work on that.

"Your mother called."

"Oh?" I pretended not to care, but inside I was a wreck thinking maybe Mom had changed her mind somehow and was willing to take him back.

"Gotta clear my things out of the storage unit."

I nodded, moving forward in line. "Well, you enjoy that." I spun around, wanting this conversation over. I'd said everything I needed to say to him over two years ago. The lady in front of me shifted away from the register and it was my turn. I only got one step away before my father's hand pulled me back, his fingers biting into my arm.

"I'm not done talking to you," he growled. "When are you going to get over your little hissy fit? Your sister didn't turn her back on her own father. Just you. Do you even know what it means to be loyal to your family?"

I gasped, at his words and his rough handling. For as terrible of a father as he'd been, he'd never laid his hands on my sister and me. "Family doesn't lie to each other for years on end. I think *you're* the one who doesn't understand how families operate."

His hand only gripped me tighter, the sneer now laced with unabashed hatred. "When you have a spouse and a family depending on you, then you can lecture me on what a family is. Until then, believe me when I say you'll never do better than I did. You're cut from the same cloth."

"Excuse me." Lawson, the owner of Crazy Beans, put his hand on my father's forearm, squeezing tight. You didn't mess with Lawson. He was a bodybuilder with tattoos that made me wonder if he got into lifting weights because of a prison sentence. "Let go of her now and get the fuck out of my shop, Hellman."

My father let go of my arm, but his eyes glittered dangerously as he sized up Lawson. Why was it that fools never knew when to back down? My father was double Lawson's age and at least thirty pounds lighter, and he was still looking up at him like he might throw the first punch. The whole shop had grown quiet. I wouldn't be surprised if this little altercation got around town before I got my much-needed coffee.

"I could sue you," my father said quietly.

Lawson grinned and I got goose bumps. "Private business. I don't have to serve anyone I don't want to. And I bet at least five people will testify that you put your hands on a woman first. Go ahead and sue. Let's see who wins."

My father tossed me one last disgusted look around Lawson's shoulder and then he walked out of the coffee shop. Everyone watched him go. And then I felt the stares. The same stares I'd gotten two years ago when the shit hit the fan with my family. Pity. Judgement. I fucking hated the weighty looks.

"How about a large mocha with all the whipped cream I can cram on there?" Lawson asked, shooting me a friendly wink.

"Sounds like exactly what I need." I reached for my wallet, but he put his hand up.

"On the house for me not seeing what was going on right away."

"You don't—"

Lawson lifted his head and speared me with his disturbing light blue gaze. He looked like he could rip a grown man apart with one hand tied behind his back. "Yes, I do. No man touches a woman on my watch. Ever."

I nodded my thanks and backed away to wait for my drink. I didn't know what had happened to Lawson before he moved to Blueball, but I got the sense that he was a good man behind all that intensity. Maybe I should see if I could hook him up with Marlo.

I had more time than I wanted to run through each line of that conversation until it gave me a headache. Lawson slid my drink across the countertop and I took it gratefully, slurping down as much as I could in one gulp. Ignoring the heads that turned my direction again as I walked out, I hustled to my car, looking over my shoulder to make sure my father wasn't out here on the curb waiting to accost me again. Would have been nice if Mom had given me a heads-up this morning when she called instead of just spreading doom and gloom about my current relationship. Then again, she'd always been a little out of touch. As long as my father came home occasionally and the bank account had money in it, she figured he was doing his job as a husband.

I hit the door locks and let my eyes slide shut. The caffeine was finally hitting but all it was doing was making me anxious. Anxious about running into my father again, about how things had been left between Boston and me, and even a little niggle of worry about the level of truth behind my father's words this morning.

Was I a hopeless dreamer wanting a happy marriage and two point five kids? Instead of examining that too closely, I drove to Paisley's house and shoved brownies in my face until my stomach hurt. Every time I texted Boston and he didn't respond, I ate another one. At this rate I'd have diabetes waiting on that man to put me out of my misery.

Paisley gently shoved away the almost empty pan of brownies and put her arm around me. She smelled like baby lotion and it almost made me cry. "I think you just came on a little strong. Which I admire the hell out of, mind you, but it might have been too much for Boston."

"You know, for how big he is, he sure is skittish," Marlo piped up from the floor where she was staring up at the ceiling fan.

"Only with emotional things." I was quick to defend him. After all, he'd taken charge up at the cabin, doing all the manual labor to get us out. "He just shut down when I pressed him on an actual relationship."

Paisley squeezed me. "I think it was the forever comment. You went from a fake relationship to talking about forever in the same breath. I mean, you've only known each other a few weeks."

I let my head fall on Paisley's shoulder. Time didn't seem to matter where my heart was concerned. "I think I love him though."

Marlo snorted. "And he probably loves you based on how intensely he looked at you the whole time we hiked our asses off that mountain. I kept looking at you to make sure your clothes weren't catching fire. But he's not ready to admit it. Gotta give him time."

Boston had made it clear he didn't think he could fit in the role of husband and father like I wanted. Was I being an idiot to ignore his warning? Could I compromise my dreams for him? Would just dating forever be enough for me?

"But what if he never comes around?" I asked, fearing that outcome more than anything.

"Then we dig a really big ditch. Little bitches get ditches." Marlo sat up, her eyes fierce and her jet-black hair a tangled mess. "I keep telling you guys I have a backhoe and the land to do it. Just say the word."

Paisley leaned her head on mine, whispering, "Marlo's kind of scary."

I nodded, both of our heads jostling.

But she was also kind of wonderful.

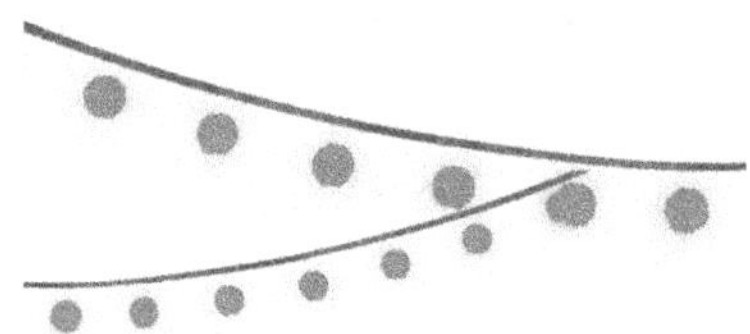

Later that night when Boston still hadn't made an appearance and I had chewed off all my fingernails, I reached out to Keva.

Me: I know you're mad at me, but I'm worried about Boston. He's not here and he's not answering his phone.

Keva: He's here.

Me: Thank God. Can you and I talk tomorrow?

Keva: Sure, but I'm not mad, babe. Boston explained how it all went down, and once I got over the feeling of being the last one to know about my own best friend and brother, I actually think you two together is pretty cute.

Me: That's a relief! I didn't intend to fall for him.
In fact he pissed me off at first. But why is he
not answering my texts and calls?

Keva: Well…we are related, after all. We
Mooneys can be a bit stubborn.

I was about to break out my harmonica just to soothe myself. Normally teasing Boston would soothe me, but he was currently scared of me.

Me: If you're fine with us dating…what the hell
is he being stubborn about??

Keva: When Linc came back to town and
wanted back in our lives, what was I most
scared of?

I thought back to that time, not exactly pleased Keva was giving me riddles in my emotional time of need. God, Keva had been so damn stubborn. She'd nearly walked away from the best thing in her life, just to keep herself safe in her little bubble.

Me: Trusting him again?

Keva: Right. Because trusting means opening
up emotionally. And that's another thing about
Mooneys. We're not so good at sharing our
hearts. I'm working on him, babe. Give him
time.

Me: Tell him I don't care about the other stuff. I
just want my cocoon back.

Keva: I don't know what that means.

Me: Want me to explain?

Keva: NO. I'm not sure what brain bleach
would do to the baby…

Me: lol I love you

Keva: I love you too. And so does my brother.
He just can't say it yet.

CHAPTER TWENTY-FIVE

oston

LINC AND ANNABEL gave me their guest room for the week. I felt bad sleeping there the first night. Like my skin was crawling with guilt for not going back to talk to Audrey. Then the next day I'd received word I'd been accepted as the renter for the cabin and Annabel kept me busy running from store to store finding all the little items I'd need for living on my own. Each night the itch got worse and with it came a weight on my chest that got heavier and heavier. By the following weekend, I wasn't sure I could even suck in a full breath.

And yet I still didn't contact Audrey.

"If that's your happy face, I'd hate to see your sad face," Annabel drawled, coming up to me while I was putting away a set of new glasses in the kitchen cupboards.

Today was move-in day and Linc, Annabel, and Lucas had helped me bring everything in and get it set up. Linc was currently cursing over assembling an Ikea dresser in my bedroom. Lucas would fall into a fit of laughter every time Linc dropped the f-bomb and Annabel hissed at him to watch his mouth. Their family antics would have made me happy, except for the fact that I wanted all of that for myself.

Audrey, and everything she had to offer, had been the only thing I'd been able to think of this last week. Every lonely hour had given me time to envision a new future and none of that could be possible until I got my life together. I couldn't keep crashing at other people's houses. I had to get a job. I had to have something other than dickish commands and survival skills to offer Audrey.

Eventually, they all left and I sat in my brand-new chair, watching the fire dance in the dirty fireplace. I had four walls and a roof that provided more amenities than my tent. Things with my sister were better than they'd ever been. Gannon and I were supposed to talk tomorrow about hammering out details of me coming to work for him. For a hermit with low needs like me, this was practically fucking paradise.

And I hated it.

Pete didn't know it, but right after Gannon and I chatted tomorrow, I was going over to check on the old man. I'd been seeing him every other day or so, feeling like I owed him that for giving me a chance. He didn't know me at all and yet he'd helped me in all aspects of my life.

So had Audrey.

I just didn't know what to do about that yet.

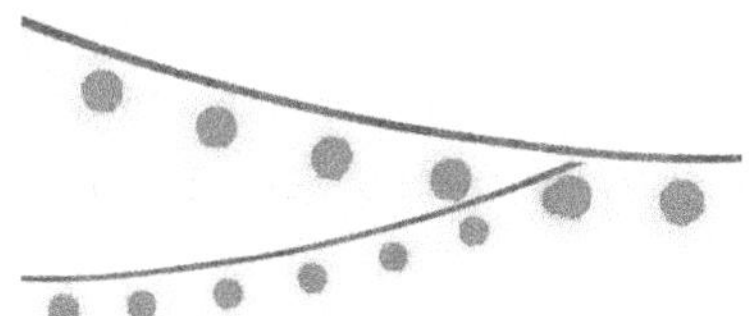

"This whiskey set me back a paycheck or two, so you better drink it sparingly." I handed the fancy whiskey bottle to Pete before joining him in the rocking chairs on his front porch.

He let out an excited yip as he eyed the bottle in his weathered hands. Then he ripped the packaging off the top, wrenched open the bottle, and took the kind of lengthy swig that couldn't possibly be healthy before lunchtime.

"Hey! I said sparingly," I groused, reaching over like I was going to grab it from his hands.

He twisted, hugging the bottle to his chest. "It's mine now. I do what I want with it."

I rolled my eyes and got my chair rocking. "Heard you signed the deal yesterday." Gannon had kept me informed. Audrey would have too. If we were still speaking. Her texts and voicemails had trailed off over the week. Not that I blamed her. Kind of hard to talk to someone who wouldn't communicate back.

"Sure did. Saw the clause you added in there." Pete gave me side eye.

I didn't want his thanks. I was just making sure we did right by him. "Wasn't me."

Pete snorted and then spit. I grimaced. It was like viewing myself in forty years if I kept up my hermit ways. "Bullshit."

"Fine. It was me, but it was only fair. The land means something to you and I wanted to make sure that even if you sold it off to Glamper's Paradise, you'd still have some rights."

I'd made sure that Pete would always have priority to rent any of the cabins that Gannon built on the new acreage. Gannon also couldn't build any structure within fifty yards of Pete's remaining land. That way Pete would always have the privacy he craved. In return, Pete promised to give Glamper's first right of refusal for any other tracts of land he put up for sale in the future.

Pete wouldn't look at me. He clutched the bottle of whiskey tighter, his gnarled hands twisting it around and around. "Well, I appreciate it."

We sat there and rocked until the awkwardness passed and our minds had wandered off to other topics. That was the best thing about Pete: he understood that talking about things out loud and with actual words wasn't always necessary. Sometimes a head nod and grunt were all you needed.

Pete finally put the bottle down on the wood planks by our feet and twisted my direction. His faded eyes seemed to dance. "Now tell me all about Audrey. You two look like you go together. Like tuna salad and fruit punch."

I shook my head, entirely grossed out. I could eat some pretty weird food when camping out in the wilderness, but that got my stomach twisting.

"Pickles and peanut butter?"

I groaned.

"Ketchup and mashed potatoes?"

"That one might actually work." I sat forward. "I mean, you put ketchup on french fries, right?" I could also admit, I was trying to distract him from his original question.

"Quit dancing around and tell me you've bought a ring already," Pete barked.

I sat back on a sigh, figuring the truth was my best course of action. "Nah. I actually haven't talked to her in a week."

Pete stood up so fast his chair creaked more than his joints.

Then he was walking away from me, slamming his front door closed. My mouth dropped open. Well, shit. I guess I pissed him off. I looked out at the pine trees and wondered if I should just go home. Pete clearly didn't look like he wanted to talk to me any longer.

I'd just stood up and fetched my keys out of my front pocket when the door opened again and Pete stood there with his legs braced apart, a shotgun in his hands. Aimed at me.

My hands flew in the air automatically. I felt like I was having a déjà vu moment. This was the exact scenario the day I'd met Pete. "Put the shotgun down, Pete."

"No!" He advanced onto the porch and I backed down the stairs. "Not until you get your head out of your ass and make things right with Audrey!"

"I understand you're upset, but there's no need to pull a gun on me. Let's just put that down and talk like two adults." Maybe that whiskey he'd guzzled was stronger than I thought.

Pete glared at me in silence, his face screwed up into a thousand wrinkles. And to think I'd put in a special clause in the contract to protect him. With escape in mind, I was thinking I could back all the way up to my truck if I just kept him calm long enough.

All of a sudden, Pete let the gun clatter to the floor. I ducked left, in case it fired on impact, but thankfully it just lay there at his feet.

"It's not even loaded, hotshot," Pete growled, sounding a lot like me when I was irritated. "Wasn't loaded the day I met you either, but it sure does get people's attention."

I stood up straight, letting my hands drop back down to my sides. "You pull your shotgun on a lot of people?"

Pete batted his hand through the air. "Only jackasses who let the best thing that's ever come into their lives slip right through their fingers."

I took a hesitant step forward. "So, only me, then?"

"You guessed it." Pete put his hands on his bony hips, losing the glare the more seconds that passed. He looked downright sad, which hurt me more than that shotgun he'd waved around. "Why, Boston? Why would you mess things up with Audrey?"

Nope. Not sad. Disappointed in me. Which was the fucking worst.

"I needed some time, Pete. I had to figure out my feelings."

Pete studied me. "Do you even know what those are?"

"Yes, I know what they are," I answered, exasperated. "Audrey wants forever. A husband. A litter of kids. I didn't know if I could give that to her because that was never my plan for my life. So yeah, I took the time to think it through."

"And?"

I lifted my hands and then let them drop. "And...I figured out I love her."

"And?" Pete growled. Like he was frustrated with my methodical speed.

"And since I didn't die in the Army like I figured I would, I want what my sister has. I want a family of my own."

Pete tilted his head to the porch with the beginnings of a smile. "Get your ass up here then and let's figure this out."

I came up the stairs, still eyeing that shotgun. Knowing Pete, it could very well be loaded despite what he'd said. "What's to figure out? I already decided what I want and it matches with Audrey's plans."

Pete sank into his rocking chair and the disgust was back. "Jesus. Kids these days are so damn stupid."

"Excuse me?" I had half a mind to pick up that shotgun and return the favor.

"She pours her heart out to you and you just ghosted her for a week? What makes you think she won't kick you right in the nuts the first time you try to tell her you finally have all your precious emotions figured out?"

I opened my mouth to defend myself, but realized with sudden horror that he was probably correct. Audrey wasn't the type of girl who would let a man yank on her emotions and then come crawling back to her without paying a steep price. For all she knew, I'd ditched her permanently without even a goodbye.

"Oh shit. I'm such a jackass."

Pete laughed, showing off the gap in his back molars. "That's what I've been trying to tell you!"

I smacked his shoulder. Gently. Mostly.

"Quit laughing and help me figure out how to show her how I feel!"

Pete's laugh turned into a glare once again. "You don't just show her, jackass. You gotta say the *words*."

The wind left my sails and I sank into the rocking chair next to him. "I'm not good with words."

Pete held up the whiskey bottle. "You better get real good with 'em real fast."

I spent the rest of the afternoon sipping whiskey with Pete and practicing what I'd say and how I'd say it. Pete even role-played the part of Audrey. He was surprisingly good at sounding like her when he used his falsetto voice. When I'd sobered up enough to drive and I felt like I had an excellent grovel plan in place, I went home to my cabin and pulled out my phone. I read through the string of messages from Audrey, each one getting shorter and more curt as the week rolled on.

I winced. Pete was right. She was going to be pissed.

Me: Hey, lusty, I'm sorry I've been silent. I've been thinking a lot about what you said and what you want. Can we meet in person to chat?

I waited another hour, staring at my phone. Finally, the little bubble appeared, showing me she was reading my message and hopefully writing me back. Then the bubble disappeared and I waited another hour. When it was clear she had no intention of texting me back, I went to bed, running over every detail of my plan while I stared at the ceiling.

This absolutely had to work.

I didn't want to be a hermit in this cabin pulling a shotgun on innocent people and drinking whiskey until I forgot about how lonely I was.

udrey

"WOMEN *all across the nation are going crazy over the news that Henry Cavill will be starring in the latest romantic comedy written by a romance author made famous last year by TikTok. More details at ten tonight.*"

The news reporter was giving me a headache with her chipper little voice and her stupidly beautiful blonde hair. I threw my popcorn at the screen.

"Shut it, woman. Don't you know men suck?" I shoved an entire handful of buttery popcorn in my mouth and glared at the screen while I munched. A girl couldn't even watch a horror flick without being bombarded with handsome men and the women losing their ever-loving minds over them.

"Whoa. I draw the line at throwing popcorn all over the house. When we eventually move out, I want to be able to get my deposit back."

My head swiveled to see Madi with another cute outfit and

dangling feather earrings that wouldn't have worked on someone my height. I'd look like the actual owl they were plucked from.

I rolled my eyes and turned back to the television that had thankfully gone back to a particularly gruesome scene that fed my dark mood. I grinned at the blood spatter and Madi sighed, plopping down next to me on the couch and trying to steal my blanket. I was not in the mood to share. She'd have to wrench this thing out of my cold, dead hands that matched my cold, dead heart.

"Goodness. You are in quite the mood, aren't you? I take it he still hasn't contacted you?"

Two nights ago, I'd taken my misery into the kitchen and blended up a whole bar's worth of margaritas. Madi had been all too happy to join me. I was two drinks in when everything came spilling out of my mouth. Let's face it, I couldn't keep a secret to save my life. Normally, Madi was on my shit list, but this week, I'd literally cried on her shoulder and used her sleeve to wipe the snot. To her credit, she'd been there for me.

"Nope." I let the "p" pop with some extra oomph. I watched the horror flick unfold, not wanting to talk about the man whose name I would not say. "Ooh, maybe I should get some bale hooks."

Madi flinched next to me. "What the hell for?"

My phone, lying on the coffee table in front of us, pinged. We both looked down to see Boston's name appear. I gasped and grabbed for the phone. Madi looked over my shoulder like the nosy bitch she was.

Boston: Hey, lusty, I'm sorry I've been silent. I've been thinking a lot about what you said and what you want. Can we meet in person to chat?

Equal parts dread and hope filled my chest. My thumbs immediately flew over the screen. I yelped when my phone was snatched out of my hands. Madi jumped to her feet and held the phone high in the air.

"No! Absolutely not."

"Hey!" I threw off the blanket and tried to jump for the phone. Sadly, I only got up to her elbow. Damn these short genetics. "Give that back!"

Madi extended her supermodel-long arm and put her hand on my sternum, keeping me away from her. And my phone. "No. Listen to me for a second. I'm on your side, okay? That man took a full week to think things through before reaching out. Take five fucking minutes and breathe before you text him back. That's all I'm saying."

I folded my arms across my chest in a full-on pout, but I had to admit she had a point. Seven long days and nights I'd stared at my phone, willing it to ring. Each night I checked in with Keva to make sure he was okay. And still that man had given me the silent treatment. Didn't I deserve better? Wasn't I falling into the same shit my mom had fallen for with my father? She'd been a doormat for that man, something I promised myself I'd never be.

"You know what? You're damn right."

Madi smiled. "Of course I am. You'd be surprised what people tell me when they're on my table for a massage. If they'd listen to my advice, the divorce rate would plummet."

That was taking it a bit far. "You've never even been married, Madi," I answered dryly.

She shrugged. "Simply waiting for the right man. Which you should too. If Boston is the one, he'll still be the one tomorrow. Or whenever you choose to reply back."

I really hated when she was right. "Fine. Agreed. I'll wait until I've slept on it before contacting him." I sank back on the couch. "In fact, take my phone for the night, will you? I don't want to be tempted."

"You got it, kiddo." Madi slid my phone into the pocket of her dress. "I'm heading to bed. I'll leave your phone on the kitchen counter tomorrow morning before I leave for work."

I watched her walk to the hallway that led to the bedrooms. "Hey, Madi?"

She turned back. "Yeah?"

"Thank you."

She smiled. "I may not be the best roommate, but women have to stick together when it comes to men." With a wink, she was gone, just a cloud of her expensive perfume left in the room.

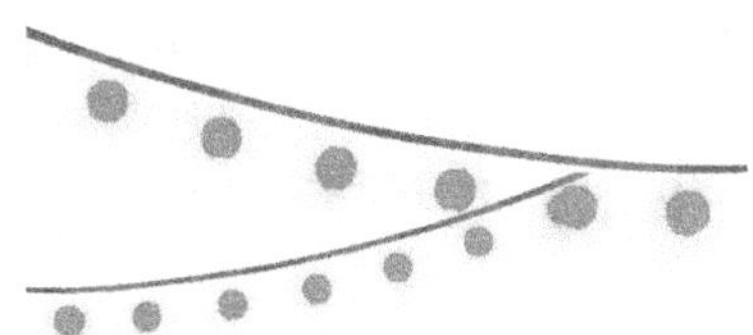

"Rise and shine, honey!"

I blinked my eyes open, disoriented. A whack on my ass had me waking up nice and angry. I sat up and pushed the hair out of my face to see Nikki Hellman sitting on the edge of my bed.

I really needed to stop giving people keys to my house.

"Nikki? What the..." I trailed off, my brain not yet online enough to string together a full sentence. I'd been dreaming about hacking my way through the forest with a chainsaw, chasing Boston down, while crying and telling myself not to hurt him. It was weird. It was confusing. And it was an accurate depiction of the state of my head this week.

Nikki looked like she'd already been up for awhile, her bob of hair perfectly coifed, light makeup on point, and her outfit looking like she was thinking about going back to the pageant world, just a few decades older now.

"Think of me as your fairy godmother."

"Isn't it a little early for sequins?" I grumbled, rubbing my eyes. And it was way too early to be dealing with Nikki Hellman when she had a stick up her ass about something.

"You're adorable when you're grumpy." Nikki's smile only intensified. "I can see why Boston adores you. Now get your ass up. We have work to do."

I was thoroughly confused. Last I talked to Jason, he said he didn't need me in the office until Monday. "Work to do?"

Nikki got off the side of my bed and waved her hands frantically in the air. "Yes! Work! Madi tells me you've been moping all week and that Boston has finally reached out."

I rolled my eyes, but tossed the covers back. "Madi's got a big mouth."

"Well, maybe you should have told me all this yourself. Blueball gossip takes a little longer than I like to reach Hell. I found out yesterday that you and Boston are engaged, much to my surprise. You didn't even tell me you were dating for real! Then Madi called, and I made sure I was over here at sunrise."

"Why?" I climbed out of bed and looked around for clean clothes. Someone, in her misery, had forgotten to do laundry this week.

Nikki grabbed my shoulders and got in my face, halting my search for clothing. My eyes went wide. Uh-oh. No one wanted to be Nikki's center of attention when she'd set her mind on making you her personal project. It was like standing on an island, facing down the eye of a hurricane hell-bent on destruction and mayhem.

"Why?" she snapped. "Because you were raised by the asshole named Richard, who has done a number on every single one of his kids' heads. And guess what else I finally heard through the grapevine?"

I opened my mouth to answer but apparently this question was rhetorical.

"You ran into Richard last weekend and also didn't bother to tell me that. Did you?"

I shook my head, almost afraid to answer now. This was a situation of damned if you do, damned if you don't.

Nikki squeezed my shoulders so tight, I wanted to ask who her trainer was. I was smart enough to keep my mouth shut, however. "We're going to breakfast and you're going to tell me every last detail about your relationship in your own words. And then I want to see where your head's at. And then we're going to unfuck everything Richard fucked up by coming back to town. Understood?"

The chaos didn't stop there. Somehow I found my hair brushed, clothes on my body, and shoes on my feet before I was able to utter a word. Nikki whisked me away from the house before I remembered to grab my phone. I figured we were going to a diner in Blueball or even Hell, but we ended up back at Nikki's place where Ace was manning the stove, bacon popping and giving off an aroma that made my stomach growl. His wife, Addy, was there with their two kids, buttering toast. Blaze was training a huge German shepherd not to lunge up onto the counter to snatch the bacon while his wife, Annie, poured juice. Daxon was being an asshole while his wife, Rita, poured pancake batter in the pan next to the bacon. Callan and Cricket were setting the table but came over to welcome me with hugs. I could hear all their kids playing in the back living room.

The chaos was a reminder of everything I wanted. I wanted the ring, the wedding, the kids. The love.

"Ethan and Andi are doing a live video on the back porch, but they should be done just in time to eat and not do any of the cooking," Daxon called from the kitchen.

"Kind of like you?" Nikki was quick to respond. Daxon shot his mama a wink, knowing he could get away with anything.

"Wow, the gang's all here, huh?" I felt a headache brewing.

I loved my brothers and their wives, I really did, but I just wasn't in the headspace to deal with a crowd. I'd already made up my mind to go see Boston and talk things through, whatever the end result would be. But I'd have steel lining my backbone.

Daxon came over, slinging his arm over my shoulder. "Listen, sis. Say the word and we'll go mess up that pretty boy's face."

As much as I wasn't pleased with Boston, I wasn't going to let my brothers interfere. Or put down the man I loved. "He's not a pretty boy, D. He's way bigger than you."

All the other brothers erupted into taunts and bickering back and forth about who was bigger and stronger. From experience, I knew this could go on until my hair turned gray. I put two fingers in my mouth and let out a shrill whistle. Blaze's dog immediately sat on his haunches and let out a whine that broke my heart. I shrugged off Daxon's arm to give the good boy some pats on the head.

"Seriously, Audrey. We don't let assholes mess with our little sister. I'll bring Ace and Blaze to help me."

"Language, Daxon," Nikki sighed.

I didn't think it wise to mention the multiple f-bombs she'd unleashed already this morning.

"He can't take three of us, can he?" Ace asked.

"Hey, why didn't you say you'd take me?" Callan looked hurt.

Blaze snickered. "You'd want to bandage his split lip and put ice on his boo-boos."

"It's my job to help people, but I can throw a punch when it's necessary." Callan wasn't backing down and now the boys were arguing about their fighting skills.

Now it was Nikki's turn to take back control. Her whistle was louder and longer than mine. "Have a seat, everyone, and shut your mouths. We're here to help Audrey, not coordinate a fight."

Daxon threw the kitchen towel down on the counter. "Well, shit. There went all the fun."

I managed to eat a decent breakfast, barely keeping the boys from getting in their trucks to track down Boston when I told them the whole story of falling in love with Boston Mooney. I didn't get any life-changing advice that would help me decide what to do or say when I saw Boston. But I did get a dose of love and family life that had me laser focused on what I wanted. Richard Hellman had fathered these boys too and they had amazing spouses and kids. No matter what that asshole said to me, I knew exactly what family meant. It was sitting around this table, willing to fight a giant of a man for treating me badly. It was the hugs and kisses and promises to have my back, day or night.

oston

I WAS ENTERING enemy territory and I knew it. Which was why I had my hands balled into fists and all of my five senses on hyper mode. There were half a dozen cars parked on the sidewalk, but Audrey's piece-of-shit sedan wasn't one of them. The property was pretty, the front yard filled with an expanse of green grass and a flower bed that looked like it yearned to be on the cover of a landscaping magazine. The porch wasn't much different except the flowers were in colorful pots. I knocked on the door and tried to fill my lungs with enough oxygen to speak.

The door whipped open and one of Audrey's half brothers stood there with a dog at his side. I couldn't remember which one he was, but the way he narrowed his eyes at me meant Audrey had filled him in on what was going on between us. Which meant this was probably a very bad idea.

The guy didn't even greet me, just twisted his head over his shoulder and hollered, "Who got dibs on the first punch?"

Before I could explain that punches wouldn't be necessary,

the doorway filled with four more brothers, each with a frown that spelled disaster for my face and vital organs. I put my hands up in peace. There was no way I could take on all five at once.

"I come in peace."

"Fuck that."

"You made our sister cry."

"Dude, you gotta tell me what protein powder you use."

They all spoke at once, but everyone's mouth snapped shut when a woman pushed her way out on the porch. She was the one I'd seen the first time I saw Audrey at The Tavern.

"Nikki?"

Her eyes gave me a once-over that had me certain I'd be found lacking, but her eventual smile was welcoming. I was both afraid of her and wanted her to give me a hug and pat my hair. It was a confusing reaction.

"You must be Boston. The man who's turned my girl's head." She held out her hand and I took it, expecting to give it a shake, but she pulled me into her before wrapping her arms around me. The five men behind her only frowned harder. I swallowed hard and pulled away from her hug far faster than I wanted. There would be no hair patting today.

"I'm actually here to talk to you about Audrey."

Nikki nodded at me to continue, but her sons had some opinions, based on their snorts and eye-rolls.

I shifted on my feet, wishing I could have spoken to Nikki alone. But I was desperate to make things right with Audrey and talking to them all at once was probably a good thing. So, I drummed up courage in the face of adversity and hoped I could find the necessary words.

"I love Audrey, ma'am. I didn't want to, thinking I couldn't offer her what she's always wanted. But it's come to my attention —thanks to a sister who isn't afraid to tell it like it is—that I do have a right to want something better for my future. And that something better is Audrey. If she'll have me."

Nikki beamed at me, reaching up to grab my forearm. "Why don't you come inside, honey, and we'll talk this out?"

"Oh come on, Mom. You don't believe him, do you?" one of the brothers whined.

"Yeah, we don't want to get blood on your indoor rugs."

The sea of testosterone parted and a woman came out, a baby on her hip. She gave the boys a sharp look that made them instantly shut up. "Oh, like none of you messed up and had to come crawling back with your tail between your legs?"

Nikki giggled and one brother opened his mouth, but shut it quickly when the woman swung her gaze to him. "If you can't be civil and hear him out, I suggest you leave."

"Thank you, Addy," Nikki added, nodding to the woman.

The mass of men moved backward and Nikki and Addy went inside. I followed, Audrey's brothers purposely bumping me as I went. I didn't mind. I'd been in fistfights more than I'd like to admit. I could hold my own. Plus, I'd done the exact same thing when I thought Linc had messed with my sister.

When we were all finally seated in a very nice living room that I hoped would not have my blood on it today, I told them the whole story of the cabin and my sister and my parents and how I felt about Audrey today. My throat felt like it might shrivel and die from all the use and Nikki had a tissue in hand to wipe at her eyes.

"Sorry. It's the menopause. I cry at everything now."

"Always have," one of her sons said out of the corner of his mouth.

Nikki cut him a severe look before coming back to me. "So, what can we do to help? Audrey seemed pretty down and out earlier today."

I sat forward, my forearms on my knees. I was nervous as hell and out of my comfort zone by a mile, but I had to do this for Audrey. "I have a plan."

By the time I'd explained it all, the women were fully invested in my plan. They shouted out ideas that enhanced what

I'd already mapped out. Audrey's brothers reluctantly got on board. Nikki gave me another hug that made me feel like I might beg her to adopt me as one of her sons.

I also felt like I'd lost my voice from talking so much. The Hellman boys each shook my hand when I left, every single one of them squeezing harder than they needed to. I understood the subtle threat and respected them for it. With hope buoying my spirits, I went back to Glamper's Paradise to enlist Linc and Gannon's help. Keva happened to be there, bringing lunch to Linc. She squealed when she heard my plan, throwing her arms around my waist.

"I knew you weren't a dumb shit!"

I grinned at the top of her head. "I love you too, sis."

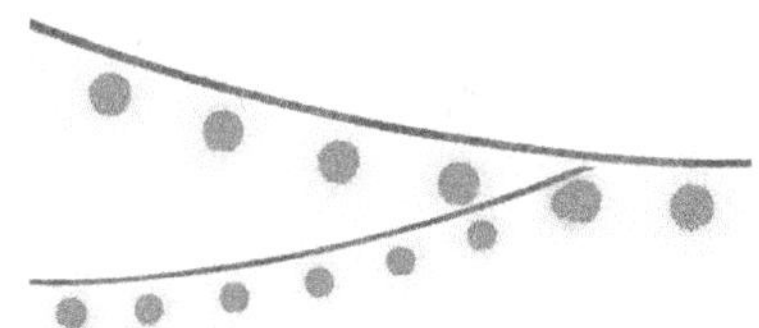

I was going to sweat through this damn shirt before Audrey even got here.

The band was setting up on the stage, each of them eyeing me like they were glad they weren't in my shoes. I'd gone over the playlist with them, ensuring they played the same songs that had been playing last time I'd come to The Tavern and met a short blonde-haired woman who'd turned my world upside down. I was so nervous I couldn't eat. Even the beer wasn't to my liking.

The door swung open and the Hellman boys and their wives

swooped in right on time. The women all came over to wish me luck and smother me in hugs, welcoming me to the family—which I thought was premature but appreciated just the same. The boys gave me reluctant head nods and fanned out to take up room at the various tables. Nikki and her husband, Jason, came in right after. Jason came over to introduce himself, also giving me a friendly warning about screwing things up with Audrey.

If nothing else, this whole plan had showed me exactly how many people loved Audrey. She said her family life was terrible and yet she could fill a bar with all the people who loved her and protected her fiercely. The woman attracted good people, and I'd try like hell for the very rest of my days to be someone who deserved to be in her inner circle.

The band began to play and Nugget started serving beer. He'd let me rent out the whole bar for a hefty sum, saying he'd bartend himself just to see a big guy like me down on his knees for a woman. He seemed just grumpy enough to be friends with Pete. I'd have to introduce them if I survived tonight's public grovel. Pete could stand to have a friend, even if he'd go kicking and screaming into the friendship.

My stomach was in knots, and I was pretty sure my deodorant had failed me, but the door opened again and it was like all the lights and sounds faded as a familiar blonde head came inside. My sister, Paisley, and Marlo were with her, the three of them pushing Audrey toward the bar where I was standing. I knew the second Audrey's gaze landed on me. Her beautiful eyes opened wide and her mouth tipped up automatically into a smile. Then the reality of me leaving her on silent mode for a week hit her and she glared at me.

I pushed off the bar and made my legs move toward her. The three girls shifted to the side to give us privacy. Audrey's head whipped left and right, realizing her friends had set her up as they slunk away. I watched Audrey's spine straighten and her head tip up. Fuck, she was gorgeous when she was standing up for herself.

"Audrey."

"Boston." Her voice was clipped, the slight red tint to her eyes making me see just how much I'd hurt her.

The band cut off mid song and started in on the song that had been playing when I'd first danced with Audrey. I held out my hand, palm up, my heart right there for her to take if she still wanted it.

"I have a lot to apologize for," I said just loudly enough for her to hear me. "Will you allow me to dance with you and explain everything?"

Audrey dropped my gaze and looked around the bar. Her family and friends were looking at us with hopeful expressions. "What's going on here?"

I kept my hand out, hoping like hell she'd give me another chance. "I asked everyone to come so you could see how much family you really do have. Everyone in this bar loves you, lusty."

Her head snapped back to me, the meaning of my words hitting her. Her eyes filled with tears. "Nugget loves me?"

My lips quirked to the side. I shrugged. "Everyone except him."

Audrey, the girl who couldn't reach the top cupboards and thought sugar was part of the four essential food groups, stood there so strongly in her convictions I wanted to kiss her senseless. "I'm not sure love is enough though, Boston. I want it all."

I dipped my head. "And just like up at the cabin, I'll give you everything you want and need." I looked her right in the eyes and bared my soul. "I would die before withholding anything you ever wanted, Audrey Hellman. If you'll give me another chance, I'll give you the love, the family, the kids, the marriage. Everything."

Audrey looked at my hand, then around the bar. "So this isn't to get me back so we can hook up in the bathroom hallway?"

I winced. This plan wasn't giving off the vibes I'd hoped it would. "No. I invited your friends and family here so you could see that I understand the life that you need. I've also found what

I need. You." I gestured to where my sister was standing next to Linc. "I want a family. I want a partner who knows everything about me and still wants to fight for a life together. I brought you here to show you that that night I met you changed everything for me. No more hookups. No more hermit. No more COTFRWB. No more CPHTFRWB. Just EFRRWAB."

Now it was Audrey's turn to fight a smile. "That's a lot of acronyms."

"I practiced for thirty times in the mirror this morning to get it right."

The grin grew flirty. "I feel like that level of patience should be rewarded."

I flexed my fingers and she finally put her hand in mind. "I feel like that level of trust should be rewarded."

"I feel like this song should be danced to before my ankles swell," my sister snarked from the bar next to us.

Audrey and I stood there grinning at each other for a moment longer.

"Dance with me?" I tugged on her hand until her whole tiny body was right up against me where she belonged. "Forever?"

Her eyes were still full of tears, but the smile made all the nerves twisting my gut wash away. "I'd hate to waste a perfectly good party with all *our* friends and family. Ours, Boston. You love me, you get the whole family too. You ready for that?"

I shrugged, wrapping my arm around her waist and breathing in her familiar scent. "I already managed to talk to your brothers without getting punched in the face, so yeah, I think I'm ready." Leaned down to whisper in her ear the words I only wanted her to hear. "I love you, Audrey."

She pulled back and a tear escaped, tracking down her cheek. "I love you too, Boston."

And then we danced.

CHAPTER TWENTY-EIGHT

udrey

DESPITE MYSELF, I was super glad I let the girls drag me to The Tavern tonight. I'd put up a good fight, whining and moaning for a solid hour before they threw an outfit at me and threatened to unalive me if I didn't hurry up. I was so depressed that even Madi failing to make good on another payment this week to make up her back rent didn't phase me. Going out to a bar wasn't even in my top one hundred list of good ideas to get my mood back to the sunny side, but things had taken a sharp turn for the best when Boston was there.

And now that I knew he loved me and just needed the time and space to think things through? I was straight giddy.

The band seemed to crank louder as Boston and I took to the scarred wooden dance floor. Our friends and family cheered us on, which should have been embarrassing, but wasn't. They'd all known how depressed I was without this man. Only fair they got to see up close and personal how things turned out.

Boston's hands enveloped my waist and back, holding me

tight against his rock-solid chest. I breathed him in, realizing just how much I'd missed him. My hands barely reached his shoulders.

"You make me feel so safe," I said quietly.

Boston heard me though. He always did. He was a man of few words, but he always trained that quiet focus on me. His grip on me tightened as he dipped his head by my ear.

"I will always protect you, Audrey. I don't love a lot of people, but when I do, I love them fiercely and will never give up on them. That I can promise you."

My eyes flooded with tears. I believed him. I'd seen the way he'd approached his sister, single-minded in his plan to make things right between them. I opened my mouth to respond, but lost the ability to speak when he took my hands off his shoulders and spun me out and then back in like he was some kind of ballroom professional.

My mouth dropped open as his eyes twinkled down at me. "What is this?"

Boston spun me back out, and right on the beat, brought me back in, continuing to sway back and forth like he hadn't just shocked the hell out of me. "Someone told me I needed to actually move my feet. I asked Annabel to teach me to dance for you. She might hate me again."

I burst out laughing, laying my forehead in the middle of his chest. I truly loved this gentle giant of a man. I may have said it out loud because next thing I knew, Boston was stepping back and kneeling on one knee on the dirty floor, his hands holding mine.

"What—"

The volume of the band suddenly dipped to a hushed background noise. I could feel the press of bodies around us, but I couldn't look away from Boston's dark eyes.

"Audrey Hellman, I didn't think I was capable of loving someone. I thought love only led to heartbreak. And then I danced with you and you woke something up inside me. Your harmonica playing broke my eardrums but everything else about you was magical."

I snorted even as more tears gathered in my eyes. I couldn't believe this was happening. All the things I'd dreamed about and planned for, but wasn't sure were actually going to happen, were happening. I was standing in the center of my dream, smack-dab in the middle of the kind of life I knew I deserved.

"I'm sure I'll make you mad a thousand times over. And I'm sure you'll pick up a thousand hobbies between now and when we take our last breath together, but I can't imagine living the rest of my life without you. I want to see you in a white dress, I want to witness our child in your arms, I want to celebrate your first gray hair. I want every last moment with you and I'm selfish enough to ask for what I want. Audrey, will you please marry me?"

Boston pulled something out of his pocket. I was sure the ring was pretty but I couldn't look away from his face. The way the tips of his ears were red, embarrassed about pouring his heart out in front of all these people and yet he'd done it. He did it because he knew I wanted the proposal, the wedding, the two point five kids. He did it because he loved me beyond his fears and insecurities. Happiness bubbled up inside my veins until I was positively drunk on it.

"Yes!" I squealed right before tackling him in the kind of hug that required both feet on the ground. He tipped sideways and got a hand on the ground to stabilize us. Always my hero. Always protecting me.

Boston shook his head, the grin turning his face from rugged to handsome. He stood up, getting us both on our feet before shouting over his shoulder. "She said yes!"

Everyone went wild and Nikki hollered for the champagne. The band picked up playing a song by Luke Combs about being crazy but also beautiful. Surely there was a subliminal message there, but I chose to ignore it. Boston picked me up and whirled me around while I held on to his shoulders and kissed the hell out of him. My brothers hollered at us to get a room and still Boston didn't put me down. I swung my legs around his waist and we swayed right there on the dance floor with him carrying me.

"Wasn't getting engaged enough? You gotta try for the baby right now too?"

Nikki's sassy voice had us coming up for air. My cheeks went hot and Boston allowed me to slide down his body so that my feet finally touched the dance floor. Nikki handed us each a flute of champagne and that's when I realized Nugget had handed out champagne to everyone else.

"To another happily-ever-after! To Audrey and Boston!"

Everyone raised their glasses in the air before sipping the good stuff someone had the foresight to bring to a bar that only served hard liquor and sticky beer.

"Oh, I almost forgot." Boston held out the ring again. The gold and the round diamond gleamed in the twinkling beer sign lights. "I had a ring made from my mom's necklace. She never took it off as long as I could remember, but the coroner brought it to me after the accident. I kept it with me the whole time I was overseas, not knowing I was keeping it safe for you. I want to give something precious to the most precious person in my life. I hope that's alright."

Now my eyes were burning again. "You are a romantic at heart, Boston Mooney."

Boston slid the ring on my finger. "Let's keep that between you and me."

I stared down at my ring, letting the diamond flash in the light. It was gorgeous and perfectly traditional, just like I wanted.

Nikki cleared her throat while Jason tucked her into his side. "I knew you'd be smart enough to choose true love with a good man. Welcome to the family, Boston."

Jason shook hands with Boston and then each of my brothers came up to do the same with varying degrees of warmth. They'd come around once they saw how happy Boston made me. Or maybe they wouldn't. I didn't exactly know how brothers handled their little sister getting hitched. I guessed I'd find out.

"Boston! You ready to belt one out, brother?" the guy at the microphone called out to my fiancé. I'd have to get used to that word.

"What's he talking about?"

Boston squeezed my waist and looked even more embarrassed. "They want me to sing the final song request I made."

"You can sing?" I stared up at him.

He shrugged his massive shoulders. "A little."

I swatted his ass and made him jump. "Then get up there! I want to hear this!"

Boston let go of me, shooting me warning looks, like he worried I might give back the ring if his voice wasn't any good. I honestly didn't care what he sounded like. Just to see him do something so extroverted when normally he wanted to crawl into a dark cave and hibernate was a sight to behold.

Gannon hollered while the band welcomed Boston to the stage. "Dammit! If I'd known you would sing tonight, I'd have brought your banjo too!"

Paisley hushed him. "Talk about your band later, babe."

"But—"

Paisley clapped her hand over Gannon's mouth while Linc burst out laughing. Those boys were up to no good and now they had Boston to corrupt.

The band started playing a slow song, another track by Luke Combs. This one was about loving a woman anyway, even if she broke his heart. I had a split second of wishing I'd brought my harmonica to join in, but then Boston opened his mouth and I lost all ability to think. His voice was rough but in tune, a melodic gruff version of his speaking voice. He locked eyes with me and didn't even blink as he belted out the song. The words flowed through me and the tears were as natural as breathing. By the time Boston sang the last line, I'd melted into a puddle right there in the middle of The Tavern.

Not only was my man hotter than all the men in the county, he could sing! And fill out a pair of jeans like nobody's business. And survive in the wilderness. Was there anything he couldn't do?

Boston let go of the microphone and hopped down from the stage to march right to me like a man on a mission. I jumped, he caught me, and our mouths fused together. His hands were everywhere, and my fingers were clutching him to me like my life depended on him getting ever closer. I didn't hear a damn thing except the door swinging shut behind us as he got me out of there. The evening air was cold against my back, but there was an inferno building between us.

"My place," Boston grunted in between kisses. He plopped me down on the seat of his truck and swung my legs in before closing the door. The guy actually ran around the front of the truck and left tire tracks as he peeled out of the lot.

"Think we should have said goodbye?" I asked, crossing my legs to help with the ache Boston had put there.

Boston ran a hand over his face and looked in pain. "I can go back if you'd prefer to say goodbye."

I wrinkled up my nose. "Nah."

"Thank fuck."

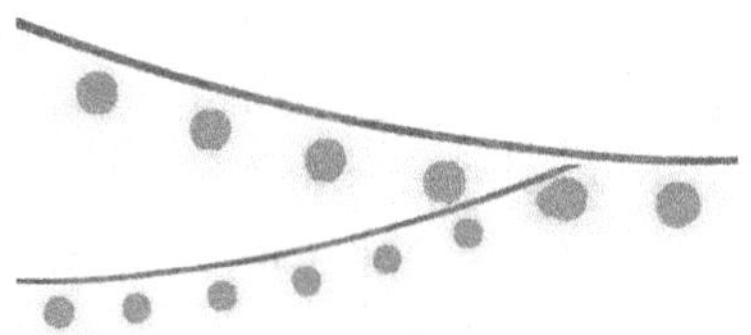

"This rug was a perfect purchase," I panted.

Boston was the one sitting on it, the log fire snapping beside us, but my heels were digging into the soft white faux fur as I sat on his lap inside his new cabin. He was buried deep inside me and our skin was coated with sweat. He kept bringing me right to the edge and then stopping, claiming he wanted to extend our lovemaking. He was going to kill me with his patience.

My arms tightened around his shoulders and I dug my heels in harder to ride him faster. Boston gripped my hips and lifted me, like he planned to pull me off of him. I was so close I could feel the electricity snapping in my extremities.

"Don't you dare stop or I'll get out my harmonica while you try to sleep tonight."

"But—"

I squeezed my internal muscles as I pulled back and smiled triumphantly when he grunted in the back of his throat. "I'm going to marry you, you know. We can make love every day if we want."

Boston's answering grin was just as smug. "Twice a day?"

I sank back down his length and my eyes nearly crossed. "Yes, beast. Every hour if you want."

And then, with a growl, my fiancé was as lost as me, his hands gripping me tight as he moved me over him, his hard length grinding against every sensitive nerve ending until we both faltered and exploded. Our stuttering breaths mingled as we groaned and clutched each other tight. When I couldn't possibly hold my head up any longer and the tremors had subsided, I laid my head down on Boston's shoulder. He rubbed my back in that calming way of his, and I couldn't think of a time when I felt more satisfied in every way.

Boston was where I was supposed to be. I thought I'd been waiting on my dream to happen, but I'd been waiting for *him*. The dream wouldn't have felt this damn right with anyone else.

CHAPTER TWENTY-NINE

$\mathcal{B}$oston

Two months later

"My two favorite Angelos are here!" I stepped outside the cabin, having seen my sister's car pull up my driveway.

Linc, Annabel, and Lucas got out of the car, my nephew running straight over to tackle me. The little man and I had gotten closer these last two months. I'd been to every single one of his soccer games, no matter how frustrating it was when the kids ran the wrong way on the field or picked their nose instead of kicking the dang ball. Plus I was always swinging by to take Lucas to get ice cream. No better way to become the favorite uncle.

Never mind the fact he only had one.

Linc flipped me off behind Lucas's back, which made me smile harder. My best friend knew I loved him, but if push came to shove, I'd choose my sister and my nephew without one damn drop of guilt. Thing is, I knew he'd choose them over me too and that made me feel good. I knew that my sister had someone watching over her in case something happened to me.

"We had a bit of an incident last night," Annabel started, instantly pulling my attention to her and the baby bump she was rubbing.

"Are you okay?" I swung Lucas up on my shoulders and came closer to inspect my sister for myself. She didn't have visible bruises and her eyes weren't red from crying. If anything, her eyes were sparkling with happiness.

Linc put his arm around her. "Nothing bad. Just had a hungry monkey in our kitchen." He looked pointedly above my head at Lucas.

Lucas began to squirm and would have fallen off my shoulders if I hadn't clamped my hands down on his little legs. "I didn't know, Mama. I'm sorry."

"I know, baby. Besides, I'm kind of glad we know."

"Know what?"

I twisted to see Audrey coming down the stairs and over to our group huddle. She'd been fast asleep when I got up this morning. She'd promised me sex every day and I wasn't going to let her up on that promise. She did need her sleep to recover though, which I was all too happy to give her if it meant she was open to my advances every night.

Annabel did a little shimmy that looked weird with a huge baby bump. "We found out what we're having!"

"No!" Audrey grabbed Annabel's hands and squealed right along with her. Linc and I just rolled our eyes and waited them out. Whoever thought best friends dating best friends was weird was dead wrong. It was awesome having spouses get along so well.

"Lucas thought the gender reveal cupcake was the dessert I'd been baking for the soccer bake sale. He bit into it and then complained about the filling." Annabel and Linc had second-guessed their decision about finding out the gender of their second baby and had left the gender reveal cupcake in the refrigerator for weeks.

"For fu—fundamentals' sake. What was it?"

Annabel gave me the hairy eyeball for almost swearing. I gave it right back for stringing out the news. Was I having another nephew or a niece?

Annabel looked up at Linc, who looked at my sister like she'd personally hung the moon and every single star that came out at night up here in the mountains.

"You tell them, babe. I already got to do this once."

Linc kissed her on the nose and then turned to us. "It's a girl. Cora Angelo."

Audrey screamed and then the girls were hugging and crying. I clapped Linc on the shoulder, trying not to drop Lucas. Damn. A little girl. Everyone talked over each other with opinions on girls. Spoiler: Lucas thought they might be kind of lame. Linc couldn't wait to teach her to drive a stick-shift truck so she'd be badass. Audrey already volunteered to sew a coming-home-from-the-hospital onesie, an offer Annabel wisely turned down despite this being Audrey's latest hobby. Then the growing little family said they had to leave to tell Paisley and Gannon the good news.

"You better call Marlo to come over when you tell them or she'll feel left out," Audrey rushed to suggest.

Annabel sobered quickly. "Yeah, you're right. She's been quieter and grouchier than usual lately."

After a round of hugs, they took off and Audrey and I stood in the driveway with our arms around each other. The birds were calling across the treetops and the sun was still peeking behind the far trees as it rose in the sky. The weather was already turning warmer and the days were getting longer. Pretty soon, I'd have to be shirtless all the time just to not overheat. Audrey would love that.

"I'm worried about Marlo," Audrey said into my chest as I held her.

I squeezed her tighter. This woman's heart was just too big.

"She'll be fine. Everyone's allowed to be in a mood every now and then."

"Yeah, but—"

I cut her off. "Look what happened with Madi. You thought she'd be mad about you breaking your lease earlier and moving in with me and she was totally fine. You don't need to worry about everyone else and their feelings so much."

That was somewhat of a lie. Madi had initially been pissed about losing her roommate, the one who always covered the rent for her, but I'd had a private little chat with her. Madi's mood had magically changed and she'd paid Audrey back for all the rent she'd missed. Some people just liked to take advantage of other people's kindness.

But they better not try that shit on my future wife. I wouldn't stand for it, and if going behind my wife's back was what I had to do to protect her, then I'd gladly do it and apologize later if I needed to.

Audrey sighed, but grabbed my ass, a move she frequently engaged in when no one was around. Apparently, she was obsessed with my ass. "I know you're right, but she's my friend. I want to see her happy." Audrey pulled back suddenly. "Wait, weren't you supposed to be leaving early to meet with the concrete guys?"

I wished I had more time with her, but she was right. I had to get to Glamper's Paradise. Gannon had not only made me a partner in the business, he'd tasked me with the buildout of the new cabins on the land we'd bought from Pete. The foundations were getting poured today and I needed to get over there. If all went according to plan, we'd have at least a few cabins ready to rent out middle of the summer.

"Yeah. I'm going. What do you have planned today?"

"Working from home on that one new contract and then wedding planning."

I stepped back carefully. I didn't get involved in the wedding planning much. In the beginning, I'd tried, but the girls always laughed at my ideas. I didn't know why an ax-throwing station at the reception was met with giggles and eye-rolls. I could guarantee every male—and probably a few females—would fucking love that at a wedding reception.

"Love you, lusty." I kissed her quick, running back inside for my keys.

She swatted my ass as I passed her again, waving as I backed my truck out of the driveway. I could get used to this, coming home to Audrey every single day of my life. She'd moved in last week and I had no idea why I thought living alone the rest of my life was a good idea. What a dumbass I'd been.

I didn't get home until late that night, exhausted but satisfied with the work we'd gotten done. When I pulled up the driveway, Audrey's mother was just climbing out of her car. She pulled her sweater tighter around her and waited for me to get out too.

"Hey, Shann, how are you?" I wracked my brain but couldn't remember Audrey telling me her mom was coming over tonight. I'd only talked to her twice since getting engaged, but both times she'd been very kind, if a lot quiet. It was hard to see that Audrey was her daughter. Clearly, Audrey had gotten all her enthusiasm and charming personality from her father. Except she didn't use her charisma for evil.

"I'm well, thank you. Do you mind carrying a box for me?"

"Sure." I stepped over to her car as she opened up the back seat. The box lying on the seat was a large flat white box. I picked it up carefully, but nothing shifted and it wasn't that heavy. We moved up the stairs and into the house.

"Honey, I'm home!" I called, my usual greeting that made me smile every damn time.

"Hey!" Audrey came sliding around the corner, but stopped short when she saw her mom next to me. "Mom! I wasn't expecting you, but I'm so glad you stopped by."

The two women hugged and Shann motioned to the coffee table to set down the box. I placed it there and then had a seat next to Audrey. Her mom stayed standing, her hands clutched nervously in front of her.

"Mom? What is it?"

Audrey and her mom had an interesting relationship. They were both guarded and a bit unsure of each other. There was love there too, but most times I wondered if Shann knew how to handle someone as vivacious as Audrey. I had yet to meet Audrey's sister, Zoey. She refused to speak to Audrey and her mother at the moment. She had sided with her father, and while that hurt Audrey, she knew Zoey had to figure things out on her own.

"I brought you something," Shann blurted out. She reached down and shoved the box closer to Audrey. "Go ahead. Open it."

Audrey glanced at me, but obeyed, opening the box and unfolding tissue paper. Then she gasped.

I leaned in closer. Oh shit. It was a wedding dress. Audrey pulled it out of the box by the heavily beaded shoulder pads. The thing looked like an exact replica of Princess Diana's wedding dress, complete with see-through material up to the neck and long, billowy sleeves.

"Wow." Audrey's eyes were round and I could tell she was holding back what she really thought. There was no way in hell Audrey would choose something like that for her own wedding dress. Did Shann want Audrey to wear it?

"Now don't get concerned." Shann put her hand on Audrey's. "I didn't bring you my wedding dress to suggest you wear it. I was hoping you'd help me burn it."

Audrey's jaw dropped. "You want to burn it? Really?"

Shann's drawn face perked up into a rare smile. "I think that's the best thing for it, don't you? I mean, the marriage wasn't even real. What am I keeping this dress for?"

Audrey dropped the dress and hopped to her feet. She pulled Shann in for a hug, which her mother reciprocated awkwardly. I knew from all the talks with Audrey late at night she was worried her mom would someday try to go back to her father. If

Shann was willing to burn her wedding dress, it was safe to say there would be no plans for going back.

I stood and clapped my hands together. "I got a pile of leaves out back I've been meaning to burn. I'll get the lighter fluid."

Shann beamed at me while Audrey tried to hide the wiping of her eyes. We went out back and we let Shann drape the dress on the pile of leaves. She gazed at it for a moment, perhaps memorizing the miles of train or the design of the millions of beads. Then she straightened her spine and held out her hand for the lighter fluid. I placed the bottle there and she almost looked gleeful spraying down the dress.

"Would you two like the honors?" I held out the box of matches.

Audrey took one and her mother took another. With a nod to each other, they each lit a match and tossed it onto the pile. The dress instantly popped into flames and Shann clapped while she watched it burn. Audrey put her arm around her mom and I could see the pride on her face. She'd been waiting twenty-six years for her mom to stand up for herself.

There were just a few burning sticks of wood under the leaves when someone honked from out front. I frowned. Why did everyone just think they could constantly stop by uninvited? Was this normal for non-hermits? I decided I needed to put a stop to it.

"I'm getting my gun," I mumbled, turning toward the house.

Audrey grabbed my arm. "Hold up, beast. That honk was for me. You and Mom wait here."

"I'm not letting you go out there by yourself," I grumbled.

Audrey lifted her nose in the air. "Do you trust me or not?"

I hated when she did that. Of course, I trusted her. It was literally everyone else in the world I didn't trust. Audrey patted my cheek and ran around the side of the house, oblivious to snakes or other animals that might have come out in the darkness that had descended on the cabin. I just shook my head and tried not to think about all the terrible things that could happen.

"You're a good man, Boston Mooney," Shann said from behind me. I turned to see her studying me in the glow of the dying fire. "I had no idea what a good man actually looked like, until I saw you with my daughter. Funny how as parents we think we have so much to teach our kids." She shook her head with a soft smile. "Turns out they have so much to teach us too."

And then for the first time, Shann came up and put her arms around me. I wasn't a big hugger unless it was Audrey I was hugging, and based off her stiff limbs, I had a feeling Shann wasn't a big hugger either. Which made it all the more sweet. I hugged her back and that's how Audrey found us as she came back around the house with something in her arms.

"Ahhh. You two are the sweetest." She bent over and put her load on the ground. "Maybe you can save some of your hugs for this lovey."

The load moved, all limbs and floppy ears and a tongue hanging out its mouth as it dashed across the yard. It was a dog. A Saint Bernard to be exact, based on the coloring. He darted over to me and sniffed my boots. I bent down to pick him up. He lunged in my arms and swiped his tongue across my face. He was a drooler already. Definitely a Saint Bernard.

"What is this?"

Audrey came up to my side to scratch the little guy behind the ears. "He's your dog. When we were snowed in, you told me you always wanted a little cabin in the woods and a dog by your side."

My heart squeezed in my chest. For the dog I already loved. For the woman who loved me better than I could ever hope for. For this life I'd found here in Blueball. I twisted to see Audrey past all the fur and swiping tongue. "Let's get married tonight."

Audrey just laughed. "Patience, beast."

I leaned down and kissed her, not caring that her mother was just a few feet away or that puppy breath had joined the kiss too. I love this woman and I couldn't wait to make her my wife.

udrey

ONE YEAR Later

"WHAT'S WITH THE BACKPACK?" Boston slashed at a bush blocking our path with the huge machete-looking thing he brought on our short hike.

"What's with the machete?"

"Never know what you're going to find in the wilderness." He held back a tree branch so I could pass without getting hit in the face. We'd gone hiking a lot the last year, finding peace in the quiet of nature. I liked the hikes best when we'd been arguing over something. There was nothing like fresh air and the scent of pine trees to make us stop being stubborn and actually talk to each other. Oh, and the makeup sex. Boston always performed his best work when he was in nature, if you know what I mean.

"Same, beast, same." I hopped over a large rock and moved further north, my thighs only burning a tiny bit. I got in better shape with all these hikes too. "First time I ever went on a hike with you I got stuck in a dilapidated cabin for days on end with a limited supply of food and firewood. I won't make that mistake again."

I came to a clearing, shielding my eyes against the midday sun. There were stakes in the ground and a slab of concrete with little tubes sticking out of it randomly.

"You got food and firewood in there?" Boston asked behind me.

What in the world was this doing way out here? Far as I knew, this was still Pete's land. I'd have to have a word with him and help him evict whomever dared homestead on his land.

"Something like that," I answered absentmindedly, envisioning a legal battle that we'd most certainly win. God, it pissed me off when people tried to swindle an old man. Pete, despite his protests of wanting to remain a hermit, had become like a father figure to me over the last year, and I wasn't going to let some land-stealing criminal take advantage of him.

Boston put his arm around my shoulders and stared out at the beginnings of what might be a house or a building of some sort. "Here we are."

"Where?"

"Here."

I huffed and turned to him, crossing my arms over my chest. "Where are we, Boston? And why is there a structure being built on Pete's land?" And why wasn't he as pissed as I was about it?

Boston grinned, clearly not catching on to what was happening here. "This, my lovely fiancée, is not Pete's land."

I swiveled my head, getting my bearings now that we'd reached the top of the hill. The view was incredible and I knew for a fact this was part of Pete's land as we'd hiked through here before. I opened my mouth to argue, but Boston had pulled rolled-up paper out of his rucksack and unfurled it, pointing here and there.

"See? These are the plans for the house. I took the liberty of deciding on the layout, but now you have to pick all the details. Flooring, windows, porch size, granite countertops. All the fun stuff."

"Boston!"

His head snapped up. "What?"

"What are you talking about?"

He paused, his face transforming into the soft smile that always had me melting at his feet. "This is our land now, lusty. Pete gifted it to us as an early wedding gift. The house won't be ready by the wedding, but—"

I clapped my hand to his mouth, heart fluttering like a crazed hummingbird. "This is ours?"

He nodded his head while I gaped. I finally let him go so I could run around the foundation and check out the view from every angle, chattering away a mile a minute. Boston just followed behind me, chuckling and nodding at all my ridiculous commentary. When I came back around to what would be the front of our little house, I threw my arms around him, like a koala with her favorite tree. Then I pulled back.

"I need to thank you properly and I brought just the right things!"

"Huh?"

I shrugged off my backpack and set it on the ground, ripping it open and pulling kneepads over my shoes and onto my knees.

"What the fuck are you doing?" Boston said from above me, shoving the plans back in his rucksack.

I ignored him, pulling the bottle of bug spray out and spraying it over me like a cloud of protection. When that was done, I shoved the backpack aside and assumed my kneeling position on my newly protected knees.

"Come here, beast," I said in my best flirty voice.

Boston only eyed me like I'd lost my damn mind. I had not, of course. I'd just come prepared. One too many encounters on the ground like this where I picked bugs, rocks, and splinters out of my flesh had spawned ingenuity. Audrey Hellman ain't no dummy. If I wanted to suck my soon-to-be husband's cock, I was going to do it with all the comforts a city girl needs.

"Get your ass over here," I barked.

Much to my surprise, Boston obeyed, coming to stand right in front of me, hands on his hips. "Seriously, Audrey. What are you doing?"

I threw up my hands and then used them to wrench down his shorts. He jerked, but didn't move away. His dick sprang free and I watched it grow right before my eyes. "Isn't it obvious?"

And then I attacked, my mouth getting around the head of him, my tongue laving the tip, and my hands gripping the base. It didn't take long before Boston not only took over the rhythm, but also grunted into the fresh morning air like a wild animal. When he shouted and the birds flew from the trees, I braced myself, swallowing hard and fast until he sagged backward and pulled from my mouth.

I grinned up at him, mouth and chin wet, more turned on and in love than the day before. My career was on fire, my relationship was the best thing to ever happen to me, and an entire house was going to be built with a stunning view of Blueball as we started our life together.

Boston stumbled closer again, tugging me to my feet and kissing me before he pulled his shorts back up. "You're crazy. And all mine."

"Fuck yeah, I am." Then a red robin flew across my vision, right over Boston's head and I jerked away. "Quick, hand me my binoculars!"

"Binoculars?"

"That bird! Did you see it?"

Boston groaned. "So it's bird-watching now, huh?"

I shrugged, reaching for the binoculars with bug-sprayed limbs and knee pads in place. "A girl's gotta have a hobby to stay out of trouble."

EVERY FRIDAY NIGHT had turned into a jam session at Glamper's Paradise. Sometimes the campers joined us, sometimes they went off on their own, but for two or three hours, our men played their instruments and entertained us. They started out rough, not going to lie, but they'd improved massively. Boston didn't like being the lead singer, but when we heard Gannon sing, we all voted for Boston to be the only one mic'd up. Linc flat refused to sing, but given his drum skills, we all forgave him.

Marlo was currently in a camp chair, watching the makeshift band with a blanket over her lap. She didn't join in on the banter back and forth with all of us girls. She'd been pulling away more and more lately, a fact we were all worried about. We'd confronted her, of course, but she'd just shrugged and said we were all paired up and she wasn't. Of course there'd be a bit of an adjustment, one she wasn't mad about at all. Still, I didn't like how quiet she'd gotten. Marlo was the dark, morbid type already, but this was entering *The Addams Family* territory.

The kids were roasting marshmallows over the fire pit with Paisley keeping watch. Keva was rocking Cora back and forth so she'd settle for the night. I kept my gaze trained on Boston, incredibly turned on when his fingers picked at that banjo and he opened his mouth to sing. Friday night sex had also become a thing in our household. I couldn't seem to keep my hands off him after watching him play up there on the outdoor stage. Last Friday we hadn't even made it home before I made him pull to the side of the road.

My phone vibrated in my pocket and I fished it out to see an unknown number calling from an Arizona area code. I got up and moved away from the stage to answer it. The life of a realtor, always taking calls no matter the day or time.

"This is Audrey Hellman."

"Hi, Audrey, this is Vander Booth. I got your name and number from my grandma, Milly Booth."

I stuck my finger in my other ear and moved even further away so I could hear. "Oh yes, Mrs. Booth always helps with the costumes for the Christmas play at church."

Vander chuckled. "Yeah, she loves to sew. Her fingers aren't as good as they used to be though. One of many reasons why I'll be moving to Blueball to help her out. And that's where you come in. I need to buy a place to live."

"You've come to the right person. That's what I do. Are you going to be searching in person or long distance?" I saw Boston looking at me from the stage with a questioning frown. I gave him a thumbs-up, letting him know that everything was okay.

"Long distance. I'll need you to do the tour and report back. Check the vibe. Make sure there's no lurking last-century ghost trying to make me move back out."

I chuckled. Vander was quite the character. "No problem. You just let me know your preferences for a house and I'll have a list we can go see. I also have a great broker in town you'll want to see about getting pre-approved for a mortgage."

There was a beat of silence. "Oh, that won't be necessary. I'm paying cash."

I blinked. That was unusual, but not unheard of. "Cash works too. I have to warn you though, there aren't a lot of properties for sale right now."

"Can I be honest with you, Audrey Hellman?"

"I prefer that you do, Vander Booth."

"There's only one house I'm interested in seeing. The old Skinner place, up on Blueball Mountain."

My eyebrows hitched halfway up my forehead. "The Skinner place is huge. Eight bedrooms and ten bathrooms. Ten acres. And it's not actually on a mountain. More like a sizable hill. But it is for sale."

I wasn't one for lying to clients just to make the sale. I

wanted my clients to find the exact right house they could make a home. I'd love to bring a buyer to the table for this particular house though. It was the most expensive house in the county by far, which meant a huge commission for me. The Skinners had been an eccentric couple, outfitting their house with the best imported goods, with zero regard for price. Not even the smallest detail went overlooked. They'd left their property to a distant relative who had no interest in living in Blueball. The place had been empty and awaiting a buyer for a few years now.

"I don't want to overpay, but just between you and me, that's the one I want."

I spun in a circle, fist-pumping the air. When I had my enthusiasm contained, I answered professionally. "If that's the one you want, then that's the one I'll get you, Mr. Booth."

He chuckled, the sound low and rumbly. "It's Vander, please. And call me as soon as you can get inside for a tour."

"I'll call you as soon as possible. Travel safe."

"Will do."

The call dropped, and I stared at my phone like a small part of me wondered if I was being punked. The commission on this one deal would be what I made all of my first year as a realtor.

"Audrey?" Boston put his hand on my shoulder, sweaty from playing for two hours straight. "Everything all right?"

I turned to him, a grin splitting my face. "Everything is literally perfect."

His worry dropped away. "Then let's get out of here."

I eyed his damp shirt. "You're all sweaty."

"I'll shower first when we get home."

I shook my head. "Don't bother. I like the sweaty-mountain-man vibe. How about we try out the hood of your truck?"

Boston's grin was cocky. "Can't wait 'til we get home?"

Without warning, I jumped. Boston caught me like he always did. I wrapped my arms around his neck and fisted his hair. "Are we going to stand here talking, or get the hell out of here so we can fuck?"

Boston spun, moving toward his truck with long strides. "I knew you were lusty from the day I met you."

I laughed, feeling light as a feather. "And I always knew you were my home."

ALSO BY MARIKA RAY

Scan the QR code to go to Marika's Amazon page!

<u>Steamy RomComs - Blueball Band of Brothers:</u>

Grumpy the Bear - Blueball Band of Brothers #1

S'more Than a Feeling - Blueball Band of Brothers #2

Home is Where You Park It - Blueball Band of Brothers #3

***

<u>All Steamy RomComs Set in Hell:</u>

Grumpy As Hell - Hellman Brothers #1

Bro Code Hell - Hellman Brothers #2

Friend Zone Hell - Hellman Brothers #3

Cougar From Hell - Hellman Brothers #4

Falling First Hell - Hellman Brothers #5

***

Ridin' Solo - Sisters From Hell #1

One Night Bride - Sisters From Hell #2

<u>Sweet Romances</u>:

The Marriage Sham - Standalone

***

The Widower's Girlfriend-Faking It #1

Home Run Fiancé - Faking It #2

Guarding the Princess - Faking It #3

***

Lines We Cross - Nickel Bay Brothers #1

Perfectly Imperfect Us - Nickel Bay Brothers #2

<u>Steamy Beach Romance</u>:

1) Sweet Dreams - Beach Squad #1

2) Love on the Defense - Beach Squad #2

3) Barefoot Chaos - Beach Squad #3

* Novella - Handcuffed Hussy

4) Beach Babe Billionaire- Beach Squad #4

5) Brighter Than the Boss - Beach Squad #5

* Novella - Christmas Eve Do-Over

Marika Ray is a USA Today bestselling author, writing small town RomCom to make your heart explode and bring a smile to your face. All her books come with a money-back guarantee that you'll laugh at least once with every book.

Marika spends her time behind a computer crafting stories, walking along the beach, and making healthy food for her kids and husband whether they like it or not. Prior to writing novels, Marika held various jobs in the finance industry, with private start-up companies, and then in health & fitness. Cats may have nine lives, but Marika believes everyone should have nine careers to keep things spicy.

If you'd like to know more about Marika or the other novels she's currently writing, please find her in her private <u>Reader Group</u>.

If you want to take your stalking to the next level, here are other legal-ish places you can find Marika:

Join her Newsletter -
http://bit.ly/MarikaRayNews

Amazon - https://www.amazon.com/author/marikaray

Goodreads - https://www.goodreads.com/author/show/16856659.Marika_Ray

Bookbub - https://www.bookbub.com/authors/marika-ray

TikTok - https://vm.tiktok.com/ZMJvnQ2Cv